JUNKE

TWIN SUNS

BOO

OLIVE J. KELLEY

PRAISE FOR JUNKER SEVEN

"*JUNKER SEVEN* is sapphic science fiction at its finest. For fans of Becky Chambers and readers hungry for more galactic adventures a la The Mandalorian—Kelley soars with their debut."

— **Freydís Moon, bestselling author of *HEART, HAUNT, HAVOC***

"In a time when queer resistance is more important than ever, Kelley crafts a galaxy of love, rage, and revolution. Trans lesbians in love and fighting back against those who want them gone - an exhilarating reminder that our community has always been about rebellion."

— **Andrew Joseph White, NYT-bestselling author of *HELL FOLLOWED WITH US***

"*JUNKER SEVEN* is the kind of sci-fi that compels you to sit up and take note. Equal parts romantic thrill-ride and striking allegory, Olive J. Kelley's debut underscores the vitality of queer community— and that resilience and hope touch every corner of the galaxy."

— **Cass Biehn, author of VESUVIUS**

"*JUNKER SEVEN* is a hopeful mission across the galaxy that sees layered and visibly queer characters prevailing over life-threatening hardships while finding love in the stars."

— Quinton Li, author of *TELL ME HOW IT ENDS*

"Junker Seven is a futuristic take on today's fight for trans rights wrapped up in an inspiring love story."

— Jessica Salina, author of the RIVERPEAK HEROES series

"I loved the setting, despite never really getting into space sci-fi books before, and the descriptions really brought the world to life. I loved the diversity throughout the book, from LGBTQ+ rep, disability rep, and more."

— Amanda N. Newman, author of *CHILDREN OF THE OUTBACK* and more

"It's rare for a book to keep me up at night. To move me to act. It's rare to see myself reflected so closely in characters. I love this book and look forward to reading more of Kelley's work."

— Milo, Goodreads reviewer

"The plot was easy to follow, the characters easy to love, the cause hits very close to home and is so easy to care about. I don't have a single relevant complaint other than I want MORE!"

— Angela, Goodreads reviewer

Cover art is by Cillian Plamp.

ISBN (Paperback): 979-8-9878246-0-3

ISBD (eBook): 979-8-9878246-1-0

CONTENTS

CONTENT WARNINGS

While JUNKER SEVEN is, at its core, a book about LGBT+ hope and love in a galaxy that scorns those things, it also reflects the dangerous world we live in, and therefore contains content that could be upsetting to some readers.

- Transphobia, including misgendering, systemic transphobic violence, and censored deadnaming
- Police brutality
- Sexual assault (brief mention only)
- Gun violence & an attempted mass shooting
- Character death
- Child death (past)
- Sexual content
- Ableism, including internalized ableism by a disabled character

for the riots & the rebels; the past & the future.

1

POWERFUL AND CONTINUING NATIONALISM

The city of Fontus is too bright for my eyes. Towering skyscrapers and sleek, high-brow architecture shine silver under the light of the system's sun, an old star named Caelus that nurtures six planets and thirty-four moons. Only one of the planets is inhabitable, and calling Janus inhabitable is enough of a stretch already.

I hate Janus. I always have. From the pockmarked, gritty streets of what are graciously referred to as the suburbs to the hundred-odd-floor glittering glass needles reaching into the atmosphere, the whole place reeks of humanity and greed. It gets even worse when the elliptical orbit of the planet is at its apex, casting the ecumenopolis into a slick, sweaty heat. My jacket feels sticky against the skin on my back, my skin feels greasier and greasier no matter how often I rinse my face, and the smell of the trash chutes only grows stronger as the day progresses.

Days on Janus are similar enough to the galactic standard of twenty-six hours, but I switched my watch over to JST when I landed regardless. It's nearly two PM now, so only a few more hours of the stifling heat. I have been waiting for hours already for my mark to pass and the sweat pooling at the small of my back is starting to become unbearable. I swallow hard and pluck at a stray thread on the edge of my jacket. Even the recycled air of the Gemini sounds nicer than the reflected gleam burning my skin by now.

I move to pull out my Zephyr pad to go over the job again, but before I can, a voice, far too loud at this sleepy hour, rings through the street.

"Honestly, I just feel like Marwood has the galaxy's best interests at heart." I turn my head subtly so I can lay eyes on the owner of the sneering, haughty voice. Well, more accurately, lay *eye*. My left, a high-tech prosthetic, zooms in and darts across the planes of the man's face until it positively IDs him as the mark I've been waiting for.

"Finally," I murmur and casually stand, my jacket's hood still covering my head and most of my face. He's a polished-looking brunet with his hair slicked carefully at the part. There's enough gel or hairspray or something similar on him that I can smell it from here, twenty feet back. I wrinkle my nose and part my lips a millimeter, just to breathe in the closer air and avoid the obnoxious scent.

"I mean, he just wants to keep the galaxy safe, right? If we keep to our own planets and focus on sustainability, we're surely going to thrive more than if we rely so heavily on trade, right?" he says loudly to the person walking next to him, a quiet woman with glasses and a thick messenger bag slung over her shoulder. There are dozens of pieces of loose paper poking out the open flap as well as two tablets, and I think back to the dossier I received upon accepting the job. Lola Mullen, my mark's assistant, fits the description.

I sigh. Another moving part means more complications, and having to get the assistant out of the way before I can get what I want out of the man at her side is one I'd really rather avoid.

They turn a corner and, twenty seconds later, I do too. My eye autofocuses on them within a heartbeat. When they turn again, onto a much less populated street, my lips curl in a smile.

"Gotcha," I breathe and pick up my walking pace. They're moving leisurely, surely between greatly important meetings of some sort or another, and I'm able to catch up quickly. The alley they're moving through is empty, save for a woman three stories up hanging laundry on her balcony, and I write her off quickly. If I do this right, I'll be in and out fast enough that, even if she does report me to the IPF, I'll be long gone by the time they arrive.

There's a trash compactor built into the wall and I drop a screw from my pocket— picked up on a junking job last week— into the slot. They're programed to sense new material being inserted and crush it into little bricks to be shipped off to facilities, but metal? It doesn't compact. The screw scrapes along the inside, the horrid screech of metal on metal echoing through the alleyway.

Assistant Lola turns to look, and the second she is distracted I rush up behind them and grab my mark's arm, twisting until he cries out and falls to the dirty cement beneath our feet.

"Robbie Carr?" I grit as I let my knee rest on his lower back, easily pinning the man.

He cries out wordlessly and flails until he can turn his head to see me, eyes wide and rolled back in his head with fear, and then, "Who sent you? What do you want?"

I push back my hood. My face is generic— round and white with a shadow of short-clipped hair across my scalp— but I know the scars across the left side of my face tend to invoke fear in men who have never dealt with anything more difficult than juggling a laptop and a coffee at the same time. His face pales and I can't help the slight smile that pulls on my lips.

"You stole something from someone," I say simply, "and he wants it back."

His mouth falls open. "What— the fucking datastick?" he gapes and struggles again in my grasp, but I hold strong. The knee digging into his back is my prosthetic one and I'm sure the knob of metal hurts, but I just press in harder. Hurting him doesn't quite give me pleasure— I don't care enough about this job for that— but his pathetic squeals almost do.

"Yes. Give it back and you walk out of here with all of your bones intact."

Something clatters to the ground beside me and I look down to see a small, silver datastick. Lola Mullen has her hands raised above her shoulders.

"Take it," she says and takes a step back. Her skirt swishes around her ankles as she moves and I can see a faint tremor in her fingers. "Just don't hurt us." It comes out almost like a question— a miserable little plea from a woman whose boots aren't scuffed from dirty work, whose skin is pale and clean, no scars bisecting her

Robbie scrabbles at the ground, his nails skirting over rugged concrete and dirt. "You don't know what's on that stick," he gasps and curls his fingers around it again. "This information could change the galaxy— It could end careers! It could destroy Marwood's campaign!"

"I don't care," I say simply and dig my knee harder into his spine. I feel and hear it in the same heartbeat— A dull crunch jolts through his chest, surely a rib breaking under the pressure. I don't let up.

I reach down and jam one of my fingers into his sweaty palm until I can uncurl his fingers, sending the datastick clattering to the cement once again. "Thanks." I get to my feet and scoop the datastick up in my hand, tucking it quickly into my jacket pocket.

"You're fucking evil," he spits out and wraps his arm around his ribs as he sits up. His assistant rushes to his side once it's clear that I'm not going to attack him again and falls to her knees beside him, cupping his face in her palm.

"It's okay, we can start again—"

"No we can't! We had once shot at this—"

"Robbie, breathe—"

I leave the alleyway quietly with the datastick tucked in my pocket.

To them, it's world-changing. To me, it's a few hundred credits. The plastic case is rough in a few spots where it rubbed against the concrete and I press over it with my thumb. I pull my hood up and duck down a smaller side street. My pocket feels heavy and I can still hear Robbie's exasperated moans as he clutches at his ribcage.

The alleyways in the dark city are jagged mazes and I dart through a few at random until his voice fades into the sounds of the city around me, then another few for good measure. When the anxiety in my chest eases, when I feel relatively confident that he couldn't have followed me, I pull open a door to a small coffee shop and head inside.

I don't buy a drink. I had a cup of coffee when I got up this morning, brewed from dried powder I have stored on the Gemini, and another would keep me up much later than I need to. Instead, I just sink into a plush chair right inside the door and pull out my pad. There are easily a dozen other people all doing the same thing; some people are looking at their pads, others their laptops, and others still just stare at their watches. With my dull colored jacket and mostly generic face— round, white— I fit in fine.

A half hour should be enough to throw off any tails. I sink further into the cushioned seat, set a thirty minute silent timer on my pad, and close my eyes.

My client's name is Mikael Anderrsen. He's a gang leader, as close as I can tell, and he owns a club in the quiet city.

Fontus spans almost the entire planet, and the quiet city is on a part of Janus' curvature that almost never sees the light of the sun. It's full of clubs, bars, and less savory places I tend to avoid. I hooked up with a girl once, a year or two ago, in the back room of one of the restaurants back here. I think she was the owner's daughter, or something similar. Her hair was blonde and she had dark makeup smeared around her eyes.

It was fine.

I didn't think of her afterwords. I never even got her name.

Mikael's club is called BLACKOUT. I've only been here once a few hours ago, and it strikes me quite plainly as the type of place I'd like to never return to once this job is over. The bar is sticky and the music is too loud. The bartender is wearing a low cut shirt and has her hair pulled back in two long pigtails, and her eyelashes are longer than any natural lashes could possibly be. She looks good, but it's the intention behind the look that makes me wince. It's a caricature of youth, a warped and blurred image of a young girl serving alcohol to men with wandering hands and lingering gazes.

I make eye contact with her when I enter and she jerks her head towards the door behind the bar. I remember the route through the club's complex backrooms from the last time I was here and quickly find my way back to the door simply labelled OFFICE.

The door isn't locked, so I don't bother knocking. Mikael

seems surprised to see me, with his eyebrows raising high into his forehead, but he lifts his fingers from his keyboard, crosses his arms, and smiles at me. He looks like a shark who smells blood. I keep my chin high and pull my bounty out of my pocket, tossing it over to him.

The datastick skitters across the table, plastic rattling against metal.

"Your information," I say as he looks down at the device between us.

"That was fast," he remarks and leans back in his seat, his arms crossed over his chest. "I heard you were good, but this is impressive. You ever consider going on retainer?"

"I work for myself," I answer shortly and hold out my hand. "My pay?"

The man's lips twist in a disappointed grimace for a split second before spreading wide in a fake smile. "Of course, Junker." He lifts a pad from the desk beside him and taps a few times before swiping towards me. My watch dings, alerting me to the credits transfer, and I glance at the notification to verify the amount.

"That's more than you said it would be."

"For... Efficiency," he says and smiles wider. "I'll keep you in mind for future work, junker."

"I won't accept," I remind him, turn on my heel, and leave. Two guards standing silently by the door let me go without objection, and I let out a breath as the door swings shut behind me. My shoulders relax and I notice a dull pain in my knee—My flesh knee, not the prosthetic hinge on my left side. The twinge reminds me that I ran out of painkillers on the ship, and I let out another, deeper sigh.

A couple dozen people are dancing between me and the door when I leave the club. The bartender waggles her fingers at me, but I give her a curt head shake and head for the door. I'm shorter than the majority of the people here— barely five and a half feet— and it makes it easy to twist around writhing bodies and duck under swinging elbows towards the exit.

I pivot on my heel just outside the door, turning right down an alleyway where I know a small convenience store is. This part of Janus is dark and maze-like, every cubic foot from the concrete ground to hundreds of feet in the air owned by a different person. I did a job for the shop's owner once, a while ago, and he often gives me discounts on purchases when I'm in the area.

"Hey," a gruff voice says, much too close to my neck, and a fist slams into the small of my back. I fall forward— right onto that same goddamn knee— and before I can react, the cold metal of a gun barrel presses into the back of my neck, bowing my head towards the ground. "Junker."

I spread my fingers wide, each palm braced against the cooling concrete. "Mikael sent you after me," I say, hoping, praying that it's true. Anything else this deep in Fontus spells much worse trouble than a club owner unhappy with my work, or my attitude.

It wouldn't be the first time an employer has found me wanting.

"The boss isn't pleased you rejected his job offer, *girl*," the man spits, and that's it.

I twist in his grip, grabbing the barrel of the gun and pushing it away from my throat right as the muzzle flashes and a deafening shot rings out beside my left ear. They both wince at the noise but I don't hesitate, twisting the pistol in my grip. The other man struggles to get his holster opened, and in the time it takes him to get his hand on his own gun, I train the barrel of my stolen one on his heart.

"Drop it," I hiss, and he hesitates, flicking his gaze between me and his partner, still kneeling with his hand covering one of his ears.

"You wouldn't shoot me," he responds, but he doesn't sound sure. I feel my lips turn up in a smile and I shift my finger onto the trigger.

"Wanna test that?"

The men make eye contact, and the bulkier one on the ground gives the other a minute shake of his head. The taller one holsters his gun and raises his hands. "Fine."

"Tell your boss he'll live a lot longer if he doesn't pull stunts like this." I eject the clip from the gun and tuck it in my pocket, then throw the empty weapon across the ground towards the men. With both their eyes on me, I grab the other gun off the ground and do the same. "Don't follow me, or I'll kill you," I say finally and part my jacket, revealing my own holstered weapon strapped to the side of my chest. The men's eyes flick from me to the gun, and then the bigger one nods.

With that, I make my way swiftly into the alley, the thudding adrenaline finally making itself known in my chest. My pulse beats in my eardrums and my fingertips flutter at my side, racing along an imaginary keyboard.

"Fuck," I hiss and curl my hand into a fist, pressing it hard into my sternum. My other hand flings through the air, inertia making the ends feel heavy. I keep moving, quicker now, desperate to get away from Mikael's club and anywhere his men could touch me, anywhere anyone hisses *girl* at me like it's something I've ever responded to.

The sound in my functioning right ear is muffled and faint and I jam my finger into it, yanking out the small earplugs I pressed in when I landed on Janus the day before. It doesn't help much. I swear again, quieter, and rub just underneath the shell of my ear as I hurry down the alley. There's a scar there, the tail end of a jagged one that curls off my jaw and darts back to end at the base of my skull. I trace my fingers over the raised skin and wince again.

I turn the last corner and see the convenience store's neon sign casting a faint glow on an old, old brick building across the street. There's someone standing outside smoking and I walk past them without a word.

"Junker!" a voice calls as soon as I enter.

"Luka." It comes out a pained moan.

Luka, a Black guy with long blonde locs that end around his hips when they're not tied up in a knot on top of his head, rushes out from behind the counter. "What happened to you? Jesus, come back here." He takes my arm and I instinctively jerk away, stepping back onto my bad leg and almost toppling over. This time, when he offers me support, I exhale and lean on his shoulder.

He leads me back around the counter and into a small back room, the walls lined with shelves and boxes of merchandise. He pulls on one of the shelves and an entire segment of the wall swings out with the metal wire, exposing another, smaller room with a workbench, a ratty old blue couch, and a dozen more boxes. Some are overflowing with merchandise, and even from here I can see a few things I know are worth more than nothing.

Luka's family owns the store, but Luka himself is a fence. I've sold to him more than once when I find things on junking jobs that aren't as legal or sellable on the proper market. Metal scrap and computer parts make decent money at a recycler or bulk warehouse, but IPF codes, black boxes from long-crashed ships, and other miscellaneous goods are safer sold to a fence. Luka pays decently, which is why I come back, but I wouldn't call us friends.

He deposits me on the grungy couch.

"What the hell happened?" he asks as he pulls a big metal

tackle box out from under the workbench. It has a crude red cross painted on top and, when he opens it, I see bandages, pill bottles, and some other things crammed into the small container.

"Client tried to kill me and get his money back after the job was done," I spit out and rub at my ear again. "My knee is busted and a gunshot went off right next to my fucking head."

Luke hisses in sympathy and turns the box around to face me. "Here. Use what you need. I'll step out, knock if you need me," he says and pushes the box along the floor until it stops beside me. Something twists in my chest, sending warm, queasy nausea through my throat and stomach.

"Thanks," I say quietly. "I'll pay you for your troubles."

He waves his hand and before he even says a word, I shake my head.

"I don't like owing people."

Luka hesitates, nods, and leaves the room. I hear him slide the shelf back into place, shutting the hidden door behind him, and I breathe a sigh of relief.

All at once, every pain comes rushing back in a goddamn onslaught. My knee throbs, sharp pain shooting through the joint and into the worn cartilage protecting my kneecap. My ear feels like it's stuffed with thick gobs of wax, sound echoing in a faint, vague way, like watching a show two floors down. My eyes prickle and I hiss out a curse.

The medkit isn't huge, but it has a fabric wrap that I can use for my knee. I unbutton my pants and shove them down to my calves, my thick boots keeping them from sliding any further. Under my kneecap, around the back, above my kneecap, around— It's a pattern I'm intimately familiar with. It's wrapped and ready within a minute, and I yank my pants back up.

There's nothing I can do about my ear for now, so I shut the kit and stand.

The door opens easier from the inside than it does the outside. I lean my body weight against it and it swings open without an issue.

"Luka," I call and move back into the shop proper. I can walk without limping if I push it— I'd use a cane, or another assistant, but in this part of the city, standing out makes you a target. If they look at my cane, then they could see my eye, or my leg, and prosthetics are valuable on the black market. I have to get back to the Gemini with as much anonymity as possible.

"You're leaving, I know." He's sitting behind the counter again, his feet propped up on a metal safe. "You know you're allowed to take a day off, right? Have friends?"

"Can't afford to," I reply simply. "Here." I tap on my watch and transfer him ten credits for the help and the bandage. "Stay safe."

"You too, Junker," he murmurs, and I leave without another word.

I almost make it back to the Gemini without issue.

Key word, *almost*.

The shipyard on Fontus— at least, the one I use most often — is wedged onto a wide, flat area between the under city and the grey city. It's a significant walk from BLACKOUT, and even further from Luka's shop. I shelled over enough credits to make it over halfway there on public transit, riding on the Fontus shuttles that barely make it down to the under city in the first place.

The shuttles on Fontus are the fastest way to get around, even if you own your own vehicle. They ride along a track situated in the center of the streets, and the shuttles themselves are raised twenty-odd feet in the air. They're wide and round, a flat disc capable of carrying fifty bodies a piece riding above the streets below. They block out the meager lighting that manages to filter through the stories and stories of city above, but they move quick enough that even the clouds blot out the light for longer.

I find a seat by the window and ride it until it stops. Normally, they stop for exactly as it takes for each rider to hop on board, but the vehicle stays stagnant.

"Hello?" a man calls, his voice thick with irritancy, "Why're we stopped?"

"There's something blocking the track," another guy calls, peering out the front of the shuttle. "It's a... Car, I think. Flipped."

"That's an IPF truck."

"I heard rumors of a riot—"

"How'd they flip an IPF truck—"

"Fucking insurgents—"

The door to the shuttle slides open and a quiet ding plays over the speaker system, drawing the vehicle silent.

"The N line is experiencing a temporary delay. We estimate to begin moving again in one hour. You are welcome to depart now. Have a nice day, and thank you for choosing Fontus Lightrail."

Complaints fill the air within seconds, and I ignore them all in favor of heading for the exit. Another few people are heading that way too, and I pull my hood up to hide my face as I wait for my turn.

Outside of the raised safety of the shuttle, the streets of Fontus are in uproar.

People are sprinting across the streets, traffic is stopped not just for the shuttles but for all vehicles, and, now that I have a clear view of the rail further down the track, I can see that not only is there a flipped Intergalactic Police Force truck halting progress, it's also on fire.

Someone screams and another person bumps into my arm, muttering something under their breath as they hurry down into the crowd. Distant voices echo through gritty loudspeakers and a thousand-voice cry calls out when the voice turns up. My gun is still strapped to my chest. I double check that my boots are tied tight, and once I'm sure, I move.

Hood up and eyes tracing the ground in front of me, sweeping back and forth looking for any obstruction, I head down the edge of the street. The storefronts along this normally well-traversed mainway are boarded shut, windows covered in thick layers of cardboard and tape to keep people from breaking through the glass. I've seen the videos on the Intergalactic News Network of this on other parts of Janus— The upper city and the heights, mostly. This is the densest area of the city I've seen them try to take over.

I turn a corner towards the shipyard, and the crowd swallows me almost at once.

There are hundreds of them. Many of them have signs, others with paint still wet on t-shirts and faces. Many have dyed hair, piercings— I see a man nearby, shirtless, the scars beneath each pec identical to my own. I pull my jacket tighter around my shoulders again.

"They can't just pretend we don't exist," a voice cries over the speakers. As I weave through the densely packed bodies around me, I can see the object of the crowd's focus, perched on top of a shipping truck. "We have always existed. We have always found ways to exist, even when those in power do everything they can to destroy us."

Juno Marcus.

Famous influencer, vocal member of the anti-Marwood

campaign, and face of the violent rebellion that has been sweeping through Janus for weeks. Her face is square, her jaw cutting sharp between her chin and ears. Her hair is wavy and dyed emerald green, coming to rest right above her shoulders. She's wearing thick boots— Saints, I note; you rarely see a pair these days with the price as it is— and torn leggings with a short skirt and a tank top. A lot of her skin is exposed, and I see a dozen-odd colorful tattoos across her shoulders, collarbones, and chest.

I look away from her as she raises a fist into the air, riling the crowd up further. It's all but suicide. As soon as she's caught — either by the IPF, or turned in by someone like me looking to make a few credits— she's dead. With her adam's apple and wide shoulders, the dark lipstick and crisp black eyeliner she hides behind doesn't keep her safe.

Not that she seems especially interested in hiding.

If she cared for her own safety, she wouldn't be standing on a stolen IPF vehicle as sirens grow closer and closer by the moment. To do this? She's either passionate to the point of recklessness, or really goddamn stupid.

The crowd gets rowdier by the minute. This close to where Juno is making her stand, her words are so loud through the dozens of speakers nearby that I don't bother to try to make out what she's saying anymore. It's reduced to a violen din, a deafening murmur in the back of my head, all noise smoothing into one loud roar pressing at my eardrums.

It gets quieter when I duck into a side alley, and quieter still when I leave that alley for a side street that goes straight to the shipyard. There are less IPF officers at the gate now than there were when I landed, and even the ones here seem agitated.

"ID," the officer asks and shoves his hand out. I offer my ID — The real one, not any of the half-dozen fakes I have hidden in the lining of my jacket and saved on my pad— and he looks between it and me a few times before handing it back and jerking his thumb over his shoulder. "Go."

I got a bad spot this time. I'm in yard H, nearly a half mile of walking from the entrance to where my ship is parked. I keep my eyes down the whole time, jacket pulled tight around my body to conceal as much as possible. When I finally see the Gemini in the distance, I relax a minuscule amount.

The Gemini is a two-sleeper Voyager class ship. I've had it for as long as I've been flying solo, and it has just enough room for my meager possessions and the junk I gather on jobs. The entrance is a round hatch in the very bottom of the ship, raised six feet above the ground by the landing gear. I pull down the ladder and open the hatch with my key fob, climbing up without a second thought. The smooth metal of the rungs is physical calm against my palms.

"Pollux, I'm home," I call as soon as the hatch shuts behind me. Pollux doesn't answer, probably because he is a goldfish, but I touch the plexiglass of his tank and watch him do a few happy wiggles. "Yeah, I know. I said it would be quick. Sorry bud." I grab his food shaker from the cabinet above him and unscrew the small hole in the top of the tank. The flakes fall slowly, so light they barely move at all, and as water soaks them through, they sink into the water. Pollux eats most of them before they hit the bottom of the tank, and a small smile pulls at my lips.

I take off my jacket then and toss it on my bunk.

It's really *the* bunk, now. I tore out the one above it a few months back to add more storage. It's not like anyone but me ever sleeps on the ship anyways.

"Castor." The voice is tinny and quiet and it says my name in a familiar way nobody else knows how to.

"Verita," I reply. Verita is the ship's AI— An old model, not the Bellona, or 'Bella', that the newest, state of the art ships use.

"Would you like to update your resume and open for jobs?"

I sigh and rub a hand over my eyes. My knee throbs again. I almost forgot that it hurt. "Yeah, go ahead. Auto-accept anything over a thousand."

"Updating."

I move from the small living quarters into the cockpit and sink into the pilot's chair. It's old leather— real leather, not the sticky plastic mimicry they use now— and it's worn through in a few places with age. My fingers go automatically to a small spot on the armrest where I've worn the fabric thin.

The cockpit is small. I can't even kick my feet out from the pilot's chair without hitting the dashboard. All the controls are just as I like them, and the Janus shipyard visible outside through the quarter-sphere windshield is quite familiar by now, with all the jobs I've done on this rotten planet.

"Job accepted."

I spin the chair around.

"What?"

"A job offer came through above the auto-accept threshold. I accepted it."

I splutter. "Yes, thank you Verita, I couldn't have figured that out. What's the job? Why— Who's it for?"

Jobs never come through this fast. It takes hours to get something for five hundred credits, let alone over a thousand. My auto-accept setting is a precaution, a safety net so I can sleep through the night without missing a decent offer. It's only procced once before and the offer was for 1,001.

"Verified anonymous user."

"Throw it up." The screen in the wall of the ship beside Pollux's tank lights up with a job posting.

CARGO TRANSPORT - JANUS TO ADRESTIA

20,000 CREDIT PAYOUT, HALF UP FRONT & HALF UPON DELIVERY

That's it. That's the whole message.

There are coordinates attached, and I feed them into Verita's nav system. The meeting point is in Fontus, in the grey city. The specific ping is in a cheap hotel lobby. Good. I fit in much better there with my dingy clothes, shaved head, and scarred face than I ever could in any of the towering metallic spires that cover each of the planet's poles.

"Castor," Verita says. "The employer code attached to this job has never posted on the job board before, but they are verified. I cannot trace the IP."

I squint at the job again.

Twenty thousand credits.

"Christ," I swear and look at Pollux. He looks back, his bulbous eyes darting on either side of his head. "I can't say no, Pol."

Twenty thousand credits could replace the grinding joint in my prosthetic. Twenty thousand credits could upgrade the Gemini's engine, get true light speed going—

"Fuck," I hiss. "Verita, send a message back. Ask when we're meeting." I stand from the chair and kick one of my feet up onto the edge of my bunk. I untie my shoes and kick them off. There's just enough room under my bunk to wedge the toes of my boots there, right underneath my pillow, and I do so.

"Response recieved."

"Read it."

"As soon as you can."

"Fuck," I repeat and yank my boots back out of their spot. "Alright." I tie my boots, throw my jacket back on, and look at my fish. "Let's go make twenty thousand credits."

I have to pay another day's docking fees when I pass back through the checkpoint. There are more guards here than before and they check my ID again on the way in. This time, they make me push my hood down. I stare straight at them, knowing that my multicolored gaze that's reflected in the plastic card is often enough for them to okay me, and they do.

The city is on fire. Traffic is at a standstill. There are more IPF officers than civilians, though the further I get from the shipyard, the less true that becomes. The hotel is close enough to walk to— Thankfully, because all of the city's shuttles are still at a stand still. I know this part of Janus well, but I still turn on the Verita nav system in my eye and have her lead me down side streets to the hotel. Every time the chanting gets louder, I turn away. It's loud and the air is thick with something— Smoke, probably, knowing the amount of burning cars tucked down every alleyway.

Rhythmic chanting echoes through the streets, a beating heart of passion in a city that bleeds apathy. Those who live on this hemisphere are like me: poor. We can't afford to feel that strongly about something that'll never change. Living paycheck to paycheck— even worse when paychecks are as irregular as they are in the gig economy.

At least the hotel is in a part of town where everyone looks like me, give or take. Gritty, tired men and women, the only differentiating feature between me and them my flat chest. With my oversized jacket pulled around me, I become shapeless. I'm nobody. People look right past me, not wanting to linger too long on an undesirable, just the same way they glaze past the human-shaped lumps of fabric curled in every corner between buildings despite the floors and floors of empty housing in Fontus.

The sign out front of the hotel is smeared with jagged rust that cuts through the name of the place: THE STRATO HOTEL. The O in STRATO is bisected with a crooked slice, turning it into a cat's eye with a lightning bolt pupil. I check my watch one last time and head inside.

The most common method for employers to show themselves to their mercenaries, smugglers, or junkers is sending a ping. We send one first, and then they send one back with a distinguishing feature, more specific location, or another way to connect. It's harder when the job is illegal.

Considering I'm currently being hired for an extremely vaguely worded, highly lucrative smuggling job means it'll probably be quite subtle. I enter the hotel lobby and stick to the shadows, leaning against the wall near the door. Someone passes me with an unlit cigarette clutched in their fingers and I can't help but stare. I haven't seen an analog cig in years; almost everyone in the galaxy have switched to e-cigs by now. They're cheaper, less regulated, and get you a better high anyways.

I send a ping as soon as I'm pretty sure nobody is watching me. Nothing happens immediately, so I shove my hands in my pockets and start walking through the lobby towards a small, old-fashioned coffee bar in the corner. The lobby itself is cramped and dingy. There's one ratty old couch and a cheap LED screen facing the check-in desk. It's playing the news and I let my gaze slide right past it. There's one man sitting on the floor with his back against the wall, but he looks unhoused, and he doesn't even open his eyes when I walk past.

"Checking in?" the single employee asks and looks me over. "Junker."

"Passing through," I respond, leaving no room for questions, and take a paper cup from the sleeve of them. There isn't cream or sugar, but I fill the cup and pop on a lid regardless. It won't be tasty, but it'll keep me up. It's hot and smells like caffeine, and that does more than enough.

I don't sit, choosing instead to lean against the wall in a darker corner, and let my eyes fall to half-lidded. My watch will wake me up if I get an alert from my client.

All I can do now is wait.

2

DISDAIN FOR HUMAN RIGHTS

After ten minutes of nothing, I decide to give it another ten before calling it quits and weaving my way back to the Gemini.

Of course 20,000 credits was too good to be true. Nobody has that kind of money. Not anymore. I lower my head, using the edge of my hood to block out the dim lights filling the room.

The bell above the hotel entrance dings just as my watch vibrates against my wrist. A man enters breathing heavily through his nose. Theres a smaller figure behind him, a girl probably about my age. Her hair is tucked into a thick beanie despite the heat and she's wearing a bomber jacket that billows around her arms, ending in elastic cuffs at the wrists. Almost every inch of it is covered in patches and scraggly, homemade embroidery, and she's wearing denim jeans with tears at the knee. Even the idea of the fabric makes my legs itch.

Her boots are brand new Saints, still shiny with factory polish, and they make my own military surplus boots look grimy and bulky in comparison. Her dark eyes are rimmed with smudged black liner that wings out towards her ears, which each have multiple golden rings through them. The lower half of her face is covered in a black fabric mask, casting the rest into shadow.

Something about her rings familiar, but the man steps towards me, and I don't have time to think much more into it. He has short, salt and pepper hair cropped close to the skull with the choppy top falling forward. His eyebrows are well-groomed and most of his face is also covered with a fabric mask, but I can see the edges of a mustache and beard peering out the edges. My hand twitches, bouncing a familiar rhythm against my thigh.

“Q?” he asks, referring to the only hint to my identity I offer on the job board. I nod and he jerks his head towards another door in the back of the lobby. It has a push bar labelled EMERGENCY EXIT, but no alarm blares when he presses it open. I run the pad of my thumb over the edge of my Equinox knife folded in my pocket. The blade is short, but it'll no doubt stop someone long enough for me to run.

The duo take a sharp turn and heads down the side alley until the three of us end up nestled against scrappy brick that line the short walls between the hotel and some club labelled with flickering, spent neon. There are a half-dozen trash cans between us awaiting the compactor truck and I can smell them even from ten feet away. I release my grip on the knife in my pocket just long enough to wipe the sweat off my palm.

"Where's the cargo?" I ask and tilt my head to the side. The man glances at the girl and then lifts his wrist, sending something over the secure communications line to my own.

"All the information is in the file I just sent you," he says. His voice is quiet and rumbling, thick and rough with age. I look between him and the girl and then down at my watch. It takes a second to unencrypt the file, but as soon as I skim it—

"No," I say at once.

"Listen to me—"

"No." I shake my head and turn away. My hand falls from my pocket, knife forgotten, and I start to leave the alleyway. A hand closes around my wrist.

"I need you," the girl hisses, and there's that goddamn voice. The same voice from the riots, the same voice screaming through the tinny megaphone in front of hundreds of similarly furious young adults with shocks of blue hair, rings in their lips, and a harsh set to their brow. It's the same voice that whips the militant police that run this goddamn galaxy into a red-hot fury, beating plexiglass riot shields with metal batons until there's a queer face in proximity they can pummel instead.

It's the same voice I heard just hours ago, the same voice I called suicidal and knew I could never afford to become.

"Juno Marcus," I hiss, "Get someone else. I don't want to be a part of your war."

"You already are," she snarls and looks pointedly down at my chest. I feel my skin flush hot with adrenaline and her dark gaze, almost black in the low light. I feel naked, exposed.

"We need her off planet now, Junker. She isn't safe here," the man says quietly. He tugs on Juno's arm and pulls her back closer to him, protective. "Please. I'll pay half up front and reimburse you for gas. She needs to get off Janus *tonight* and I can't get her where she needs to go."

I meet his eyes, and then Juno's again. They're colored with that familiar fury skimming across the surface, threatening to pull me down with her the second I get too close. I shake my head and pull away.

"I won't." I turn away from the girl, from a 20,000 credit suicide mission, and I look up where the nearest bar is.

I hide away in the back.

The bar itself stretches across one side of the dark room and then cocks to the side, leaving a little tail with one lone barstool pressed up under the sticky surface. With my hood up and face low, nobody will even notice I'm here.

I lift a hand to the bartender and order a vodka cranberry. I've never had an actual cranberry before, but I was always fond of the ridged jelly in a can that mom used to buy at near the end of the year. The juice works well as a vessel to get liquor into my system, at least. I know they're not grown on Janus—almost nothing is. Most food is imported.

The bartender slides my drink over and I tap my watch against the pad in the table to pay. I swallow back the instinctual nausea that bubbles up from spending credits unnecessarily, but when I remember Juno and the danger I had been in just minutes before, I down the drink anyways. I hold up the glass when I'm finished.

My second drink is stronger than my first. I've never been to this bar before, but the bartender seems to understand the types that do. Desperate, depressed, thirsty.

The spot I picked affords me a nice view, a good people-watching position, and I take full advantage of it. There are a couple of crowded tables and the length of the bar itself is almost full of people, the only open stool the one directly beside me. On the far end there's a group of three, sitting and laughing: a pretty blonde woman, a guy with a shaggy, light brown haircut, and a man with dark reddish-brown hair wearing sunglasses. Behind them is a table full of women wearing crowns and sashes cheering on their friend, who is currently chugging a margarita the size of her head. I wrinkle my nose— I'm not a tequila person.

There's a pool table closer to me and three men are

currently betting on which of them will sink the nine ball. One of them has his jacket tossed over the back of a chair and he rustles in the pockets to pull out his pad. He frowns as he replies to a message.

The bartender lines up a couple of shots for a woman with shoulder-length black hair. She knocks one back and then takes the tray with the rest to a table in the far corner crowded with happy twenty-somethings.

Someone else walks in wearing a hoodie and a jacket, their hood pulled up to conceal their face the same as mine. I ignore them, or at least, I try. It's harder when they take the very last available stool at the bar, settling in right beside me. I lower my chin until my hood shrouds my face in shadow and take another slow sip of my second drink.

"Junker," they say in a quiet voice. I tilt my head a few degrees, just enough to look back. They tilt their face up just enough for me to see a curl of green hair falling out of a beanie and a golden ring stabbed through their right nostril, mask abandoned.

I stand up. "No," I mutter and down the rest of my drink in one sour swallow. "I'm leaving."

She catches my wrist the same way she did in the alley. Her fingertips are smooth and her nails are polished black and unchipped; she's never done a day of hard work in her life.

"Hear me out, at least," she pleads. "I'll buy you another drink. Please." I look at my glass, empty now save for the melting ice remaining in the bottom, and I scowl. I slowly slide back onto my barstool and tilt my glass at the bartender.

When she comes back by, Juno orders her own drink, a short glass with two fingers of amber liquid. I've never been able to stomach straight whiskey, but I'm not sure she can either. Her face twitches at even the first sip.

"If I don't get off this planet tonight, I will be killed or imprisoned," she says quietly. I take another sip.

"That's not my problem, princess."

Juno purses her lips and looks at the huge TV hung up behind the bar. "Look." I raise my head and look. INN is playing, this time with a thick red bar bisecting the screen proclaiming this story as breaking news.

"*—Riot on Janus has claimed three lives, one of which was a dedicated IPF officers trying to protect the people of the city from these violent insurgents*," the anchor says. They show three faces: A white man with short hair a little bit longer than mine and gaunt cheeks; a young woman with red hair smiling in a social media profile picture; and a boy no older than fifteen with pink hair and thick-rimmed glasses. "*Sources here at INN believe that this riot was started by influencer Juno Marcus, also known as* █████ *Marcus, in an attempt to spread further lies about Walter Marwood's 2292 campaign.*"

Juno pales at the use of her deadname. Even I wince. She's a fool, but not even the most idiotic person deserves for the intergalactic news to spout lies about them using their deadname.

"I'll die," she repeats. "If not by the IPF, by Marwood's men. If not by them, by the people the INN and Marwood are radicalizing with their words. I have people on my side— We have information, Junker. Information that could change things."

"Do what?" I hiss, "He's got the highest ratings of any presidential candidate in decades."

"Discredit him," she says and the expression in her eyes is painfully earnest, embarrassingly genuine. "Show the people of the galaxy what he and his people are doing. Do everything in our power to make him lose the election and then keep on his ass until he disappears back to whatever hell he came from. Show them that he's killing people, ripping children away from their family. Expose all the atrocities his party commit every day."

I laugh. I can't help it. It's a pathetic fantasy, one that could never come to fruition. A couple hundred gay twenty year olds do not a revolution make, especially not against 53% and counting of the galaxy.

"Don't you dare laugh at me," she snaps. "I have thousands of people behind me that all want the same thing, and we're going to get it. This revolution has been over a century coming and a junker like you won't make any goddamn difference."

"Then why do you need me so badly?" I retort and cock my head to the side. I'm sure my smile is condescending, teasing, but I don't adjust it. "If I'm really so irrelevant, if I'm really just getting in your way, why are you so desperate for my help?"

"Because the chances that I could find a trans pilot—"

I cut her off. "Don't call me that."

"But you—"

"You don't know anything about me."

"Tell me, then."

I'm silent. There's an earnestness in her eyes, an eager glint that makes me feel that if this godforsaken galaxy had any chance to change, she could be the one to do it.

"The galaxy is too set in its ways for any one girl to make any tangible difference," I say quietly.

"I don't care if you believe in me. I don't care what you do after I'm off your ship. I just need to get off this planet," she replies. "We will pay you. We're good for the money. I doubt you've seen more than five hundred credits in one place before in your life."

I only scowl in response.

"Ten thousand up front. Four weeks of your time."

"And if I get arrested or shot for helping an enemy of the

state? If I get taken to prison and discovered to be—" I cut myself off and gesture vaguely.

"You won't," she says and yanks the linings of both of her jacket pockets inside out. "I'm off the grid."

"Nobody's off the grid. Not anymore."

"I am. As of an hour or two ago, Juno Marcus is impossible to find. I've disconnected from my online presence. I don't have a pad, or a watch. I'm untraceable and nobody will see us together or ever know I'm on your ship. I'll stay aboard on refuel stations, I just need to get to Adrestia."

I look at her. There's a harsh pit in my stomach. I trace 20,000 and all four of its zeroes into the bar below my fingertips. I could go days without stopping with that kind of money. I could upgrade my ship. I could—

If I don't... She could die.

I don't care about Juno's life, not really. It isn't worth pretending I do. Her death wouldn't affect me. Millions of people die every day. It wouldn't change anything beyond maybe making her a martyr for the doomed movement itself, giving them a surge of momentum. Marwood would celebrate and the gun-toting members of the so-called freedom movement would see it as a win. There would be riots. More people would die.

I would continue on with my life, collecting junk and doing odd jobs. I wouldn't make a difference.

I groan and tug the straw out of my final drink, setting it dripping on the already-grimy bar top. I knock back the last inch or so left in my glass and wince when an ice cube brushes the tip of my nose. I close my eyes and let the alcohol sit low in my stomach.

Later, I'll blame the drinks.

"Fine," I bite out. "I'll take the job."

The girl's face curls in a fierce smile. "You won't regret it."

We meet with her handler again and he transfers me ten thousand credits. I squint at my watch. It feels like a dream, but the number is legit.

"I can send more for fuel," he offers, and I accept. He does so without hesitation, another two hundred credits. He turns back to Juno then and pulls her into a tight hug. I swear I see his eyes glistening in the darkness, tears reflecting the neon from the shady hotel signs. I turn away and glance in the corners and alleys around us. There is still a surprising amount of people out and about, what with the news advising everyone to stay inside, and everyone still at the riot are blocks away.

I wait as the duo exchange quiet words and goodbyes before turning back.

"Juno Marcus," the girl says and holds her hand out. I don't take it.

"I'm just your pilot. We aren't friends." I turn on my heel and start walking down an alley towards the shipyard. "I'm docked at the main yard, dock E." There's silence behind me for a few steps and then I hear the heavy footfalls of her shiny boots rushing to catch up.

"We don't have to be enemies, you know," she says. "We have more in common than we do that divides us." I don't spare her any acknowledgement. I can't start planning our route to Adrestia— which is clear across the goddamn galaxy— until we're off planet, and we won't ever get off planet if we don't pick up the goddamn pace. I stick to the main streets and ignore Juno's solid presence at my side. It works pretty well for a while, and she stays quiet, but when the roads start getting smoother under our feet I know we're getting closer to where the riot was happening.

"Stay close," I mutter and tug on my hood. Juno nods.

"Is now a bad time to mention that I'm officially wanted dead or alive?"

I slow to a stop and look at her. "Excuse me?"

"We have access to their radios," she says and bites down on her lip, dark purple war paint pulled taut under pure white bone. "They'll kill me if they see me. They're blaming me for that IPF officer's death."

I grab her by the jacket and yank her into a side alley. I press her into the sheet-metal exterior of some kind of pawn shop and gnash my teeth in her face.

"You declined to tell me this *why*, exactly?" I hiss. She's shorter than me by a few inches and I leer over her, clutching her arm tight.

"You wouldn't take me if you knew," she retorts, and that's fucking true, but *hell*.

"You're right," I start, but then I hear the telltale jingle of bodies armed to the teeth moving our way. Fuck. "Police."

"We're mostly covered here," she says. I nod. She's right. There's a gutter that juts out just enough to hide us, but if they look any closer than not very close at all, they'll spot Juno in a heartbeat. I swear under my breath and look down at myself. I'm not recognizable, but she is. I quickly yank off my jacket and thrust it at her. She's smaller than me so it should cover her own brightly embroidered one pretty well. She shrugs it on. I feel naked, laid bare in just a long-sleeved, hooded shirt, but I'm not the one they're looking for.

I know at first glance I can pass for male if I have to. My hair is buzzed and my chest is flat— The only part of me that betrays my femininity are my hips, and even those are disguised well by my wide leg pants.

As long as they don't see my face, or hear my voice.

The compacted beam of a flashlight blares into the alley-way, sweeping over both of us. My hands fly up and I clutch at the knit beanie over Juno's hair, pulling myself even closer. They can't see my face, they can't see Juno's face.

If I pull back, they'll see us.

If we draw apart, we'll look like enemies.

"I'm sorry," I breathe, and then I press my knee between her legs and cup her cheek. Without waiting for a response besides the wide-eyed, quizzical look on her face, I lean in and press our mouths together. Juno stiffens on first touch but quickly realizes my intentions and kisses back, even groaning softly against my lips. I press my hips closer and kiss her harder, her lips parting against mine, and listen desperately to the voices of the police behind us.

The flashlight beam glares in my periphery, but then Juno presses her tongue against the seam of my lips, and my mind short-circuits.

I press back and shove one hand under her beanie, scratching at the brown roots of her hair with blunt fingernails. Her mouth tastes like whiskey and bubblegum and I kiss her far beyond an appropriate time for a distraction, but by the time I pull away, the flashlight glare is long since gone. The sirens fade into downtown and I pull my hand from her hair reluctantly.

"Sorry," I pant, my chest heaving. Her mouth is kiss-slick and her lipstick is smudged on one side. I bring a hand up to touch my own lips, feeling where the waxy makeup transferred onto my skin. I rub at it roughly with the back of my hand.

"Don't apologize," Juno murmurs, her hand still flat on my chest. Her eyes are half-lidded and her lips quirk up in a cheeky grin. "You can kiss me any time."

I sigh and wrap my fingers around her wrist, ignoring the way my heart is still trying to beat out of my chest. "Follow me, and quickly."

We make it to the shipyard without any issue. The crowd of people Juno had drawn before have dispersed by now, the couple dozen IPF officers holding the courtyard now surely the only reason they haven't reconvened.

I lead us around back alleys and through walkways and overpasses to avoid the majority of the remaining conflict. Cars burn on every street, debris and protest signs fueling every blaze we pass. Juno is oddly quiet for the rest of the time back to where the Gemini is parked.

By the time we're near enough to see the shipyard, the police presense has nearly tripled. Juno still has my jacket and she pulls the collar up to hide her neck, her hair tucked back into the beanie since we... Since we kissed.

As a distraction.

"Do you have a fake?" I ask quietly as we meld into the crowd gathered around the entrance gates, hundreds of people trying to get off planet all at the same time.

"No. I don't have anything," Juno replies, her mouth right beside my ear. I feel eyes on us, and I turn casually to look across the crowd around us.

There's a young woman with long red hair in two braids. She has green eyes, and they're focused right on Juno.

"Excuse me," I say and step over to her, gently leading Juno to stay behind me. "Is there any way to get through? I just have to get to my ship."

Her gaze flicks from me to the shadow behind me. "No. They're checking everyone for ID. Anyone that could've been at the riot, they're detaining." Her voice is lilted, accented in a bouncy sort of way. I don't know where on Earth the accent originated from despite knowing that Earth must be it's origin;

most accents have blurred together into one near-galactic accent that almost everyone you meet shares.

"Why?"

"That girl," she says and looks over my shoulder at Juno again. Despite her glance, I feel my shoulders relax. Anyone against Juno wouldn't call her a girl, plain and simple. "She's their priority."

"The one who led the riot?"

She eyes me warily. "Aye. I don't know much more."

"Thank you," I say and turn around, nudging back into Juno's space. "We need to get out of here."

Juno looks over my shoulder and then presses close, her cheek resting against my shoulder. My hood conceals her face and she wraps an arm around my waist. "Sorry," she breathes, "IPF behind you."

I try my best to look bored. With the sheer amount of advertising both printed on the walls and projected into the air around us, there's basically no way to ever be bored, but I glance at my watch and then casually wrap my arm around Juno's shoulders.

"No problem," I breathe back as I try to mirror the anxious waiting postures of those around us. I'm well practiced in mimicry, both from my brain not quite catching the subtle cues that social situations tend to throw at me, as well as from the decade of practice I have with blending in.

The group of IPF officers moves past, elbowing a few people into a more cohesive crowd. They look right past us, not even sparing a glance for the tired couple waiting to get off planet. It's a good cover.

I can smell their sweat and it takes everything I have not to wrinkle my nose in distaste. They're all men, all with batons in thigh holsters. They're all but a soothing presense next to the pistols and assault rifles strapped to their backs. I know they're not afraid to use them. Historically, despite the law prohibiting them from shooting bystanders, they're protected more often than not— Sometimes, they're even promoted.

"You're good at this," Juno murmurs and pulls back, her arm still around me.

"It's my job," I reply quietly. We move up a little and I return to scanning the crowd, trying to find an opening.

"Do you transport fugitives often?"

"You're not technically a fugitive." She smiles and I swear I can still taste whiskey when I look at the dark lipstick smears on the corner of her mouth.

"Maybe. The question still stands."

I take a deep breath and shift my stance. She's still touching me and I can't find it in me to ask her to stop, especially since her moving would reveal my underarm holster. It's... Cover.

"No. Most of my jobs are simple stuff. Requests for ship parts, fuel cells... Bounty hunting, sometimes. Not often though. Too many moving parts."

"I know bounties and escorts pay better than junking," she replies.

"They do. I just prefer to work alone. I'm a junker by trade, I only take jobs like this when they seem especially worth my time."

Juno smirks. "I'm worth your time?"

"Shut up."

She nods, though the smile doesn't leave her face. "Fair enough." She's quiet for a few moments, and then asks, "You're really not going to tell me your name?"

"I'm a junker first and foremost. You don't need to know my name."

"Even now that I've had my tongue in your mouth?"

I feel my face flush red hot, my body betraying me. She grins back, her lipstick slick and alluring despite the danger that lurks in every sharp angle of her face. I pull my eyes away and shake my head.

"It's not important. What you need to know is this. I have a five star rating on the job board. I get my work done, and I do it well. My ship is big enough for two, but I've been told that I snore. I will transport you wherever it is you need to go, but I'm just doing it for the money. I don't believe in your cause and I don't intend to become your friend. Do you understand?"

She cocks her head to one side and squints at me. "I don't buy it. I think you feel a whole lot more than you let on."

"You met me less than an hour ago."

"Still," Juno insists, "I can tell there's a heart in there, deep down. You would've walked away without the money if you truly didn't want to get involved."

"If I truly didn't care, I'd take the money and dump you on Doda."

She laughs at that, a real, genuine laugh. It startles me just enough that I don't move with the crowd as it writhes around us. Her smile fades but doesn't go entirely, instead just a little subtle grin pulling at her cheeks. She takes a step closer and tugs me further towards the gates. "Why did you apologize for kissing me?"

"I didn't ask first."

She's quiet for a moment, and then, "I suppose that's a good reason."

I don't respond, and she doesn't ask any more questions.

We don't make it to the gate before another huge truckload of cops erupts into the crowd outside the shipyard. The lighting changes all at once, shifting from an ambient, all over lighting to a sharp green. I look up and see the cause: all the holo-advertisements have changed to one image.

Juno's face.

"Fuck," she hisses, and I can't help but agree.

"Don't move," I breathe, "I'll find us a route to the ship." I watch the crowd shift as everyone is swiftly affected by the presense of heavily armed police, the energy in the air going from antsy to scared in moments. A hand clutches at my side and I look back at Juno.

She's shaking.

I spread my fingers at her waist and squeeze. "It's okay," I say quietly, even if I don't believe it myself.

"You," a voice says from behind me. I turn around and see the woman from before with the braids and the accent and I pull Juno close at once.

"Can I help you?" I ask.

She glances around, and then holds a hand up in a gesture I don't recognize. Another figure comes out of the crowd, a much, much larger man with wide shoulders and a shaved head. My free hand shoots to my knife and I flip out the blade in my pocket.

"Back off," I hiss, trying to imbue any lasting confidence into the words.

She holds her hands up, palms facing me, and the other man draws closer. I run my thumb over the shoddy engraving on the hilt.

"We're on your side," she says quietly. "I was..." She swallows and starts again. "I'm a friend of Juno's." She gives me a firm look.

Juno tenses in my grip. She shifts and peers over my shoulder, seeing the two figures. "I recognize him," she breathes in my ear and jerks her chin at the man. "He was at the riot. He helped me get away afterwards."

"I'm Nova," the girl says, "This is Mars. We can get you to your ship. We— We know a way around." The way she hesitates gives me pause, but Juno looks at me so earnestly, almost pleading. I nod. It feels unnatural, trusting someone other than myself. The only person I've ever believed would save my skin was myself, and this goes against every instinct.

"I trust them," Juno murmurs. It takes me a moment to realize she's speaking to me.

"I don't," I respond on instinct. Juno snorts a laugh and looks over my shoulder.

"They're getting closer," she says. "We have to go if we're going to go. We don't have time for your loner bullshit." The woozy heat of embarrassment curls around the back of my neck. "If they can get us off planet, we need to trust them."

"This way," Nova says and starts moving. Juno catches my hand and tugs me along behind them. We weave through the crowd, darting back and forth in seemingly random patterns, always ending up heading in vaguely the same way. The crowd riles up and begins to scream just as we duck inside a guard station. I don't turn around, even when Juno glances back. I've seen enough evidence of what these men can do to a civilian body to last a lifetime.

Juno feels steady, though. I suppose it makes sense that she's seen horrible things happen to good people the same as I have.

"Put these on," Nova says and shoves a trunk full of thick plastic-casted armor our way. I frown.

"There's no way they would believe either of us," I gesture to me and Juno, "are IPF. We're tiny."

"I'm not much taller, and I've gotten away with it," Nova says with a grim set to her mouth. "It's what we have." I sigh and nod, handing pieces of armor to Juno as I separate out the two sets. The bulletproof vest sits heavy on my chest, an unwelcome pressure, and yet I feel protected. The industrial grade vests the IPF have are impenetrable— This thing could stop ten assault rifle bullets and I would barely feel a thing.

Investing in the technology that protects those in charge while slowly leaking more and more leniency to the holders of weapons of mass destruction is a favored hobby of the intergalactic cabinet, and it's never more clear than seeing how clean and expensive looking the IPF gear is up close.

We're both handed blue bandanas to tie around our faces and plexiglass riot masks to cover up even more. Juno tugs her beanie tighter over her forehead.

"Hang on," I murmur when she stills and reach over, tucking a small curl of dark green away under the knit fabric. Any glimpse of her signature color could betray our disguises in a heartbeat.

I yank on gloves and pick up a baton and a folding riot shield. Everything feels heavy. My body is weighted down by the sheer amount of material between me and them. It isn't the first time I've stolen armor or a uniform to get by unnoticed, but I've never had the figurehead of everyone trans and angry beside me before. It feels a lot riskier, and I tend not to take risks any less calculated than *very*.

"We'll split up," Nova is saying and points at me. "You come with me, and Juno will go with Mars. We'll—"

"No."

Nova grows silent and looks at me. Only her green eyes are visible through the layers of cover, and she squints.

"I won't leave her," I say and jerk my thumb at Juno. Mars nudges Nova's shoulder and signs something at her, gesturing between me and Juno. Nova hisses under her breath but sighs heavily at whatever Mars said to her.

"Fine. You and Juno go straight for your ship. We'll

distract," she amends and then gives me a heavy look. "If anything happens to her—"

I shoot her a look and she purses her lips, but reaches out her hand.

"Give me your pad, and I'll put in my number. Just in case."

We exchange numbers quickly and I tuck my pad back away.

"Go, then," she says and meets Juno's eyes one more time before taking Mars' elbow and heading off towards the crowd. I see a group of IPF officers between here and there making a wall, riot shields up and batons beating rhythmically against the plexiglass.

An order rings out and they begin to slowly move forward, a hundred of them pressing the undulating mass of desperate people just trying to get off planet into a condensed mass. Someone screams.

"Come on, Junker," Juno breathes in my ear and grabs my hand. We rush past the unknowing backs of the IPF officers and hurry down the mainway of the shipyard. It's empty—They haven't let anyone through the gates in almost an hour—and it's strange being in such a large city port when it's all but empty, only a few maintenance robots still rolling around near-silently from ship to ship.

The empty metal platforms are lined with ships upon ships of varying shapes and sizes. It reminds me of a picture I saw of a harbor on Old Earth, hundreds of boats owned by the wealthiest of them all lined up side by side covering the sea in a wave of glinted metal.

The Gemini is docked between a single-seater star cruiser and a family ship barely bigger than my two-sleeper. I find it in yard H, right where I left it.

A loud, industrial crash echoes from somewhere behind us.

I don't turn, instead pulling the keyfob from the inside pocket of my jacket, but Juno spins around.

"They rushed the pigs," she says, "The gate is down."

"We need to hurry," I hiss and unlock the ship with the push of a button. I pull the hatch open and yank down the folding ladder from inside. "Get on. We'll blend in with everyone else running, they won't know which ship you're on."

Juno climbs up without hesitation and immediately pulls down the rarely-used second seat attached to the wall just beside my bunk. I climb up as well and we both, as if in sync, throw down the face shields we had donned as disguises. The cockpit chair is big enough to fit me even with my bulky armor and I fling my body into it. The thick, plasticine armor is still pressing and prodding in ways I don't like, jutting into my ribcage and pulling up on the back of my shirt, but we don't have time for the luxury of comfort until we're out of the atmosphere.

The engine starts without me pressing a button and the ship shudders, a dense vibration shaking me to my bones—

No, that's not the engine.

That tinny, desperate trembling in every crevice of the Gemini is from the footfalls of hundreds of angry people running down the length of the metal shipyard.

I bite my tongue hard and disengage our landing gear, starting the engine with the press of a lit button.

"Hold on!" I pull back on the wheel and jerk it hard to the left, cutting the Gemini through the air above the cruiser parked at our side. Juno whoops and I feel my face split in a smile as well despite everything as we lift out of the port, my windshield full of dozens of other ships all taking off beside us.

We leave the atmosphere astride them all and within minutes we're in open space, falling into one of the regulated transport lanes alongside hundreds of other ships. The artificial gravity engages with a distinct *clunk* and my stomach drops back into its place in my torso.

"We lived, bitches," Juno calls from the back, "Take that! Fuck you!" I glance in the rearview mirror just in time to see her kick her discarded riot shield with one shiny boot. Janus disappears into the black of space out the side window and I let out a long breath.

We lived, yes, but this is only the beginning.

3

IDENTIFICATION OF ENEMIES AS A UNIFYING CAUSE

As soon as we're out of radio range for Janus, I set a course for the nearest refuel station and leave the cockpit. I strip my armor off, down to the same shirt and pants I put on to do a job for a man in a club what feels like days ago. Juno unbuckles herself as well but stays sitting, examining the inside of my ship.

It feels oddly exposing. The Gemini is everything to me, everything I've ever had and ever lived on. It's my home. Her gaze doesn't weigh with judgement and yet my skin prickles and I feel a distinct urge to hide everything.

"Go ahead and get that shit off," I say and jerk my head at her disguise. I walk over and yank up on the grate that conceals my storage area, a round room underneath the floor of the living space that I tend to use for junk, scrap, or bodies. "Toss it in here. It might be good to have later." She strips quickly, tossing vests, shields, batons, belts, and everything between over to me.

She also yanks off my jacket and then her own, revealing a thin black tank top she was wearing underneath. Her exposed skin is pale with a couple of moles dotting its surface. Along her collarbones are two dark tattoos, but she turns before I can make out the designs.

The ink doesn't stop there, though— Across her sharp shoulder blades and down both of her biceps are dozens of smaller tattoos, everything from bold, colored florals to black, thin-line symbols. I pick out a carefully done piece of two Venus symbols linked together, dainty violets surrounding them and covering the spot below her left shoulder in purple and pale yellow.

On the apex of the same shoulder are two fish, one orange and the other blue, swimming in a mesmerizing circle with a round, dark shape in the center: Pisces.

She flicks her collar-length green hair over one shoulder and looks back at me.

"Something wrong?"

I shake my head and look away. "No." I don't apologize for staring at her— With the way her hands rest on her hips, unashamed, I get the idea that she doesn't mind much.

I shovel all of our discarded gear into storage and put the grate back in place.

"Do you have anything to wear?" I ask her. Juno lifts an impossibly small duffel bag she's managed to hang on to through all of our running. "That can't be more than one change of clothes."

She shrugs. "I'm used to travelling light."

I know my face is twisted in a way people don't like, a crass frown that tends to be the default expression to inhabit my face. "When we stop at the refuel station, you should get yourself a few things. The Gemini can't hold much water," I say and gesture to the wall next to the door to the small restroom where the washing machine is built in.

"Where do you keep your clothes? This thing is tiny," she says and gestures around at the Gemini. I step around her and kneel to pull out the drawer underneath my bunk. Inside are folded pairs of identical underwear and socks, a dozen or so shirts of the same style as the one I'n wearing currently, and four folded pairs of pants.

Juno raises an eyebrow. "Don't branch out much, hm?"

I bristle. The words echo through my memory in my mother's voice. "I know what I like," I respond. My tone is short, I know it is, but I don't take it back. I've tried other shirts, other pants, other underwear. It all digs in or sits awkwardly or the fabric makes me itch. If I wear these shirts, these clothes, I don't feel them, it isn't a distraction, and I don't have to feel every inch of my own skin all day.

"I get it," Juno says. "I have one brand of boxer briefs that I like best, too." I know she doesn't get it, but nobody really does. I huff out my tense held breath and nod. I don't want to get impatient with Juno, not this early into our journey. It isn't her fault her brain isn't wired like mine is.

"Here," I say and scoot my stuff to the side of the drawer. It fits in half of the drawer easily, and it isn't like Juno has much. Also tucked in there are a couple little pieces of scrap I've collected— One etched with a leaping rabbit, another metal ring I twisted into a spiral— and a folded scarf. I take those and set them on the bunk, leaving plenty of open room. "You can put your things here." I point at the door on the opposite wall, between the washer and Pollux. "That's the bathroom."

"Who's this?" she gasps and rushes over to the wall I pointed at, peering into Pollux's tank. "Oh, hello little friend!"

"Pollux," I answer shortly. She left her bag on the ground next to the drawer and I stuff it into the drawer without looking inside before shutting it again. I sit on the bunk then and watch her watch Pollux. She put her black jacket back on so I can't see her tattoos, but I still look over the patches, buttons, and embroidered words trailing across the fabric. One shoulder says

'TRANS RIGHTS ARE HUMAN RIGHTS' in pastel pink and blue, and the other is covered in smaller patches. I read one that says 'THIS MACHINE KILLS FASCISTS' with a cartoony image of a gun, and another with a combined Venus and Mars symbol overlaid with 'DOWN WITH CIS'.

For a brief moment, I envy her passion. Her fearlessness.

Not all of us have the luxury to be as up front as her.

"How's he do in space?" she asks and drags a finger across the glass. I wince, knowing it'll leave an oily smudge, but ignore it for now.

"Fine."

"Can I feed him?"

"No."

"Why not?" She turns around now and puts her hands on her hips.

"He already ate today."

She wrinkles her nose but steps away from his tank at last to investigate the rest of the ship. She peers into the bathroom and then steps inside to set a small leather bag she pulled out of her backpack inside the medicine cabinet. She relocks it behind her and then looks around the rest, circling the small ship in just a few steps.

The Gemini has a simple layout: the main chamber is a twenty-ish square foot rectangle with the bunk built into one wall and the bathroom and utilities built into the other. In the front, there's the rounded cockpit, and the back mirrors it in shape but has a second story below for storage. The rear of the ship is mostly taken over by my meager hobbies, including a small workbench and a punching bag.

My bunk is simple. It has just enough headspace to not cause claustrophobia. There's a light in the low ceiling and a small shelf in the wall closest to the exterior of the ship, harboring my few prized possessions. It has a slight lip to keep anything falling, though the artificial gravity on the Gemini tends to keep us pretty still no matter what direction we're flying in. A small stuffed rabbit, an old knotted bracelet, and my e-reader are wedged in there.

"How far out are we?" she asks after she finishes her examination, ending up in the cockpit.

"Verita, how far is the refuel station?" I ask into the air.

Verita chirps back, "We are thirty minutes at sub-light travel from refuel station Redhawk."

"You still have Verita? I thought most ships ran on Bellona by now," Juno asks and trails a finger— The polish there is chipped at the tip, now— along the dashboard of the ship.

I feel my face twist into a defensive frown. "I like Verita."

Juno shrugs. "I don't care. Verita doesn't sell your data like Bellona does, at least. Basically everything ever said to a Bellona assistant is in a database owned by Zephyr. Verita is safer, it's not owned by a selfish megacorp," she remarks. "I wouldn't trust your ship if it ran on Bellona."

I don't really know what to say to that. "Good," I finally decide on, cringing at how dull and tight it comes out. I clench my right hand into a tight fist. I turn away from her and hold my hand to my chest, tapping a rhythm against my sternum. I collect my pad and pull out the small folding table beside Pollux's tank. I roll over the stool set into tracks in the floor, normally pushed underneath my workbench, and sit down, opening the nav app.

I put down a marker on refuel station Redhawk. If this is where we're going, and our end goal is... I zoom out and scroll past planets, moons, and systems until I find Adrestia on the very edge of the outer rim. I plug it in and have Verita auto plot a course there: three weeks worth of flying at near-light speed. I sigh and start dragging the line this way and that, grabbing a refuel station, inhabited planet, or a moon with somewhere to gas up every so often.

"What're you doing?" Juno asks and leans over my shoulder. She smells like vanilla and sweat.

"Plotting our course," I say tersely and drag on the line again. Some of the stops we'll have to make are less than ideal, but we'll get there.

"Can't we just..." she says, and then makes a motion with her hand, fingers held together in a mimicry of a ship engaging their FTL drive, "Zoom?"

"If my regular routine gets wildly disrupted, someone's bound to notice. If we do what I normally do and stop at a few refuel stations, take a few junking jobs, we shouldn't be noticed," I explain and drag the line out of refuel station Redhawk onto a moon where I know for a fact a Zephyr hauler crashed a few days ago. "If we get caught, we revert to the direct route, but for now, we're taking it slow and steady."

Juno nods slowly as she looks over the course I've plotted. "I've never done any junking."

"I never would've guessed," I say flatly and she laughs. The proximity of her mouth to my ear makes it feel loud and sudden and I jump.

"Sorry, sorry," she says, still grinning, and moves away to sit on my bunk. There's still a little bit of lipstick smeared on the point of her cupid's bow from our 'distraction' earlier. I feel a warmth in my gut and watch her tuck a strand of hair behind her ear. I notice for the first time that her earlobes are slightly gauged, a matte, black circle stretching the skin taut. It suits her. "I just didn't know you had it in you to be mean."

My frown deepens. "I'm not mean," I say.

"I think you could be," Juno retorts. Before I realize what she's doing, she pinches my cheek with two black-nailed fingers. "With a little bit of my influence, we'll have you insulting people in no time."

I roll my eyes and look back at the map, but my face tingles where she touched me.

"This is impressive," she says and gestures down at my work. "Have you been to all of these places before?"

I scroll down the route and point at a few places. "Not these, but most of the government-funded refuel stations have the same layout and shops. I'm not sending us anywhere something unexpected could happen, really. All the planets I know well."

"You're good at this," Juno says and meets my eyes. I flick my gaze away from hers at once, but I preen a little at the praise. My lips turn up in a little crooked smile— It feels wrong, smiling at someone half the galaxy wants dead, but something deep and contrarian in my brain wants to do it even more because of that.

"Thanks," I say softly, and then swallow. "I'll hop into the cockpit when I'm done with this, get us docked at Redhawk."

Juno nods and leaves my side, stepping into the small restroom.

I try not to notice the distinct feeling of loss when her warmth moves away.

Redhawk isn't too busy, thank stars. Docking is near-instantaneous and I send over the ten credit docking fee without hesitation. Juno borrows a jacket and a beanie to hide her hair and we both don fabric face masks when we disembark.

"What are we getting?"

"Clothes, for you," I say and hold out one finger. "Fuel." Two fingers. "Leads on junking jobs on our route."

"What for?"

"It's what I'd do if I was alone."

"Where do you get those?"

I shrug. "Depends on the refuel station. Some have bulletin boards with tips, others I just ask around. It's not illegal, not technically, so most non-junkers don't mind sliding along any information they may have."

As soon as I say that, I see what I'm looking for. Right by the exit of the dock is an encrypted bulletin board attached to the wall between two bathroom doors. I walk over and hold up my watch so it can read who I am; I'm not a member of the official junking guild, the only protected group of junkers in the galaxy, but Luka got me hacked clearance a few years ago, so a small light blinks green. It'll be good for me to check in at a few places, anyways. Leave a paper trail. As long as there's no evidence that Juno is with me, everything should seem perfectly normal.

Plus, if I don't give them a reason to look, they never will, and all of this will be a precaution.

Juno steps up beside me and grabs something on the wall beside the bulletin board. A piece of paper— not super common, not anymore— with her face on it. It's a younger picture of her. Her hair is maybe an inch shorter and her nose is un-pierced. Even her eyes seem different despite being ringed with the same dark eyeliner as they are right now. More open, maybe. More... Hopeful.

Juno looks at the poster for a few seconds before gripping it in both hands and tearing it directly down the center. She walks over to a trash incinerator in the wall a few feet down and shreds each half into smaller strips, then each strip into tiny, confetti-like pieces before dropping them into the incinerator. I leave her to it and turn back to the bulletin board.

The holographic interface lights up with dozens of notes, messages, warnings, and other, smaller things I don't bother to pull up. There are a couple of personal ads, a couple of missing persons posters. I shuffle through them all until I find what I want: a tiny note scribbled in the notes app of someone's tablet, that just says 'ZPHR HLR' and then a set of coordinates. I select the note and send the information to my own inbox.

"I'm ready when you are," I say and shut off the board. Juno nods, drops the last few tiny shreds of paper into the incinerator, and we head through the open door to the mainway of the refuel station.

Refuel stations are all just about the same. They're strategically anchored in gravity wells sending them orbiting either a large planet or a star, intended to be a pitstop between other, larger settlements across the galaxy. Redhawk is extremely average in terms of layout. You park in the center, a large shipyard with tiers and tiers of huge, metal platforms for landing on and receiving maintenance. From there, a mainway circles that, branching off into short halls that lead to stores, rooms for rent, restaurants— An orbiting, capitalist spire in the middle of nowhere, space.

The Redhawk mainway is quiet. A few people call out to us, offering samples of food or beauty products. Juno starts to walk towards one woman holding jewelry, but I grab her wrist and tug her back.

"Don't," I say under my breath. Juno scoffs and pulls her arm out of my grip, crossing her arms.

"Just trying to be nice," she mutters back.

"Don't be. We need to get in, get out," I reply in turn and lead her into a clothing store. It's not one I shop at— It's a more alternative, younger-leaning style— but Juno's eyes light up. I gesture to a rack of brightly colored clothes. "Maybe get some color, it might be a good disguise, considering."

"Considering what?" Juno asks absently and thumbs through a rack of strappy black tops.

"*Considering* that they'll expect to see you in all black, maybe," I reply and gesture to the jacket she borrowed from me — Grey.

Juno wrinkles her nose under her face mask, but nods.

After that, shopping goes quickly. Juno picks out some plain garments and I grip a few pieces of appealing fabric between my thumb and forefinger. She pays with physical cash — an oddity these days— and I appreciate the care. We leave with one plastic bag of white, grey, and green shirts and two pairs of black pants.

Not exactly what I meant by colorful, but it'll do.

There are a half dozen screens lining the mainway and they all switch from bright, colorful advertisements to the same, identical breaking news story.

"Anti-government terrorist known as ██████ Marcus has reportedly fled Janus. We have no news on what type of ship this violent criminal has used to escape, but we do know that Marcus, as well as their compatriots, are armed and dangerous. Please report any sightings of Marcus to the proper authorities."

It shows the same picture from the printed wanted poster. Juno, hair green and chin-length, is animated this time, rotating a full 360 degrees.

I turn to Juno. Her face is sheet-white and her lips are parted. She's clutching a piece of paper in her hand, a smudge of green still visible, and she throws it to the ground. All at once her posture changes and she stiffens. Her jaw snaps shut and her brow shifts back to its focused furrow, the open-eyed, fearful expression dissipating.

"I need to call my brother."

"On a payphone," I say, and she nods. "Alright. Before we leave."

"What the fuck else do we need to do here?" she snaps. I don't react, and I'm glad I don't when she immediately softens and bites her lip. "I'm sorry, Junker."

"We need to refuel," I say, "I can head back to the ship—"

"No!" she says and reaches out for me, stopping just before she touches my arm. She swallows hard, her adam's apple bobbing gently in her soft throat. "Stay with me?"

There's that twitch in her expression: that odd little wince that I don't know what to do with.

"Refuel first, then," I concede, "Then we can find a payphone. I think there's one in the shipyard." She relaxes minutely and nods. I start walking with her at my side, and if her knuckles are white where they're clutching her new clothes, I don't mention it.

✦

If someone didn't know we were travelling together, they'd probably think that I'm a real jackass for standing so close behind Juno while I wait for her to get ahold of her brother. My arms are folded and my chin is down, and I know how I look. I could almost be sleeping against the wall if not for the way I'm scanning the crowds of people moving around the refuel station.

Normally, refuel stations are safe. The people who work here and stop here on their way elsewhere in the galaxy are the every day sort, the working class of the galaxy. We're the type to mind our own business, not the kind of people who turns someone in just for existing.

Though, even as someone who doesn't watch the sorts of

news channels that are talking about Juno right now, I know what they're saying. Every death from a protest or a riot— and there have been multiple confirmed, just since Janus— are on her.

Most were shot. Some reacted to tear gas. Another four were beaten bloody with government-issued batons.

Juno doesn't have any blood on her hands. Not really.

They want us so badly to believe she does, so they won't stop saying it until it's believed. A lot of people love a scapegoat when the alternative is dismantling everything they thought they knew about their government. It's much easier to make a young girl the enemy than it is to address the problem itself.

I just don't care either way.

"Gideon," Juno whispers into the phone. Thank god. "Yeah, yeah. It's me."

I tune out. Juno seems close with her brother— at least from the way her shoulders sink in relief when his voice comes through the earpiece— and I don't want her to feel like I'm snooping.

All I care about is her safety. What she talks about with her brother is none of my business.

We stand there for a few minutes as Juno quietly speaks to her brother. Every second that passes makes me more anxious with the thought of someone tracking her location, finding the two of us, shooting down the Gemini— I press the pads of my pinkie finger and my thumb together until the stretch across the back of my hands hurts. It calms me down.

"I love you," Juno murmurs into the phone. My stomach flips and I press the flat of my wrist against it. "I'll call you again when it's safe. Yeah, I know. I'll see you soon, Gideon."

She hangs up.

"You good?" I ask. It comes out a little flat, a little dumb, but before I have time to overthink it, she nods and starts walking towards the Gemini.

We take off without issue, but Juno feels amped up beside me. As soon as I can, I ask Verita to navigate us to the next spot on our route and unbuckle to head back into the main cabin. Juno is sitting on the ground with her back against my bunk, clutching something in her hands. I can't see what it is, but I don't pry.

Instead, I open up the fridge.

"You're not a vegetarian, are you?" I ask. That would be inconvenient. Juno shakes her head. "Any preference between mac and cheese or chili?"

"Mac and cheese, please," she says. Her voice is quiet. It's unsettling. The Juno I've seen on the news, the one I've barely gotten to know in the last day, she's tough. She's loud and unapologetic. This is a new side to her that I don't think I like much, and I'm not quite sure how to marry the two in my head.

I pop her meal in the reheater first. Within thirty seconds, I have a tray of bubbling pasta and cheese ready for her, and I hand it over. Every ration pack comes with a little plastic fork, and I hand that over too. She meets my eyes and smiles. I can't help it— I flick my gaze away almost at once— but I try to smile back anyways. It comes out a little crooked and unnatural. I turn back to the reheater and nuke my own food. When it's ready, I sink to the ground beside her.

We don't touch, and the only noise in the ship is the dense silence of infinite space and the quiet noises of two people eating.

"Verita," I say after a few moments. "Put on that show I hate."

Verita does so and angles the screen to face us. A horrible, horrible game show starts playing, one I've watched seasons upon seasons of despite the gnawing irritation that grows inside me every time.

"You hate this show?" Juno says after a minute.

I laugh. It bursts out of me like a geyser, pushing hot spray high into a thin atmosphere.

"I really, really do," I say around that same crooked smile. It feels so odd on my face, but Juno smiles back and its forgotten. "It's dumb. There's basically no way in this or any galaxy that the contestant is going to know more than a literal computer. The best case scenario is a stalemate, and even then, the contestant doesn't get any money. It's a scam."

"But aren't there questions about human stuff?"

Aha. I've heard that counter before. I shift to face Juno and set my chili on the ground.

"Yeah, but they all still have a correct answer. Like, they might ask about love, or desire, things a computer can't feel— Which, by the way, is a whole other thing, because how the hell do we know? There are computers like Verita, or Bellona, who form genuine relationships with the people who live in their systems, so who's to say that they're not sentient? They could know what love is. Even if they don't, they could still answer the question, since love, desire— they're all just chemicals, right? If they really wanted to alienate a computer, there would be a physical aspect for the contestant to take on to get an advantage." I stop to take a long breath and hold up a finger. "Even then, they'd find some way to change the show to let the computer have a robot body, and we've seen how advanced those are now. I mean—" I gesture to my leg, and then quickly realize she probably doesn't know about my prosthetic, so I kick off my boot. "They can make shit like this, so I'm sure they can make a robot that can do challenges on TV by now, if they haven't already."

I pick back up my chili and take a bite. Juno is nodding, an unreadable expression on her face.

"So in your world, the only way to make it fair is... To not have the show at all?"

"I'm just saying," I answer with a shrug, "A show where two computers compete to pretend to be human sounds a lot more interesting to me." Juno's mouth is curled in a smile now, even as she takes the last bite of her food, and she turns back to face the screen.

We're quiet for the rest of the episode unless one of us knows the answer to a question. Juno knows more than I expect, and I pull out a few obscure facts myself. The human contestant loses, and it isn't even close.

"Verita," I say after the episode ends. Me and Juno both have our legs kicked out in front of us now, our little dinner trays stacked and pushed away. "How far are we from our next stop?"

"Eleven hours and seventeen minutes," Verita says. I nod and stand, using my bunk as a handhold. I offer my hand to Juno and pull her up with ease. She's short and quite thin, the bulk of her being in her hips.

"Well," I say and release her hand. "I'm going to sleep for most of that, I think."

Juno looks back at the small bed built into the wall behind her. "Here?" she asks and pats the mattress. "Is there another bunk?"

Oh.

Right.

"I... No," I admit and gesture to the sealed off space above her head. "It's storage. I... You take the bunk, then."

"No, it's your bed," Juno argues, her brow furrowed low.

"You're the valuable cargo," I say and press on her shoulder gently. "Sleep. I'll be fine in the pilot's chair. I've slept there plenty before." She doesn't step back.

"Is there— Do you have spare blankets, or something? I can sleep on the floor," she says, but I shake my head.

"Let me grab—" I lean past her and grab the ratty old plush rabbit from the shelf in my bunk, and then a folded blanket out of the storage compartment above. "Take the bunk, Juno. I'll be fine."

Without giving her any more room to argue, I move into the cockpit and tug shut the thin fabric curtain that separates the cockpit from the living area of the ship. I don't change clothes— I'm already in a soft enough shirt, so I just pull off my pants as well as my prosthetic and settle into the pilot's chair.

It's a large, tall-backed leather chair built for a fully-grown adult. I'm grown— I'm twenty years old, I stopped growing when I was twelve— but I've always been small. I'm barely five foot five and slender, so I can curl up comfortably in the seat of the chair, especially with one less leg than the average pilot. I push the seatbelt straps out of the way and clutch the stuffed rabbit to my chest, letting the fabric touch my cheek. The material is worn through with fingers and mouths over eight years of messy childhood and, when I press it to my mouth, evokes a warmth in my chest that lulls me to sleep, just as it does every night.

I wake to a silent ship save for the whispered breaths of Juno Marcus asleep in my bed.

I smile despite myself. It's admittedly nice to not be alone in the Gemini all the time, even when the person I'm travelling with is a wanted fugitive, and she's only here because she's paying me. I climb out of the pilot's chair quickly and reattach my prosthetic before heading into the body of the ship.

"Good morning, Pollux," I whisper. I feed him quickly and watch as he does little spins and loops to nip at the floating food. I drum my fingers against my thighs and hum quietly to myself. As soon as he's done chasing the pellets and, eventually, my fingertips against the glass, I tug my sweaty shirt off and toss it in the laundry. I check our course on my pad as well— We're an hour out from the moon next on our route— before setting it back on the table.

Damn, I slept longer than I thought.

I hear Juno rustle behind me, but I focus on checking everything that needs checking when you're hurtling through space at near-light speed. I even glance at INN, but there's no further word on Juno's escape from Janus. By the time I'm done, my shipmate has been in and out of the restroom.

She's sitting at the small pull out table with my pad in hand. Her hair is pulled back in a messy bun and the bangs that normally swoop over her forehead are sticking out at odd angles. Her eyeliner is smudged but her lips are bare, wiped clean with some sort of makeup remover, and there are pink creases in her cheeks where her pillow— My pillow— pressed into her skin. I look away from her face the second I realize she's staring back, tracing her gaze over my bare chest.

"Go ahead," I mutter and run my thumbs across the matching pink scars under my pecs. "Say it."

Juno sets the tablet down. "What are you expecting me to say?"

"Ask about it. Ask about my scars, or my leg, or— I know you've noticed my eye is fake, too. Ask me why I can look like this—" I point to my chest— "And think so low of your movement."

Juno shrugs.

"Your body isn't my business, neither are your politics."

I... Okay.

Okay.

I nod slowly and kneel to the ground to open the drawer under my bunk where our clothes sit. Her black shirts and thick pants are a shadow next to my all-neutrals wardrobe. I pick out a long-sleeved shirt in heather grey and a pair of pants with many pockets, as well as fresh socks and underwear. I pile them in my arms and head for the bathroom.

When I pass her sitting at the table though, I pause. *Your body isn't my business.*

She is so much better than so many people in this godforsaken galaxy just for that, just for not trying to control me.

"Thanks," I say before I can convince myself not to.

Juno shrugs like it's nothing, like I didn't have to go to the furthest reaches of the outer rim to find a surgeon who would take me. Like I didn't have to anchor the Gemini in his moon's orbit and sit there for days while I recovered, cold and alone.

"If I tried to police you," she says finally, "I'd be no better than them."

"You could never be like them," I murmur and it comes out too soft, too warm. Vulnerable. Longing.

I wince and move into the bathroom like I had intended to. We have enough water in reserves for a quick shower, so I turn it on and shove my pile of clothes into the small shelf above the toilet opposite.

I shower quickly. It feels good to get clean, even if I spend the whole time distracted by the pale pink color of Juno's bare lips. Stars above, it's embarrassing how quickly having someone to keep me company has softened me.

"Stay focused," I whisper to myself. Once I'm dry and dressed, I head back out and, to my surprise, her face is completely bare now. Her eyelids are white and delicate, eyelashes fanning down towards her cheeks in soft-looking fans. There's a small scar just beside her left eye.

"Where are we headed today?" she asks.

"Junking. A Zephyr hauler crashed into one of Miranda's moons a couple days ago, so we're gonna stop by and see how much scrap we can get out of it."

"Cool," she says. I toss her a protein bar and and set my reheater to make us two cups of coffee.

"How do you take your coffee?" I ask and then rip into the protein bar with my teeth. Juno doesn't respond immediately, her mouth slightly agape as she stares at me. "What?" I ask after I spit out the plastic shred from the wrapper.

She shakes her head and licks her lips. "Nothing. Milk and two sugars, if you have it."

I'm struck for the first time with how young she looks. We both must be around the same age, at least the INN report that played said she was born barely a year after me, but with her war paint she seems so sure of herself. So confident with a microphone held so close to her mouth that I'm sure there's a smudge of purple on it even after she's left the planet. With her face bare, I can see the freckles that dot her skin, the mole under the arch of her right eyebrow, the early-twenties-ness of her cheeks. She's all whip-cord muscle, I can tell just from her shoulders, but her face has a touch of roundness, a softness that isn't mirrored in her expressions, her words.

I want to touch her.

I jerk one of my hands on instinct at the unwanted thought and pull it close to my chest, curling my fingers into a tight fist. She gives me a look, but I shake my head and simply set her coffee down in front of her. She smiles, a genuine, kind little thing, not the teeth-in-your-throat grin she gives when leading riots and whipping hundreds of angry people into a rage.

I want to know her.

I turn away. That's the one thing I can't do: I can't like Juno. I'm glad she's turning out to be a decent travelling companion— and I know she's beautiful, that's just objectively true— but being anything more than acquaintances is deeply, deeply off limits. Not that she'd ever be interested in me to begin with. Her type is surely everything I'm not: confident, strong, impassioned. She's probably femme for femme, or we're flying to Adrestia to meet up with her hotter, stronger butch.

These feelings, at least, add some context to her war. If Juno Marcus promised me change, I'm sure my naive younger self would have jumped at the chance to orbit her.

I sip my coffee. It's bitter, but I let it wash away the sweet words lingering on the tip of my tongue and with them, any inkling of affection I might be beginning to hold towards Juno.

"I have a spare bag," I say after I swallow the hot drink and with it, that train of thought. "I can show you how to pull junk, but knowing what's valuable is a skill learned over time, so I'll go through your finds before we leave. I'd normally spend a couple days here, but I figure two will do, and we'll head to a refuel station tomorrow night."

Juno nods. "I trust your judgement. I'm good at a lot of things, but this strategy stuff is your strength, not mine. If we need to be loud, or... I don't know," she laughs, and there's that stupid, twisting stomach feeling again, "Make a viral video. I have a lot of practice at those."

I give her a little half smile. "If I need to hit someone, I'll call you."

Juno's smile fades. "I'm not actually... This is stupid," she says with another little nervous titter, "but the only times I've punched someone, I've hurt myself worse than I hurt them."

"You're kidding," I respond. It comes out flat, almost accusatory. I hear it, but I don't know how to fix my tone and by the time I've registered that I should try again, Juno is talking.

"I just never learned how!" she exclaims and bites down on her bare lip. "My brother is a lawyer, not a fighter. We... I genuinely believe that there is no legal way to reverse the decades of damage done to the ruling force of the universe, right? But at the same time, I'm just a voice. I can get people fighting and get people passionate, but I don't... I don't follow through. I don't see action, I just incite it and leave."

"I'll teach you."

It's out of my mouth before I even register the thought. It's not what I meant to say, coward being the first thing that sat behind my teeth instead, but it's out there all the same. Juno seems as shocked as I am at the offer. Her eyebrows raise almost to her hairline and her mouth falls open.

"You know how to fight?"

I nod and pull open the storage cabinet above the bunk. Tucked in the side is a small safe and I press my thumb against the biometric scanner. It unlocks quickly. I gesture for her to look inside at my own gun, not the mass-produced pistols the IPF carry. It's a small, easy to hold pistol with C.Q.— Castor Quasar— carved into the grip. It's one of the few things to survive my tumultuous past, but it's also a symbol of everything I've pushed off: The willingness to enact change, the death of people like me in the galaxy, and the memory of my family dying and every life I've taken with it since.

"Ever fired one before?" I ask her. She shakes her head. "I'll show you. I'll teach you how to throw a punch, too. It seems like the kind of thing you should know in your line of work."

Juno is quiet for a second, looking between me and the gun, and then nods slowly. "Alright. Teach me how to win a fight."

That startles a laugh out of me. "I can't guarantee victory, only that you won't break your thumb on the first impact," I reply. "C'mon, get ready. We're almost there."

I slide my belt on with the gun's holster sitting comfortably at my hip. I'd wear my under-arm harness, but this gives me more maneuverability, and that's a number one priority as a junker. Getting into tight spaces is half of the job, and it's why I've found so much success. Most other junkers are bigger men. They're stronger, sure, so they can pull harder on panels and mechanisms, but I can fit under the dashboard, in between the walls, and inside of consoles.

Juno disappears into the bathroom with some clothes in her arms and, by the time we arrive at the moon, she has emerged again. To my vague disappointment, Juno has washed her hair and redone her makeup. Her lips are a matte black today and her eyeliner is crisp at the corners, winging out towards her temples with careful dots decorating the bottom of the line.

I offer her an oxygen tank to strap onto her back with a cord attached to a plastic mask. This moon has its own atmosphere and gravitational pull, which is why the Zephyr hauler slammed into it in the first place. Its partially oxygen, sure, but it isn't the right composition for us to breathe longer than a minute or two.

I take over for Verita for the landing. She's programmed to pick the safest, most open landing place, while I want something a little more concealed while Juno's on board. When I find a spot behind an especially tall and rocky outcropping, I land quickly.

Juno moves out of the way while I pull the latch open. The ladder unfolds automatically and I gesture for her to go first.

"So," she says as she does so. "This is just stealing shit from Zephyr, right?"

I huff a quiet laugh, fogging up my mask, and climb down after her. "Technically, I guess. It's not something they prosecute over, but they might give you a ticket."

"You ever gotten stopped?"

"A few times, when I was really young," I answer and

gesture in the direction we're heading after double checking the coordinates on my watch. "After... Well. I've been doing this a long time."

Anything more is too personal. Juno doesn't need to know that. I take the admission and curl it, twist it, instead giving her the result of the story, not the words themselves.

"When I started, I mean. I was thirteen, I had no idea what I was doing. I got stopped before I even pulled a single bit of scrap."

Juno stops walking and looks at me. I can't read her expression. "Thirteen?" she echoes.

I nod. "Had to pay for gas somehow."

"You were piloting at thirteen," she says. It doesn't quite sound like a question, but I nod again anyways.

"Yeah. I've been living on the Gemini for almost a decade. I bought it when I was eleven," I say and check my watch again. We didn't land too far and we're already halfway there, I just turn of a degree or two to the right before we continue on.

"Alone?"

"Well, I have Pollux."

"The fish."

"Mmhmm."

"And you're how old?"

"Twenty, give or take a few months."

Juno is silent for the rest of the walk. I welcome the quiet and focus on not tripping on the rocks under our feet. The gravity is slightly less than the standard artificial field modeled after old Earth that most ships and refuel stations project these days, but not so much that we're bouncing with every step. When we find the hauler, I prop my hands on my hips and heave a sigh.

It's about what I expected.

Junkers have already been here. The door on the side of the

ship is off its tracks, leaning limply against the ruined fuselage. Bolts and bits of metal are scattered across the rocky surface of the moon. From what I can see, all the good stuff is almost certainly gone already.

"We're going to have to dig deep to find anything of value," I say to Juno. The entrance is covered in a fine layer of dust and I step carefully through the ragged opening. Juno follows behind me, slower around the sharp edges than me, but she keeps up. It's dark inside so I pull out the pop-up lantern in my bag and light it up.

We enter into the main storage area. It looks like they were hauling rations, most of which are spoiled from the crash. I see smears of reddish sauce and splatters of a thick, brown substance all along the inside of the ship. I'm grateful for the oxygen mask; without it, I'm sure this place smells awful. I deftly move around the smashed crates until we reach the airlock, which is also busted open. I have to squeeze a little to get through the gap, but I make it pretty easily.

"Hey Junker," she says, a strange, strangled laugh following her words, "Is now a bad time to tell you that I'm pretty claustrophobic?"

I grimace and look around at the small hallway I'm in now. It's meant for one person max, maybe the pilot, or a technician fixing the airlock. Me and Juno are both pretty short, her even smaller and thinner than me, but it'll still be a squeeze with us both inside.

"Hang on," I call back through the gap in the door. I feel around the edges of the hall, looking for any signs of... Aha! An uplifted corner of sheet metal, probably dislodged during the crash, is letting in the faintest stream of light from outside. I reach into my junking bag and pull out a shortened crowbar. I jam it into the little opening and wrench it back as hard as I can.

It takes a couple of hard yanks, but the piece of metal pops off and clatters to the grating under my feet. Sweat drips down my neck, but the hallway is decently enough lit now.

"Look," I say. I see Juno's face appear in the little gap I squeezed through. Her lips spread in a small smile behind her oxygen mask.

"That's better, yeah," she nods. I hold out a hand. She stares at it for a second, and then reaches through, takes my hand, and squeezes her body through the gap. Her lips are pursed and I can feel the muscles in her hand tense as the broken doorway presses against her chest.

"You good?" I ask. She takes a deep breath and nods.

"Yeah. Let's move."

Once we're both all the way through the airlock, there's a large panel of glass letting light through and I can feel the tension bleed out of Juno beside me. The main cockpit of the hauler is probably the same size as the Gemini in its entirety, so there's plenty of room to move around. I immediately head for the dashboard.

"The best bits are normally in here," I say as I feel around for any lifted corners or unaligned pieces. "Computer parts, motherboards, any kind of intact wiring. People who homebrew their ships like being able to buy parts at the microscopic level, so we can make a good chunk off these at a fence or a parts shop." My fingernail catches on a bit of metal and I poke at it until I can see where the panel is screwed in: at all four corners with a flathead screw. I pull out my Equinox knife and flick open the screwdriver attachment, letting each screw fall to the ground with a quiet sound as I loosen them.

I jam the same attachment underneath the panel and wedge it off. There are faint bits of a strange, rust-like grit rubbing off around the edges of the panel, but with a few tugs it comes off in a puff of dust.

"Put this somewhere out of the way," I say and hand it to her. She nods and steps away to do so, so I hunker in. I set my lantern down on the undamaged part of the dashboard and pull out a more focused laser penlight. I switch it on and hold it in my mouth, reaching in with both hands to shift wires and bits out of the way until I can see deep into the electronics of the dash.

"Let me know if I can help," Juno says, and I nod.

Around the penlight, I murmur, "Get the bag open." It comes out muffled and stretched, more like 'geh 'he bag ope', but she seems to understand and opens the messenger bag I lent her. I pull a few chunks of wiring out by the plug and hand them off to her, where she picks a pouch in the bag and sequesters them away. I pull a hand out and take the penlight between my fingers. "You always want to find the base of whatever you're pulling, especially wires. Grab it there, not on the length of it."

"Makes sense."

I can feel the warmth from her body right up against mine. It's distracting and dizzying, the knowledge that the most wanted woman in the universe is breathing soft puffs against my neck and learning how to junk from a nobody. I pull a little too hard on a piece of wiring and snap the plug off the end. Swearing under my breath, I throw the broken wire to the ground.

"You always want to keep wiring separate from the rest of the tech, and most industrial batteries need to be separate too," I tell her and shove my hand back into the hole I've made. The back of my hand brushes against something cool and I feel a jolt of electricity shoot up my arm, jittering the bone inside.

I yank my hand back as a lazy trail of smoke spirals out of the hole, a bubbling blister just beginning to ooze up across the ridges of my knuckles.

"Fuck," I spit and push at the shiny burn on my hand. "Ouch."

"Here," Juno says and hands me a pair of gloves that I recognize as my own from my bag. "Are you alright?"

"Fine," I reply tersely and yank the gloves on, ignoring how the rough material rubs against the burn. That fucking hurt. I reach back in, penlight aiming deep into the hole, and find a small blue glass plug. I pull it out without further issue and hold it up in the light to examine it. It has a connector similar to an ethernet cord and the body of it is a pale teal glass concealing some kind of mechanism inside.

"What's what?" Juno asks from behind me.

"I don't know," I reply and hold my hand out to her. "Is there any scrap cloth in your bag?"

She wordlessly drops a piece into my hand and I wrap up the plug at once.

"I'll find out, though," I add and tuck it into my bag. "Go over to the other side of the dash, see if you can get a panel up." Juno nods and leaves my space. I feel her loss against my side like an itch on a phantom limb.

I discard the glove on my burnt hand and examine the mark again. There's no way the glass could've carried the charge on accident, which means that whoever placed that plug there intentionally set a current through it, probably intending to shock whoever tried to pull it out next. I rub over the burn, sending dull notes of pain through my nerves, but I barely register it. Questions swirl through my brain, none of them easily answered.

Why was this ship booby trapped? Who put this blue plug in the dashboard of a Zephyr owned ship? What does it do?

I sigh, yank the glove back on, and return to collecting scrap. All that matters, really, is how much it's worth.

4

SUPREMACY OF THE MILITARY

At the end of the two days, we leave with a fairly good haul. I suppose it makes sense that two people would be able to collect more than one could on their own, but I've never had anyone at my side to test the theory before now. Juno does a decent job for someone who has never done it before and both of our bags are stuffed by the time we leave the moon. The refuel station I picked for our next stop is only two hours away, so I take a quick shower.

There's a fold-out seat in the Gemini's shower so I don't have to balance on one foot while I wash off. I built it myself out of bits of scrap and an old chair I got from Luka's shop. All it needs to do is support my bodyweight, and it has done that job well enough. It doesn't need to be pretty, so it isn't.

I smear burn cream over the back of my hand and wrap it in a clean bandage. It'll surely scar no matter what I do, but what's another scar on an already marred body?

While Juno takes her turn in the bathroom, I check fuel levels, water, and oxygen. Everything seems as it should be, at least decent enough to get us to the next stop, so I let it be and feed Pollux while I wait on Juno.

She comes out of the bathroom with her cheeks flushed red

and a towel wrapped around her body under her armpits. My mouth falls open; I can see the two tattoos inked into her collarbones, now. Birds in flight. I turn away after just a second too long's hesitation.

"Sorry, I forgot—" she says, not even bothering to finish her sentence. I close my eyes tight and try desperately to will away the blush crowding my face. Her pale skin, still shiny with drops of water and smudged with shocks of bright color and harsh blacks, lingers in my mind, and I squeeze my eyes shut even tighter. "You can turn around now."

I exhale softly and turn around. She's wearing pants now but her top is only covered by a black sports bra. I see the curve of her small breast as she bends down to pick up a shirt and I look away again, suddenly deeply, deeply aware of the distant warmth pooling in my gut.

Okay, sure.

Juno is hot.

I knew that.

I also know it would be wildly inadvisable to ever let her know that I feel anything but a neutral sense of responsibility for her, even if that 'more' is just this thumb on my pulse attraction, beating in my veins and itching at my fingertips.

But...

Seeing her now, all skin and stark lines and sharp black clothing, I can't help but think about how her lips tasted that night on Janus.

"Are we almost there?" she asks. It pulls me from my thoughts and I'm grateful to see that she's wearing a shirt now as well as her bomber jacket. She's twisting her wet hair into two braids, her bangs styled just enough to look intentional. It distracts me from thoughts of her bare skin just enough for me to shake my head and clear it enough to hum an answer.

"Yeah, just a few minutes out."

"Let me see," she says and peers at my pad where our course is pulled up. "Isn't Vestav a mining planet?" she asks and leans into the restroom to apply her lipstick, cocking an eyebrow at my reflection in the mirror.

"Yeah, for fuel components," I reply and it comes out smooth and easy, not like the way her hips are canted in the mirror is making me slightly dizzy for reasons I don't care to explain.

Well.

I'm a young lesbian and Juno is an attractive girl my age that I've been forced into close proximity with, so maybe I already have my explanation.

I'm human.

"Why are we stopping here, then?" She pops her lips and tilts her head this way and that, checking every crease and corner for missed spots.

"Fuel is cheaper when they mine it miles from where you're pumping it," I reply absently, still watching her in the mirror. She doesn't seem to mind. If anything, I feel like she's preening under my gaze, dragging a gloss applicator over her dark-colored lips.

"As opposed to light years, sure," Juno says and turns around, leaning against the sink, "but is it really *that* much cheaper?"

"You'd be surprised. They want to draw tourism and business to the planet while it still exists, before they've mined it so hollow the planet collapses in on itself," I respond. "Not much value in a black hole."

"I suppose," she says and taps her fingers against her hips. Her jeans sit lower than mine do, accentuating the gentle dip of her waist. I'm sure it would be soft to the touch, just the right size for my hand to curl into the crook there. "You'd think they'd have learned after what we did to old Earth. We can't just eat planets whole for whatever industrial bullshit we think we need or deserve. We— Humanity, I mean— Had our planet, and we killed it. We can't just do it again and again."

I shrug. "It's not like there's anything we can do to change their minds.

Juno smiles, but it doesn't reach her eyes. It feels worse than any cutting remark, anything she might say at a protest or a riot.

"There is if you aren't afraid to get your hands dirty." She steps away towards the second seat as we approach Vestav, letting the sentiment sink into my skin. I sigh and push off the conversation. Her optimism is nauseating and I don't know if it'll ever sweeten. I push through the cockpit and buckle in, but her words stick in the back of my head.

We land without a problem. I pull my hover caddy out of the under-floor storage and show Juno how to load our junk onto it. She pulls a beanie over her hair, tucking each of the two braids up into it. Her face looks younger without the shag of green that covers her forehead.

The refuel bot chirps that they're running a bit behind, so it'll be an hour or so before they'll get to the Gemini. I remember what I saw on the computer: While Vestav is mainly a stop along the way for travelers, it also has a massive observation deck to view the mining operation. It's as close to a tourist trap this side of the galaxy has.

I haven't sold to this fence before so I know the prices won't be as good as Luka's, but it'll do. It's not like I'm hurting for money, not since the ten thousand credit deposit from picking up Juno. Before we leave the Gemini, I tuck the carefully wrapped blue plug into my pocket. I might as well ask if they've seen it before.

We move through the spaceport unnoticed and unstopped. There are a dozen other junkers dressed in similar neutral tones to us both, hover caddies and duffel bags carrying their bounties, moving through the man-made structure. We blend in easily, especially with Juno's mouth shut and hair tucked away. We get to the fence— Once again, essentially running out of a pawn shop— and I lift a hand in greeting.

"Junker," she nods back. "What do you have for me?"

I pop open the top crate and start showing her. She has grey hair streaked with pure white tied up in a messy bun on top of her head. Her skin is tanned and pockmarked with wrinkles and texture you don't normally see from someone who lives and works in a spaceport, but this planet is dirty enough and close enough to its sun that I can imagine spending even a few years here would age you in much the same way.

Juno helps, and within a few minutes this woman has separated out a small pile of goods she won't take from the overall haul. It's not a big deal, mostly frayed wiring and a bit of scrap, but I can't help but notice the glittering blue plug tucked alongside the rejects.

"Do you know what this is?" I ask and hold it up. She shakes her head.

"Never seen a battery like that before."

I hum and tuck it back into my pocket. A problem for another time.

We get just over three hundred credits for the lot. It's decent. Not great, but decent. I accept the deal and pile crates and bits of scrap back onto the hover dolly. Juno helps, but there's a slow hesitance to her movement, a quiet and sluggish set to her shoulders. We leave the pawn shop and I point out a poster for a restaurant further down this level of the mainway. Juno nods.

We walk in quiet for a minute, and then she finally speaks.

"Is that it?"

I glance at her. "Is what *what*?"

"That's all? You spend whole days doing something extremely difficult that you're obviously very skilled at, and it nets you barely three hundred credits?" Her lips are twisted down.

"It's work, Juno. I get what they'll pay me, and I loot another crash. That's it."

"How long before you'll find another place to go junking? How many days do you have to make that three hundred credits stretch for?"

"Depends on the day. I have a lead right now, so the three hundred might just need to get me to the next coordinates. Forty for gas, forty to restock rations every two weeks or so. Eighty minimum for my credit bill, thirty to forty for docking fees, fifty kept aside for repairs, ten for water—"

Juno interrupts. "Do you spend any on yourself?" she asks, and I know my face must do something, because she waves her hand as if to scrub the question away. "I mean, do you ever have money just to spend? For clothes, or your ship?"

"If I get an especially good haul," I start, "I'll replace some of my older stuff. Most improvements I make to my ship or my gear, I make myself."

Juno shakes her head. "I... That's crazy. Do you have a savings account?"

I can't help it. I laugh in her face. "Are you kidding me? I haven't had a savings since I drained my parents' to get this." I kick out my prosthetic leg, "And this." I point at my eye. "It's the economy. I live off whatever gigs I can get my hands on. Why do you think I was so easily swayed to take you on board?"

Juno is silent then and I steer us finally into the restaurant. It smells amazing, all spicy, peppery sweetness and savory warmth. It's a counter service kind of place with a couple of tablets built into the counter. I tap through the menu until I know what I want, then gesture for Juno to do the same.

"I can pay for myself," she says. I shake my head.

"Paper trail. Go."

She hesitates, but steps up and taps on what she wants. I press my watch against the payment terminal and it spits out a little plastic card. I take it and lead Juno over to a secluded booth in a shady corner of the small restaurant.

There aren't many others here. We are here between meal times, at least on the galactic clock, so I suppose that makes sense. I'd rather it be quiet anyways. I feed the plastic card into the slot in the table, and within a few minutes our food is brought out by a small drone. It's similar in shape and size to my hover dolly, but this one has an LED face and the brain of an AI chirping platitudes at us. We take our plates quickly so it'll leave and I take a deep inhale.

There's something about food not made in the Gemini's reheater that hits differently. Sticky rice smeared with a thick, savory curry sits pretty in the center of my dish; hunks of lamb, carrot, onion, and potato surround it, dripping in a yellowy gravy that makes my mouth water. It was also served with another plate full of hot, fluffy flatbread that sits in the center of the table between us.

"I think this might be the first time I've seen you smile."

I look up. Juno has an odd expression on her face. It's almost a smile, but there's a weary sturdiness to it that I don't quite understand.

"No," I say and shake my head as I rip a hunk of flatbread with my thumb and forefinger. "I smiled when we were watching The Climb."

Her eyebrows twitch into a frown for just a milisecond before her face splits in an open, easy grin. "That horrible trivia show? Of course you remember that."

"You've smiled at me plenty," I note. Her grin fades, lips wrestled back into careful neutrality, and I shake my head. "It's not a bad thing. People in this galaxy could stand to be a little looser sometimes."

"What about you?" she retorts and dunks the half of the flatbread I left on the plate into her own food, a similar curry but with peas and some kind of fried meat on top.

"I don't talk to enough people to justify loose lips and easy smiles," I respond. "I don't have any friends. I don't have any family. The only people I speak to are those paying me to, and my fish."

"I don't think your fish counts as a person," Juno says. That little smile is still tugging at the corners of her eyes, but there's something else there too now.

Pity.

I take a big bite of food to keep myself from snapping. "He keeps me company well enough," I say after I swallow.

"Why don't you have any friends?" Juno asks. The second it's out of her mouth, her eyes widen and she shakes her head. "That came out rough. I meant—"

"No," I interrupt. "It's fine. It's true, why would I take offense to that? I don't have time for friends, and I... You have to have noticed by now that I'm not the most trusting person."

Juno nods slowly. "I did."

"I don't trust you. Not really," I say. Juno's face does something strange. "I trust you enough to let you on my ship, to sleep when you're on board." I try to make it sound like acquiescence, but her face twists further and she looks down at her food. "I don't need friends, and I don't need trust. I do just fine on my own."

She looks at me for another long second. "I understand," she says finally, and we eat in silence for the rest of our meal.

We return our bags and the hover dolly to the Gemini and are told by the same refuel bot that it's going to be another half hour. Juno takes me by the wrist and tugs me gently towards the observation deck where we find a stretch of plexiglass and railing to stand by and look down.

The pit is endless, or as near to it as you can get without being in space itself. There's no way to see the bottom, even though it's well-lit with dozens of hanging lights around every area a miner is working. They have huge, gurgling machines boring deep into the sides of the cavern, thousands of long, dirty conveyor belts moving minerals and stone from where it came from to massive vats glittering full.

It's quiet on the observation deck, but I can feel the vibrations from the drills in the floor under my feet. I take a step back and read a sign that explains the process from mining the solid, highly compacted carbon all the way to it becoming fuel or other materials, most of which are also used to make fuel cells or batteries.

"You fit in here."

I look back at Juno. "Hm?"

She's leaning heavily against the railing and peering down into the abyssal mining operation slowly consuming the planet Vestav. There are a dozen-odd other tourists around us and two armed guards leaning lazily against their respective walls. They aren't IPF, and their guns only carry six bullets a piece. I could take either of them in a fair fight.

Juno sniffles. The air is thick with smog and dust and I realize suddenly that the Gemini is going to be caked in the stuff when we leave.

"Your boots," she says finally, "look just like theirs."

The hundreds of visible miners working around the edges

of the cavern below are all dressed in nearly identical garb: grey, stained jumpsuits, respirators, goggles, and, sure enough, thick-soled work boots covered in soot and dark carbon.

Juno steps into my space and nudges our feet together, putting her boot down on the ground beside me to show the differences in our shoes. I notice that my feet are just a hint smaller than hers, even with my wide, rubber soles. Her boots still gleam faintly with shoe polish, the black leather almost purple in the LED lighting emanating from small strips warning us of the edge of the deck.

Mine, by contrast, are dull and ripped. There's a tear in the suede toe and one of the laces hangs loose and fraying at the end. The soles are caked irreversibly in mud and I'm sure the insoles are nearly flat.

"Not all of us can afford Saints," I say and bump her foot with mine. It leaves a small scuff of old mud on the toe and Juno clicks her tongue at the sight. She kneels to scrub at it with her thumb, removing the offending mark with two quick swipes.

"Saints aren't even that good for working in," Juno says as she straightens herself up and laces her fingers again over the railing. "They're hard to break in, and the traction isn't as good as— Yours are military surplus, aren't they? IPF?"

"They are," I confirm. I wiggle my toes, feeling the individual worn-out spots under each digit.

"Saints are a status symbol. Did you know, the guy who founded the company— Luc St. Aldwyn— He was a staunch anti-Federate," Juno says and lays her cheek down on her folded arms. Her hair falls into her face and my fingers itch to push it out of her eyes. How can she stand that? One spare hair on my neck after reshaving makes me feel crazy.

"No, I didn't know that," I say finally when I realize she's staring, black-lined eyes boring into my skull. Her gaze feels weighted, but not like the iron in the toes of my boots. More like a thick blanket, cocooning me and drawing me close.

She nods and sniffs again. "He was. He died, actually, in one of the first riots, before the IPF was even the IPF. Back when every loose group of old Earth colonists were just spreading across the galaxy, no government, no rule," she says. Her voice is fingertips on my spine, gentle caresses I don't know what to do with. She's looking at me and, despite the vertigo it brings me, I look over the edge to avoid looking back.

"How'd he die?" I ask.

"Trampled. They found him with a perfect, boot-shaped bruise on his chest and eight broken ribs," Juno says and finally, finally looks away from me. I chance a look at her profile and look at her slightly upturned nose, sharp jaw, long lashes. She looks wistful, like an old painting. "You know what the boot print was from?"

"Saints?"

The set of her mouth turns grim around a tired smile.

"Shit," I breathe and shake my head.

"I bet I'll die like that."

"Under the crushing weight of your own creation?"

Juno huffs out a quiet, breathy laugh and shakes her head. "Maybe. No, I meant... Rebelling."

"You probably will."

She laughs again. Something metallic clangs against stone deep below us and she shifts her posture until she's leaning harder against the railing. It makes my stomach turn. "Probably."

"You chose this, though," I say before I can stop myself. She raises her perfectly shaped and filled eyebrows in question. "You chose to speak out, I mean. You could have just made your little videos, your makeup tutorials and reality show recaps, but you chose to speak out against the IPF and Marwood and all of the people voting to make our galaxy a worse place. All two hundred members of the senate, all two thousand-odd in the house... That's a lot of enemies, Juno."

Juno presses her forehead against her arm and lets out a long breath. "I know."

For some reason, I was expecting her to fight back.

In fact, I was hoping she would.

"I was sixteen when I started this," she says and pulls back, a red mark on her forehead from where her skin pressed together. "I was barely three months on hormones and I thought I was indestructible. Now I'm a fugitive."

"You became an enemy the second you decided to start estrogen," I murmur. "I became an enemy when I got top surgery. You just don't hide it."

Juno snorts and looks out again. She seems younger somehow in the flickering, muggy light that Vestav's pitiful atmosphere barely contains. "You're so quiet about it you won't even tell me your name."

I swallow. "That's not fair."

"You know my name," Juno says pointedly. "You know my deadname, too."

"I wish I didn't," I say instantly.

"I wish you didn't either." She sniffs again and rubs at her cheek. My name— Castor, the name I chose; Quasar, the only thing I have left of my parents— sits hot in my mouth, but I can't make myself say it. It feels sour, nothing compared to the confidence with which Juno always says her own.

Juno Marcus. World saver, life changer.

"I don't want you to know me as him," Juno says quietly.

"Who?"

"██████."

My mouth falls open and I take a step back on instinct. "What the fuck? I never would."

"I know," she murmurs and scrubs her fingers over her cheeks. They're pink and streaked with little bits of soot and her fingers draw pale lines through the grey dusting. "I... Forget I said that."

"Juno," I say and move back to stand beside her, if not closer than before. Something burns in my chest so hot I can't reach out for it, can't touch it without being burnt. I feel it and I let it consume me. I reach out and touch her lower back. "Juno."

She looks at me and her gaze is even hotter, steam licking at my skin and blanching me bright red. It's the metal covers on the Gemini's engines moments after landing against my fingertips, even through thick leather gloves. "Junker," she replies quietly, and there's no malice in it. It's open and vulnerable and I swear I can see a part of her I shouldn't peeking out from behind her eyes.

"Juno," I repeat. She nods and takes a deep breath.

"Juno."

She's intoxicating. The clever self-awareness and honest fear she holds so, so close to her chest are just as much parts of her as her green hair and witty comments and I find myself watching her as we walk back to the ship. Someone smiles at her as we walk past and she wiggles her fingers in a vague wave. Her black-painted nails are shiny in the faint light and I swallow. I feel drunk, almost, distantly aware of all the chemicals we surely just breathed in from the mine.

That makes me think of Juno's soot-streaked face, the careful lines of her purple lipstick that she draws on so neatly and then covers so often with a mask: color just for her to feel, just for her to see. I look away as we approach my ship. The lights dim as the night cycle begins on Vestav and, in the dim, warm light, everything feels different. I hear her voice saying she's going to change the galaxy, and for just a second, I believe her.

The Gemini is ready when we return and we climb on board without a word. I keep the lights similarly dim inside and quickly strip out of my clothes, now sticky and dirty with coal and ash, and pull on a pair of shorts and a loose tank top. Juno takes her clothes into the bathroom to change, and then we strap ourselves into our respective seats for takeoff.

I have Verita send us off to our next destination, a planet a full night's flight away. There, we'll refuel, and continue on. I stay in the cockpit until we're out of atmosphere and then I head back into the main cabin.

Pollux eats what I feed him and by the time I'm done with him, Juno is back, wearing a soft looking t-shirt and loose sleeping pants.

"You want the bunk tonight?" she asks, but I shake my head again. She looks at me for a beat too long, but then climbs into my bed and places her head on my pillow. Her green hair splays against my cream pillowcase as she turns away from me.

"Verita, shut off the lights," I say quietly and duck back into the cockpit to settle in. I tug my blanket up over my lap, press the ratty stuffed rabbit to my chest, and lean the chair back, staring up through the top of the segmented windshield. The stars are bright and blurry as we begin to pick up speed, so I shut my eyes tight.

I shift and adjust my grip, but everything still feels wrong, like the seat prodding into my shoulders is too heavy and pressing at all the wrong places. I roll the other way, but nothing changes. Juno's soft breathing in the other room is even and slow and I can't help the frustrated sigh that comes out when I realize that she's asleep already and I'm not.

Historically, when I can't sleep, I just... Don't. There's no obligation to keep your circadian rhythm synced with galactic standard time anyways, so I stay up, maybe search online for junking leads or watch a few reruns of old trivia shows.

With Juno asleep just a few feet away, that's not an option. I wouldn't dare wake her. Whatever we breathed in on Vestav is still making me feel a little floaty and loose and I roll onto my back and clutch my rabbit tighter to my chest. I listen to Juno's quiet breaths, let my mind wander to the places it can't in the day time, awoken by Juno's soft skin and open words, and I make a list.

KISSING JUNO MARCUS

PROS:

1. I get to kiss Juno.
2. Maybe, for the first time since the crash, I'd have reason to stay somewhere for any reason other than money.
3. I get to kiss Juno.

CONS:

1. I would have to admit that I don't always want to be alone.

I cross that one out as soon as I think of it and rewrite it in my mind.

1. I AM AFRAID OF EMOTIONAL VULNERABILITY.
2. She could reject me.

I'm fairly confident that Juno would accept my advances, based on the way her eyes drag down my form when I undress and how she seems to crave closeness. She's been vulnerable with me, which, from what little I know about her, doesn't seem like something she would do with a complete stranger, or at least someone she doesn't trust.

Despite the facts, there's still a gnawing doubt.

Why would someone like Juno like me? I know I'm... Odd. Even before the crash, even before I was a junker. I've always been strange.

I sigh and go back to the list. I add a con: having to put trust in another person.

Pro: *Getting* to put trust in another person.

I wince and roll again, pressing the rabbit against my cheek. There's a reason I don't date anybody. Really, there are a few. I stare at the thick glass above me, where only a few inches separate me from infinite space. I crumple my list into a ball and start another one.

Well, really, I rephrase the original one.

REASONS CASTOR QUASAR DOESN'T DATE (ANYMORE):

1. I never stay anywhere long enough to meet people.
2. I never know anyone long enough to get attached.
3. I'm off putting to most 'normal' people.
4. I am scared of emotional vulnerability.

The fact that I know that fourth one so plainly doesn't change the fact that it's true. I'm not brave, not like Juno. I'm not one to face my fears.

I shift in the leather chair again, my eyelids finally starting to get heavy, and I think: Would it be worth it to start now?

Would it be worth it to let Juno know me?"

The decision is made for me.

I know I'm dreaming almost instantly because Apollo is there. I don't dream every night, but in every dream I *do* have, Apollo is at my side.

This, however, isn't just a dream.

It's a memory.

We're sitting in our parents' four seater ship. Me and Apollo are in the back, strapped into a harness and a booster chair respectively. Apollo's rabbit is clutched in his chubby, childish fingers and we're laughing about something I can't quite make out. It sounds like we're underwater— murmured, bubbling words spilling out of Apollo's red-stained lips. His hair is dark like mine but it's longer, springing out in perfect curls all over his head.

He's nine, and he's my best friend.

The ship slows. We're about to enter the atmosphere of some planet I've never been back to. I hear my parents talking to police over the comms, but I just watch Apollo. He's a ray of sunshine beside me, the brightest star in the whole goddamn sky. He reaches out for me with his empty hand and I smile, taking his sticky fingers in mine.

Crystal clear, I hear my mother say, "Thank you officer, but we'll make it just fine."

In the dream, I'm silent, but the other me— Castor, the grown-up who knows how this ends, who knows the feeling of their brother's blood on their face— is screaming.

We enter the atmosphere. Our ship is ripped apart within seconds.

In reality, I went unconscious the moment the ship began to plummet towards the dense forest that blankets the planet Dasos.

In the dream, I see it all.

Apollo squeezes my hand tight and closes his eyes. My

mother and father hold hands too and I see my mother's fingers snap when my father is flung through the windshield, so small against the backdrop of infinity. Our ship slams nose first into a 500 foot tree trunk, a dark brown skyscraper with spiky limbs barely swaying upon the impact. I feel every tendon tear and bone snap in my left leg as I'm twisted in my seat.

The explosion casts itself over me. Fire claws at my eyes and bites through the skin of my left side until I'm dripping in my own flesh.

The ship is mangled. It's barely held up by the branches speared through it, one less than a foot from my skull. One wide branch trembles and snaps, finally sending the ship plunging hundreds of feet through the air just to crunch into one lower branch, and then, finally, the forest floor.

I woke up then and clawed my way over to Apollo. I'm a bystander in my own body now, even as I grab his stuffed rabbit from where he dropped it. The ship has turned on its head and he's hanging by the seatbelt of his booster seat, both arms hanging limp with gravity's pull. I feel blood drip off one fingertip and onto my face, splattering into my left eye— I can't feel it. I don't see it.

He's staring at me, but he isn't. His eyes don't focus. They're glassed over and his mouth is open, blood dripping form the corner of his lips.

Apollo has been bisected by a sharp panel of metal biting into the plush seat behind him. His torso stays, but his legs slide limply out of the booster and crumple to the roof of the ship beside me.

I reach out. "Apollo," I try to say, but my mouth is full of blood and burnt flesh.

The faster-than-light drive bursts into a green fireball. I'm blasted away through the remnants of the windshield, Apollo's rabbit held close to my chest, I land on my left side in a puddle of fuel and tree sap that eats at my skin like acid. I can smell myself burning, the acrid scent of flesh eating at flesh the only sensation left until I fall unconscious, every nerve aflame.

I wake with a desperate, clawing gasp, tears sticky and too much, *too much* against my face. My chest is heaving and it feels like a planet rests on me, crushing my lungs and ribs into a familiar paste. I shove off my blanket and sit up, looking searchingly out the windshield at open, empty space ahead of us.

I can see the lights of a refuel station glimmering to the galactic west and a planet even further off in the same direction with three moons orbiting it in long, concentric circles.

I can see a thousand stars, light years away, each one host to a dozen or so planets with even more moons and even more refuel stations. I can see open space, and I can see the gentle contrails of a couple of other ships heading this way.

I can see darkness, and I stare until I'm absorbed by it.

"Junker?" Juno says from behind me. I startle.

"Juno," I respond dumbly. I realize vaguely that my head is pounding and my mouth still tastes like ash, mirroring the trembling in my hands and the nervous sweat at the small of my back.

"Do you want me to stay, or do you want to be left alone?" she asks. I can't see her, but I've spent enough time with her in the past few days to know the face she's making. It's the same face she makes when faced with a difficult challenge, when lines upon lines of police have guns pointed at her skull with nothing between them but fierce determination. It's the face I saw on TV the day we met, and again when I refused her job.

I open my mouth but nothing comes out. I press myself

against the outer reaches of my skull, saying the words again and again in my thoughts until I'm screaming them.

I was in a spaceship crash.

I was in a spaceship crash, and I lost my brother.

I hear her sink to the ground behind me. She doesn't talk and neither do I. I can't make the words form in my mouth. I think about my brother and I think about my father, and I whisper the words in my head.

Nothing comes out.

I was in a spaceship crash, and I dream about it all the time.

I look out the windshield and count the stars until finally, when I open my mouth, I feel like I can breathe.

"Dream," I manage, hoarse and trembling. I fall back into the captain's chair and close my eyes, succumbing to a different kind of darkness.

Juno exhales softly. She's quiet for a moment, and then she says, "Do you want to hear about my dreams, instead?"

I nod. Anything but the riot in my head.

"I dream about the day my parents left me. They took one look at my lipstick and left me for dead."

I'm silent, but I reach down and unlatch the mechanism that keeps the chair facing forward. I slowly push myself around until I'm facing Juno, but I stare at the ground near her socked feet.

"Gideon came with me and he never looked back," she says.

"Brother."

It takes me a second to realize that it came from me, that my mouth is willingly forming words again, but Juno just nods. *I had a brother*, I say in my head. *His name was Apollo.*

"My twin," she responds.

I've always felt my brother's heart like he was my other half, I say in my head. *I named myself Castor so I would always feel near him, near my twin flame.*

"Gemini," I manage.

She hums and scoots forward until there's less than a foot of space separating my feet from hers. I dare to lift my eyes up to her bare shoulder, tracing the two well-detailed fish that swim there in an eternal dance. I point to it, and she nods.

"Pisces. I always liked that there were two of them, two matching. He has the same tattoo."

I smile despite myself and drop my gaze down to her knee. "Rabbit," I say.

"Your brother's rabbit, in your bunk."

I nod.

He held it every day. He couldn't sleep without it. After the crash, I grabbed it first, because I knew he wouldn't be able to sleep without it, and he cried when he couldn't sleep.

"You miss him."

I nod. I can't speak anymore, not even in my head. I feel exhausted. I miss him every second of every day.

"Do you want to come down here?" Juno asks, and I slide bonelessly out of the chair until we're sitting together, our knees pressed against one another. "Let me know if you want me to stop. Just tap me a couple times, okay?"

I nod again. She detangles her legs and pulls me between them, curled up against her chest. I press the hollow of my eye socket against the spot on the front of her shoulder where it juts out just enough. It lays a perfect pressure onto my eye and I hum, a quiet little noise in my quiet little ship. I can hear her heartbeat, but it's quiet too.

She brings a hand up and gently scratches her black, blunt fingernails through my shown hair. It feels good, sends pleasant reverberations through my scalp, and I can't help but curl closer. Despite her small size, Juno is warm and solid and I feel like I could lean against her at the heat death of the universe and she wouldn't for one second hold it against me. She is the sun and everyone else surrounds her, reliant on her steady gravity.

This is why she's the one who's going to save the universe. She can handle it, and she doesn't resent anyone who can't. She accepts them into her orbit and keeps them alive. I snap at her, and she still holds me when I wake up crying.

Juno leans closer and I feel something soft press against the top of my head. I touch her waist with one hand and keep my other curled tight to my chest, my hand bent nearly in two against my collarbones.

We fall back asleep like that, and my last thought before I slip away into a dreamless rest is this: Juno Marcus now knows me like nobody has since Apollo, and that thought scares the shit out of me.

5
RAMPANT SEXISM

When I wake up, I'm wedged between my chair and the dashboard of the ship. The bunk is empty and my blanket is draped over my shoulders. Apollo's rabbit is wedged in between my hand and my chest.

Juno is nowhere to be seen. The ship isn't very big, and we haven't stopped, so I pull myself to my feet and knock on the door to the tiny restroom.

"You can open the door, if you want," Juno says through the metal. I hesitate, but I dig my fingers into the latch and swing it open. She's standing in front of the mirror with wet strands of dark green hair clutched between her fingers. Her dark roots are showing at the base, a little strip of brown touching the green right at the hairline.

Even more startling than her natural color peering through is her completely bare face. Her eyelids are pale and soft looking, but even without the vicious wing of her eyeliner she still cuts a sharp look my way.

"Do you need something?" she asks. I shake my head, but I leave the door open.

"Just looking for you."

She squints at me, but drops her hair and picks up a small

black tube from a pouch sitting in the sink. She pops the cap off and balances it on the small shelf below the mirror before leaning in, her bangs pushed off to one side, to carefully draw the dark wings she wears every day.

I know I'm staring, but I'm too exhausted to make myself look away. Her movements are practiced and perfect, and within minutes of subtle lines and confident scratching she has crisp points on either corner of her eye. She recaps the pen and picks up a thicker tube, a clear one with a shimmering purple gloss inside.

Juno starts right at the top of her cupid's bow and drags the pad of the applicator down to the left, then to the right, and finally across her plush bottom lip. She fills in the color and examines herself in the mirror.

When she seems satisfied, her gaze turns to me, and she cants her head to one side. "Like what you see?" she says. It's loud in the quiet ship, the only sound between us the hum of the engine puttering us across the galaxy.

"Irrelevant," I respond. My desire, my weakness from last night, it's gone, right alongside my inability to help words leave my mouth. "We're stopping today."

"Where at?"

"Doda." She winces, and I agree. Doda sucks. It's a hunk of rock and ice coated in an unending storm, peppering any exposed skin with needle-sharp drops of ice water. The rain never ceases and never slows, and despite the fact that it's such a light storm you can barely see the drops in the air, it wears on your psyche. The last time I was there, I forgot my gloves, and even just the rain on the strip of skin that still showed on my wrists between my jacket pocket and my sleeve was mind-numbing within minutes.

In addition to the chill, Doda is eaten through with worm-like tunnels, leaving a swiss cheese grid of holes and caverns across the surface. That, combined with the wind, creates a low whistle that permeates even the best earplugs and rattles you to the bone.

Doda sucks.

"Why can't we just stop on a refuel station or something?" Juno asks as she leaves the restroom, her face stretched in cartoonish disappointment.

She doesn't mention last night, any part of it, and I'm grateful.

"Doda is the best place to refuel without leaving our course," I say with a shrug. "Sorry."

Juno curls her lips and yanks open the fridge where the rations are stored. She selects one and raises an eyebrow at me.

"Whatever is fine," I say, so she grabs a second. I get the two little stools set up around the table and sit down.

"Do you want to talk about last night?" she asks and slides a piping hot tin of spaghetti across the table to me before shoving her own food into the reheater.

Fuck. I spoke too soon.

"It doesn't matter," I say and shake my head, but I meet her eyes anyways. "Thank you, though." I flick my gaze away before it can overwhelm me.

Juno shrugs and sits down with her own food. We're going to have to restock rations on Doda, I realize. Ugh. I understand the need for discretion, but not telling me that my payload required sustinence really messed up my internal catalog of supplies.

"I don't want to press it, but... I'm here. I think I would understand more than you think I would."

I shake my head but otherwise don't bother to reply. Instead, I ask Verita to put on the TV. It automatically skims through a few channels, but nothing good is on. At least, not until—

Juno's fork clatters to the table. "Shit." On the screen is a blurry shot of her fleering Fontus. Two figures, dressed in police garb, stand with their backs to the camera, but a curl of green hair is floating out of the face shield she had been wearing. That, combined with her slight build and shiny Saints, makes it nearly impossible to pass this off as anyone else.

"If you or someone you know has any information about the escape of violent terrorist ██████ Marcus, please call the hotline below."

"At least I got my own hotline," Juno says, but the attempt at humor falls flat. I purse my lips and peer at the TV closer.

"That's... Definitely you," I sigh, "But they haven't ID'd me, and nothing on the Gemini. There's no reason for them to suspect anything beyond the fact that you've left Janus, which they knew. If we keep to my route and keep doing the things I'd do, we shouldn't draw any further attention."

Juno nods slowly but there's still a nervous glint in her eyes and a tense set to her jaw. I reach out and rest my hand on her shoulder. Her skin is buttery soft and, even with all of the dark lines and soft colors, perfectly smooth and unblemished.

"I'll get you to Adrestia," I say, and I mean it.

She looks at me and I can almost feel the fear and tension ooze out of her.

"I believe you."

Doda sucks just as much as we both anticipated.

Juno is in a spare jacket of mine and I'm wearing a turtleneck sweater, gloves, a beanie, a face mask, and socks that go halfway up my calves under my pants. We're both covered as much as we can be, and I even dig out some goggles I looted off a mining ship a few months ago. They cover the last vulnerable bits of our skin and keep our eyes from being pelted, but they dig in uncomfortably above my ears.

Right before we disembark, I tuck two pairs of earplugs into my pocket. I know I'll need them, and maybe Juno will want them too.

When we step off the Gemini, we're immediately shocked with a rush of cold. I wince beneath my layers but Juno fully recoils back into the ship at the temperature.

"Okay?" I ask. It's significantly muffled, so I offer a thumbs up as well. Juno nods.

I nod back and we make our way from the ship to the long walkway from the docking port to the enormous glass bubble easily a half mile away. Doda City is covered in an enormous bubble of thick glass that protects the buildings and people inside from the horrible weather, as well as soundproofing the interior. The shipyard was built first, but the surface of the planet is so drilled through with holes and caverns— hypothesized to have come from long-dead creatures, finding shelter from the rain— that the nearest place to safely build a city was a while off. The walkway is lit well and smoothly paved, but the low, constant drone of the wind rattles me to my core.

Within half a minute, I pull out my earplugs and squish them into my ears. I offer the second pair to Juno, who quickly accepts them with a cupped, gloved hand. The noise is still there, rotting my skull through and through with the dull sound even through the masses of foam in my ears, and I fold my arms tight in an attempt to alleviate some of the buzzing in my chest. Whoever decided Doda was going to be the biggest hub in this quarter of the galaxy deserves to be drawn and quartered. Juno's shoulder bumps mine, warm and solid in a sea of dissociative chill, and we walk on.

As soon as we make it through the airlock, Juno pulls her goggles down to hang around her neck. She doesn't take off her hat or mask, and neither do I. I pull out my ear plugs and stuff them into my pocket, gesturing for Juno to do the same.

"Alright," she says and rubs at her ears, wincing as feeling and color returns to them. "We're doing what you would usually do, right? So, if you were here alone, what would you do?"

I look around. Doda is a necessary stop for a lot of long-distance travelers due to being the only planet with a breathable atmosphere, albeit manufactured, within over a day's travel. Because of that, Doda City is huge. Towers of neon signs advertise shops, restaurants, entertainment of... Various levels of ethicality. Shopkeepers lean out of colorful, decorated booths, calling out for people to stop and peruse their wares. Every inch of the place is lined with holographic advertising, even the inside face of the glass dome. From this close, it barely looks curved.

Above the entrance, a massive, holographic dragon swirls through the air. It's thin and spindly with long, trailing wings and scales that glitter even though they're simply projections in the air.

"Well," I finally say, my chin tilted up as I watch the dragon's flight. "I'd get food, but we already ate. We need to restock on rations... I don't do much else." The dragon flips and dives into the ground, scattering into a thousand particles of light.

Juno doesn't seem surprised. In fact, she smiles. "I figured. How about you let me pick something out? Something fun." She raises one eyebrow at me and I bite my lip.

"That sort of defeats the purpose of sticking to routine," I say, but there's that little tug in my gut, the same one from Janus that makes me feel like I could never deny Juno anything.

"Sure, but we'll hide it in between stocking up."

"We really shouldn't—"

"Please, Junker," Juno says and there's something in her eyes, something almost... Desperate. Hidden.

I take a long breath.

PROS:

1. It might be fun
2. We'll both get to spend a little more time on an actual planet instead of in the artificial gravity of the Gemini.

CONS:

1. We could be caught.
2. It's a waste of time and credits.

I sigh.

"Fine. What do you want to do?"

Juno shakes her head. I can tell she's grinning behind her mask by the way her eyes are crinkled at the corners and her cheeks are rounded. "That's the whole idea," she says, "I don't know. We're just gonna pick something."

I shake my head, echoing her movement from just a second ago. "You're a bad influence," I mutter. I don't say no, and she claps me on the shoulder when she realizes.

"That's the spirit. It'll be great, c'mon. Let's go get our rations first."

Juno decides on a casino. I can't swallow the laugh that erupts out of me when I realize.

"This is the stupidest thing you've done so far," I tell her as she pulls me by the sleeve towards *GUNNAR'S BIG WIN*, a pretty sizeable casino in the city. It's nearly blinding with neon lights, some proclaiming '*100% WIN RATES*' and others touting '*HIGHEST JACKPOTS IN THE GALAXY*'. I roll my eyes and fidget with the wadded up earplugs in my pocket.

The sounds of ringing slot machines and tumbling coins ring in my ears. Juno says something in my ear as we enter, but the roaring gambling accoutrement makes it quiet and fuzzy, feeling light years away. She walks ahead and looses her grip on my sleeve, so I tuck my hand into hers. Just to stick together. We're still wearing thick, wool gloves, but even so, I can feel the warmth from her palm. It's grounding. I use my other hand to push my earplugs back in, only twisting them halfway into my ear canal. They muffle the sound pretty solidly and the weight in my chest eases.

"Just a couple games," Juno decides and pulls me over to lay on a bay of machines. They're themes around some old Earth show, one I've seen merch for briefly in the past. There's a man in a blue shirt with pointed ears and a very 2050's new wave haircut standing next to another man in a yellow shirt with creases dug into his forehead and wispy brown hair curling around his ears. It says, in huge letters, '*THE FINAL FRONTIER*'. There are two open next to each other and Juno tugs me by the hand until we're sitting side by side.

"I've never done this before," I say and squint at the machine. Juno laughs, loud and warm, and it almost makes up for the fact that she releases my hand.

"I could have guessed," she says and yanks down her mask, allowing me to see slightly smeared purple lipgloss and a happy, crooked smile. I recognize the words that I said what feels like a millenia ago and I can't help but smile back. "Watch." She grabs my hand again— I don't think too hard about the way my stomach lurches— and pulls my glove and sleeve until my watch is exposed. "I'm just gonna start with one credit, to show you."

I nod. That's fine. One credit doesn't even buy a pack of gum these days. Juno taps my watch against a plate on the front of the machine and the chunky wheels on the screen begin to spin. They flash between icons, some I recognize and others I don't— an apple, a silver disc, an old, retro looking flip phone— and it spins, and spins and spins.

"We won! Look, look," Juno says and taps at the screen with the hand not still holding mine. Sure enough, it says: *WINNER! 5 CR. PLAY AGAIN?*

Juno looks at me with a question in her eyes and I can't help it. Her enthusiasm is contagious. "Sure." She taps the screen and releases my wrist. I flex my hand and realize for the first time how hot it is in here. Sweat is sliding down my back and my palms are clammy and warm under my gloves, so I pull them off and stuff them in my jacket pocket. The wheels spin again, and land on different symbols. None of them match.

SORRY, TRY AGAIN! 0 CR. PLAY AGAIN?

"I don't even get my one credit back, huh," I mumble to Juno.

She shakes her head. "It's an all or nothing kind of system."

"Okay," I say, "I think I see the appeal. Go again." I hold out my hand, hoping the soft tips of her fingers will brush my pulse point again. When she takes my hand, I don't try to swallow the quiet exhale that escapes me. Her skin is so damn soft. It's hard to imagine a life without injury, without scars and burns littering her knuckles and wrist, but I find myself twisting my hand to link our fingers. She brings my hand over to the machine and taps my wrist again before allowing our hands to fall, still clasped, to rest on my knee.

I can't help it. I stare at our hands. I swear, they fit perfectly together. My knuckles are thick where hers are thin, her nails are clean where mine are ragged.

I swear at all the romance books downloaded onto my pad. They're rotting my brain.

Juno is off limits.

That doesn't mean I pull my hand away.

We win a 10 credit jackpot.

We sit there for around a half hour. By the end of it, we're up thirty credits. It isn't much, and Juno confides in me after a while that she picked a machine she knew had no minimum bet so we could keep our wins and losses alike quite small.

The whole time, she's touching me. Her thigh pressed against mine, her fingers threaded through my own, her laughter warm on my cheeks.

"I have an addictive personality," she says, and *stars* do I relate. "I know if I ever get really into that kind of thing, it'll kick my ass. It's why I don't smoke, too. Tried it once, knew it would ruin me, so I never touched another cigarette."

"At least we came out on top this time," I offer. Juno nods and reaches up with the same hand I've been holding on and off for an hour to scratch her forehead. A bit of green hair slips out of her knit beanie. I go to tuck it away, but she meets me halfway and takes my hand again. The pad of her thumb smooths over an old scar. Our shoulders touch.

Juno brings our linked fingers to her lips and kisses the back of my hand.

My eyes shoot wide open and I snatch my hand back, pressing it flat against my sternum.

"C'mon, Junker. Let's get a drink. How long until they're done with the refuel?" Juno asks, unaffected.

I open my mouth and then close it and I look like goddamn Pollux, I know I do. "Another half hour," I croak. I don't know if that's true, not at all, but if it means I get to spend another half hour with glittering neon reflecting against Juno's pale skin, I'll take it.

"Plenty of time for a drink," she says with that wide, bright smile, so out of place on a rock like Doda, and tugs her mask back over her face. Juno starts walking towards the bar and I'm stuck, rooted in place. I watch her go until she turns and looks back, beckons for me to come with her, and waits for me. I follow instinctively.

She orders a drink for herself, but I shake my head. My mind is on fire enough without booze— My skin is still tingling from the touch of her lips. I look down at my hand and see a smear of purple lip gloss across the knuckles. A shiver rakes through my body.

"Here," Juno says and scoots a pale yellow glass across the bar to me. "Lemonade."

I look at her. "How did you know—"

"I'm psychic," she responds and wiggles her fingertips at me. I must make a strange face, because she laughs and glides her hand down my back, resting it at the base of my spine. "I saw the cans in the Gemini's food storage."

"Ah." I pick up the glass and take a long sip. The acidity of the drink wakes me up as it drags across my tongue. I feel warm all over, warmer even where Juno's hand rests on my jacket, but the cool drink helps. I let my eyes fall closed.

POP. *POP POP POP*.

Juno and I both hit the ground immediately.

I'd know that sound anywhere, and I don't have to imagine why Juno would too. It's inescapable in Marwood's galaxy.

Gunshots.

We're belly down, face to face, and we squeeze ourselves

as tight under the bar as we can. My heart thuds a horrid staccato rhythm in my chest and I turn my face away from the sound. Juno's glass is shattered on the ground beside us, a sticky, pink liquid oozing over the tacky tile, and I narrowly avoid resting my palm in shattered glass when I shift closer to her.

"We need to hide," I breathe right beside her ear. She turns her head just slightly and I tilt my chin past her at a sturdy, wooden card table that had been empty when we walked to the bar. It could take a few bullets and, with any luck, the shooter wouldn't look behind it.

Juno nods, a jerky little motion that matches the scared flutter of her eyelids, and pulls her mask up higher on her nose. I reach out, but I'm historically bad at comforting people in a crisis, so I just hover above her shoulder until she nods again, exhales in a little puff, and makes a mad dash for the card table.

POP POP POP POP.

I stay close, close enough that I'm sure she can feel my breath on her ankles. There are dozens of other people similarly curled underneath tables and pressed against slot machines, all looking just afraid as Juno. I ignore them. I look out for me, and for Juno, and we're barely halfway across the floor to our chosen shelter.

Suddenly, an alarm begins to blare. It's the same emergency alarm they use on refuel stations, the same one I heard echo through the halls of the medship that saved me after my parents' crash. It's a sound I know well.

I reach up and jam my earplugs into my ears, but despite that, I can still here pattering, rhythmic gunshots echoing through distant areas of the casino, growing closer every minute.

Juno keeps crawling even as distant rattling and yelling gets louder and more dangerous. She gets underneath the card table right as a bullet whizzes past my head and I force myself underneath with her.

I don't know what game is played here, and really I'm just glad that there's enough space underneath the table for decks of cards, chips, and two small adults.

Juno's face, so close to mine, is pale. A bead of sweat drips down her temple. Each gunshot— less frequent now— makes me jump, but she just curls further in behind the table and meets my eyes. Wordlessly, she reaches over and takes my hand. I let her twine her fingers with mine and somewhere, distantly, I realize that I'm shaking.

Her touch helps, but there's still something buzzing in my head louder than any bullet. I've heard gunshots before. Hell, I've been in an active shooter situation before. It's not like they're uncommon, what with the unregulated sale of military-grade weapons across the galaxy. Juno leans closer to me and I squeeze her hand tight.

"Not how we thought we would be spending our time on Doda, huh," she breathes against the side of my face in a long gap between shots. I swallow hard and squeeze her hand. I can feel where her body is touching mine— her hand, pressed palm to palm against my own; her ankle on mine, warm even though our socks; the heat of breath against my ear.

"No," I whisper, "It's not."

Her gaze shifts and she gasps in a little breath, letting go of my hand to touch the inside wood of the table behind my head. I shift until I can turn and look, finding a small, round sticker stuck to the wood there. I have to squint and allow my prosthetic to adjust to the muddled darkness again, but when I see it, I gasp too.

Stuck there in a clear but hidden sign of rebellion is a sticker that says JUNO in rainbow, pixellated letters. I don't recognize it specifically, but based on Juno's response, I can fill in the gaps. I look back at her and see that her mouth is curled in a big smile. She parts her lips s if to say something, but her face simply falls and all the color drains from her cheeks.

She tilts her head towards the opening behind me, and I listen. The heavy, steady footfalls we've heard since the first shot are growing closer and closer, near-imperceptibly shaking the floor under us. I could swear that, if the table wasn't covering us, I could reach out and touch them. Juno's face is pale in the darkness and I meet her eyes despite my usual constant urge to look anywhere else.

"Give me the masker key for the slot machines," a voice says, way too fucking close for comfort. I freeze, and Juno does the same under my touch.

"It's a kid," Juno hisses.

Sure enough, the voice is that of a boy, *maybe* 15. It's high pitched and crackly even as the boy repeats his words to the kind bartender who had been serving us drinks just minutes before.

"There isn't a master key," she replies, a distinct quiver in her voice.

I shake my head and close my eyes as she signs away her life, saying no to a petulant child with an assault rifle.

"Hand it over!"

"I have to go out there," Juno breathes. I snap my eyes open at once.

"Absolutely not," I hiss and shift until I'm between her and the open side of the table. "Juno, no. That's not our responsibility."

She shakes her head and her jaw juts forward. I recognize the expression. She's not going to be persuaded.

"Maybe not yours," she says and reaches up, tracing over the sticker stuck to the inside of the card table. "But it is mine."

"You are under my protection," I insist.

"I don't need you to protect me, Junker."

I push my hand between the crook of her neck and grab on tight to the storage shelf behind her head. "Juno, please don't do this," I whisper. It comes out needy and wanting, betraying just how fast my heart is sputtering in my chest at the thought. I see her in my mind, bullet holes torn through pale skin and mottling her beautiful tattoos with dark, oozing blood.

At least she's wearing black. No stains.

"I have to," she breathes. "If I don't, I'm nothing." She stares me down, her eyes dark as endless space and darker still in our shadowed cave of protection. I wince and try to hold her gaze, but within seconds I drop away and stare into the smudged shapes of the table around us.

You're everything, I want to say, but the words press against my skull. *You're everything, and you need to stay here, stay safe. Stay with me.* Juno touches my cheek softly with her palm and uses her other hand to push my arm down. She space between our safe haven under the table and the open air above, still thick with the echoes of gunshots elsewhere in the casino, is suddenly open, empty, and light streams in without my body to block it.

Juno drops her hand from my cheek and climbs out past me. I get a whiff of that soap she uses, vanilla sickly sweet with gunshot residue hot on the air, and then she's gone.

She speaks to the shooter. It's blurry in my mind. Hazy. The words go in one ear and out the other. I don't know what she says to him, but I see the assault rifle clatter into sight on the tile floor beside me. Gunshots are still echoing in further areas, other massive rooms of *GUNNAR'S BIG WIN*, but they're far enough away that I can hear people start to quietly leave their hiding spot and make a run for the exit. Muddled, horrible sobs echo and I hear Juno's quiet murmur, comforting this fifteen year old kid who thought he should shoot up a casino to make ends meet, or make a statement.

She's so goddamn stupid, I think, but immediately push that away. She's not stupid. She's a foolish idealist who won't make it another year in this galaxy if this is how she perceives the people around her. She's unflappable, and it's going to get her killed.

"It's okay," I hear her say to the child that fully intended on killing us both if that's what it took to get his point across. "It's all going to be okay."

The Doda police show up within ten minutes, but it takes them another thirty for them to enter and subdue the other three shooters. Juno is taken in for questioning but the cops here are local contractors, not the pigs running the government that'll shoot Juno in the forehead on sight. Every time I see them within a hundred feet of her I feel dizzy, but I remind myself.

She chose this.

She made the decision to put herself in between the barrels of their guns and a fifteen year old kid with a death wish.

He's not the only one, it seems.

It turns out that it was four kids, all under seventeen. Three of them were disabled, one in a way that rings a little too close for comfort. Prosthetic she'll never pay off, burn scars, autism.

She's brought out in a body bag. Apparently, her hand twitched on her rifle when the police entered. I try not to look as they wheel her away.

She chose this, too.

I repeat the words to myself and try not to think about what I'd do if it was Juno in that bag instead. Guilt leeches into my bones, the same way it always does when I see queer people on the news being tracked down and killed. It rises like bile in my throat, but if I intervene, it's my life.

I'm checked over by a medic and led to a corner where a bench is set up where they tell me that Juno will be needed for questioning for at least another hour. I press my ear plugs dangerously far into my ear canals and close my eyes to wait, trying desperately not to think.

Juno is gone for over three hours. They took her into a small security room off the side of the main floor. I wait the whole tine, even when the cops tell the other gamblers caught in the crossfire that they're allowed to leave. I sit and I flick my equinox knife open and closed in my fingers until I nick myself between the second and third knuckle. I flick it closed and jam it deep in my pocket, pressing the round palm of my hand against my ears. I push my earlobes up and fold them over, trying desperately to block out the cheery noise echoing through the casinos, the slot machines up and running and hundreds of people gambling away like three children weren't killed or arrested here just minutes ago.

The slot machines are still on, and the infinite ringing presses even through every attempt I've made to block out the noise.

When Juno steps out after three and a half hours, I spring to my feet and start walking out of the casino. She follows silently all the way out into the rain and droning blur of Doda's atmosphere. I yank my hood up, my mask, my goggles. I pull up everything around me to block out each prick of freezing debris.

I block out Juno too, even as I see the faint movements

under her mask that imply speech. I shake my head and cross my arms tight against my chest.

Holding hands in front of a retro slot machine feels years away, worn away with adrenaline and time.

The rest of the walk to the dock is quiet. I can still feel the bone-deep reverberations in my chest but I focus on each step: one foot in front of the other. There's something in my head that won't go away, a buzzy, desperate ache that makes me want to flap my arms and kick my feet out. I push back as hard as I can and tap a rhythm on my elbow, gritting out quiet, breathy noises that nobody should be able to hear.

When we get within eyeshot of the dock, I realize that something is wrong.

Dozens— Maybe even hundreds— of people are waiting to board their ships and leave. It reminds me of Janus, the desperate mass exodus after Juno's riot. I frown and turn to my companion, but she's already turned to speak with someone else, her facemask pulled down over her chin. I pull out one earplug.

"What's going on?" Juno shouts over the noise.

The man, also dressed in dark, warm clothes, with every bit of his body covered save for a thin strip for his eyes, looks at us with resigned boredom in his eyes. "We're stuck until they decide it's safe for us to leave," he grunts.

"Who?"

"Cops. Apparently there was a shooting," he says and shrugs loosely. "Another day, another death."

Juno pulls her mask back up and nods, but I see something glistening in her eyes. I walk over to the edge of the raised passage where there's a three-foot railing and sit down against it beside dozens of others doing the same. Juno sits beside me, so close our thighs brush.

"You stayed," she says. The words are quiet, just for me, and I take a long breath.

"You're my cargo," I reply. Juno nods, claps her gloved hand against my knee gently, and then curls in on herself while we wait for the Doda police to clear the exits. I listen for a minute, not to the torturous sounds of the atmosphere's breath through this hole-ridden planet, but to the other people waiting with us. There are kids crying with women and men alike trying to calm them down, some older couples standing so close to each other their coats blend into one mass of fabric. There are other young people, solo pilots like me and groups like the sort I imagine Juno is used to. I see a long pink braid peeking out of a hoodie and I hear the person attached to it laugh, loud and jovial, but then quiet themself and huddle closer to the taller person beside them.

It's a perfect microcosm of the human existence I've come to distrust so deeply. People are filled with joy, people are hollow with sadness. Babies cry, people die, and still, people like me and Juno and this person with the pink braid have to hide ourselves, fit ourselves into tiny boxes to keep from drawing attention.

I've spent the decade since my parents died hiding, and Juno has spent it becoming the face of the revolution. Only one thing can happen to a figure that public: martyrdom.

I sigh and press my forehead against my knees. I put my earplug back in and try to quiet my brain, but Juno's thigh pressed against mine, the only warmth on this planet of frozen rain and roaring wind, keeps me from resting.

Juno doesn't try to talk to me again until we're on the ship.

It takes a full hour before the cops decide they've caught all the perpetrators of the attempted robbery on the casino, and then it takes us another hour to make it back onto the ship. By the time we're both on the Gemini with the hatch shut tight, I'm dripping with built up rain and all I want to do is fucking hit something.

I pull off my outermost layers, the ones soaked through with freezing rain, and drape them over some crates down in the storage area. Juno waits until I'm done and back in the main cabin and then climbs down into storage to do the same. I turn the temperature on the ship up a little bit and feed Pollux, checking his water temperature as well. Once I'm satisfied, I move to the cockpit. I gather up Apollo's rabbit and set him on the dash, staring back at me with black button eyes.

"I'm tired," I whisper.

He doesn't reply. I sigh and figure out where we're going next— refuel station Tortoiseshell, which is a full 26 hour day's flight from here. Our fuel is completely full and we're good on water for a while yet, as long as we keep up the rate of use we've fallen into. We got rations on Doda, but it's probably a good idea to pick up some more at the next stop. I groan and rub at my eyes for a second, crusted with salt and exhaustion, and then I strap myself in.

Juno wordlessly sits in her own seat and buckles up. As soon as she does, I pull back on the steering apparatus and lift us off this horrible planet, through the thick layer of cloud that separates Doda's atmosphere from open space, and set us on a course for refuel station Tortoiseshell.

As soon as the artificial gravity clanks on, me and Juno both silently unbuckle.

"Are you okay?" she asks.

I.

Well.

That's not what I expected her to say.

"What?"

"I realized that Doda must be like hell for you, with all of the, uh." She rubs at the back of her neck. I see a tattoo underneath her armpit, a long shape in black ink smudged into her skin. "Stimulation."

My face must do something awful, because her eyes widen and she shakes her hands.

"It's just so loud," she says. She must realize how silly it sounds, because she bites down on her still-purple lip and doesn't say anything else.

"Everywhere is tough for me," I say. It comes out scratchy, like I just woke up. "Everywhere is loud, everywhere is bright. It gets under my skin no matter where I go, and Doda is no different. I don't want your pity."

"It's not pity, Junker—"

"It is, and I don't want it. I..." I let out a noise, a nonsensical, frustrated grunt, and I press the palms of my hands into my eye sockets. "I don't need to explain myself to you."

"But you waited for me."

"I waited for you because if I left you, I wouldn't get paid," I snap and pull my hands down, pushing them harshly against my ribs. Juno doesn't retreat at the volume, just steps closer to me, all green hair and sharp black lines right in my face.

"You waited for me because, some part of you, deep down behind years of loneliness and trauma, behind your fake fucking apathy, some part of you *cares*!" She's yelling and my hands go back up to my ears. I press a knuckle against my eardrum on each side and close my eyes tight.

"I don't," I say. "I don't, I can't. I can't care about your galactic war, not when it could kill me."

"That's when you have to care the most," she spits. It's muffled through the bone and flesh between her lips and my ears and I shake my head.

"I don't have the privilege to, not like you do," I murmur and press harder at the side of my head. The pressure makes the twitchiness in my fingers fade, the urge to scream and smash my fists into the thin metal separating us from the vacuum of endless space fade into nothing but a dull twinge.

Juno scoffs. "Junker," she says, "Look at me, please." I open my eyes, but I can't look any closer than her shoulder. She seems to accept that, because she says, "I'd give my life to keep others safe. I will do anything in my power for the rest of my life to make the people who will come after us have a safer and more comfortable existence."

I shake my head and slowly pull my hands away from my ears. The sound of pure nothing breathing against the outside of the ship soothes me, wraps me up in the only safety I've had for almost a decade. "You're wasting your time," I manage. Juno sighs and turns away. She runs her fingers through her hair and tugs on a little knot, loosing it within seconds.

"Believe that if you will. Maybe you're right. We're nothing, anyways. I'm just cargo." Juno steps into the bathroom and shuts the door behind her. I let out a long groan and sink down into the pilot's chair. I sit for about eight seconds before I stand up, the need to be active and work some of the energy out of my system more compelling than the urge to rest. My legs are itching, desperate for something to do, but we're going to be stuck on this ship for over 26 hours and there's nowhere to go in a barely two hundred square foot box hurtling through space.

I pace.

I grab Apollo's rabbit and I rub it on my face. That helps a bit, but not enough. I tuck it back into the seat and keep walking back and forth, my boots heavy against the metal floor. I can hear Juno in the bathroom but the shower isn't on.

I do another lap, and then I kneel in the main cabin of the ship and pull up a grate that covers part of the under-floor storage. There's a punching bag down there, one I bought a year or so ago when I decided to stop using the gyms on refuel stations after my top surgery. I hoist it up and out of the storage compartment and hook it onto a carabiner clipped onto the ceiling in the ship. It's in the back, opposite the cockpit, so I pull off my shirt and toss it into the laundry chute. From the drawer under my bunk I produce a pair of bike shorts, nearly knee length and skin tight, and I change into those quickly. In socks and shorts, I wrap my hands quickly with two long pieces of cloth.

The thud of my fists into the bag sound good to my wanting ears, but even more so the sharp impact of my knuckles, even through the wrist wraps, sends reverberations up my arm into my shoulder that feel *good.* I know I'll be sore tomorrow but right now, I can't find it in myself to care. Right now, the rhythmic thuds of my fists against the bag are all I need to feel okay.

I distantly note when Juno steps out of the bathroom, but my attention stays on the bag. It doesn't seem relevant that Juno is behind me, or at least, it doesn't until she catches my wrist mid-swing.

"Watch out," I manage to say as my fist continues in its course, jerking her hand along with it. She pivots with the movement until we're shoulder to shoulder, her left hand clutching mine, our faces inches apart. She drops my hand and cocks her head to the side. As she pulls a little black rubber band from her wrist, she licks her lips.

"I know we're just... Crewmates, if anything," she says and thoughtlessly ties her hair up in a messy bun, "But will you still teach me how to fight?"

I watch one loose strand of green hair fall down to brush her shoulder and, before I can stop myself, I pluck it from her skin and offer it to her. She takes it in her fingers and stuffs it into her messy updo, securing it away.

"Yeah."

Punching Juno, the stupid, tattooed, broad-shouldered object of every single one of my current frustrations can't hurt, right? "In the drawer with my clothes in it, there's another set of wraps."

She crouches down and I watch as she rummages through to find the wraps. I let myself look at the pale skin between her jeans and her tank top, and promise myself that I'll hit the bag extra hard later to make up for it.

Turns out I wasn't in the worst of it yet, because as soon as Juno has the wraps held securely in her hand, she stands up and shucks her jeans off onto the floor. I'm aware in some far-away capacity that I'm staring, but I can't make myself look away. Down her right thigh in stark, black ink is an enormous octopus with tentacles and detailed suckers curling all the way around her kneecap and up her hip under her black underwear.

"You have a problem?" she asks me and I look back up to her face. There's a little smudge of pink on each cheekbone and I shake my head, sure I'm flushing in much the same way. I clench my jaw.

"When you're dressed," I say, and thank infinity it comes out clear and strict when my stomach is busy doing that horrible, traitorous thing it likes to do when Juno shows skin, "I'll show you how to wrap your fists."

She nods and pulls on a pair of leggings I remember buying back on Redhawk. I don't watch. Instead, I open the fridge and get two bottles of cycled water. I set one down on the table and crack open the other, taking a long drag. The icy cold soothes me, tamps down all of the terrible unwarranted heat that Juno makes me feel, god *damn* her. When I turn around, she's fully dressed, and she holds out the white strips of tape. I take it, careful not to brush her palms with my fingertips.

"See how mine is?" I say and hold out my own hand, palm up, for her to look at. She nods. "The goal is to protect the joints. If you throw a bad punch when your hands aren't taped, you're much more likely to break something. So..." I trail off and hold out both my hands palm up in a gesture for her to do the same. She does, and I grit my teeth as I take a step closer to wrap her knuckles.

I loop the end of the wrap around her thumb and start twisting it and winding it, going between each finger until I finally twist it back around and connect it, tucking it under itself at the base of her palm.

"See?" I say and it comes out so quiet and tender that I want to rip my hands away and never look Juno in the eye again. Instead, I move to her other hand and do the same motions. Juno's eyes never leave her hands and she nods again when I'm finished.

"Got it," she murmurs. "I bet I could do it on my own, next time."

"Probably," I say.

I hope you don't, I don't say. *I hope you don't so I can keep accidentally brushing my fingertips against your pulse.*

I pivot and walk over to the bag, gesturing for her to take a stance. She does, and I immediately correct her posture, her form, the way she's holding her fists.

"You'll break your thumb if you punch like that," I say softly — too fucking softly, I'm supposed to be mad— and take her hand, unfolding her fingers and refolding them with her thumb on the outside. I press on her hip until she isn't leaning forward anymore, and then I step back. "Watch me." I shift into a fighting stance and slowly throw a punch, and then another, telegraphing every movement. I'm barely hitting the bag, but

Juno's eyes on my body feel better than the pressure on my knuckles did to begin with. The anger I felt at her has fizzled out, shifted to a warmth deep in my gut.

"I understand," she says and shifts back into posture, this time much closer to correct. I nod approvingly and look at her hands.

"Good," I say and touch her shoulder. "When you throw a punch, use the force from here," I move my hand to her shoulder blade and trace over the muscle, "Not just your arm." She nods and twists her body again, punching out with her right hand.

I tap her thigh. "Don't keep your feet locked. Be fluid with it. You want to move with the punch, be ready for the kick-back." She shifts and bounces up on the balls of her feet. I nod approvingly and step away. She throws a few punches at the bag and I give her a few more tips, but she's a natural. It makes sense that she can run a riot as effortlessly as she does, as confident and unflinching as she is now up on a car, or a podium, or a rooftop. Her body is made to be the force that changes things, she just didn't know how to use the parts other than her voice.

"Do you ever practice with other people?" she asks as she takes a sip of water.

"I used to." I drink too, and the cold water feels good going down. "I used to go to a gym on a refuel station, in a huge rec center a lot. That was before I... Well." I gesture to my bare chest, and she nods.

"What about now?" she says and wiggles her fingers at me, "I'm right here."

I snort. "Yeah, and you learned how to throw a punch an hour ago. I'm not going to hit you."

"I can take it," she replies, a frown creasing her cheeks and brow.

"I know you can, princess," I say and I can see her jaw do

that thing again, that little 'I can do anything I set my mind to' thing. "Maybe I don't want to pummel you, is all."

"Please," she says and steps forward, into my personal space. I screw the cap back on my water and set it down on the table.

"This isn't exactly the safest place to spar, either," I say but she shakes her head.

"We're not really sparring, just— You'd just be helping me to judge distance and stuff for if I need to get in a real fight," she says, and then, "*Please.*" She looks so goddamn determined.

"Fine," I spit out before I can stop myself. I move us into the center of the cabin so there's no chance of either of us missing and slamming our fists into hard aluminum alloy. It's a decent enough open area and I shift back into my fighting stance. "If you aim for the spot next to my head, you'll get a good idea of—"

Before I can even finish my sentence, Juno throws a wild punch in my direction, definitely not aiming for the air surrounding me. Her fist thuds hard into my collarbone and I gasp out a forced breath. She bounces back and shifts between each foot, her eyes wild and ready.

"C'mon, Junker," she taunts. I squint and adjust my posture again, and then we're off.

I haven't thought much about having sex with Juno, but I'm pretty sure if we did sleep together it would feel a lot like this. Our fists are hard yet fit perfectly into the squishy flesh of each others' bodies, all while sweat drips down our chins, our chests, our backs. I try to hold back at first, but Juno makes it clear within the first minute that she wants me to hit her, so I do.

I hit her for every stupid thing she's done since she started riding on my ship. I hit her for every time she flicked her hair my way and the faint scent of vanilla shampoo wafted through the recycled air of the Gemini. I hit her for every time I've wanted to kiss her.

So, really, I hit her a lot.

She hits me just as much, and we both dodge just as many times as well, and by the time she pins me on the floor of the Gemini with her knees straddling my hips, we're both panting and dripping with sweat. I wriggle but she's holding my wrists tight and my body is drained.

I'm too tired to fight back, so I don't. Her skin isn't even touching mine, but the heat I can feel through her leggings, through the wraps on her hands, the sweat falling from her chin onto my bruising collarbone— My mouth falls open, and the room smells like sweat, vanilla, and Juno.

"I think I won," she gasps above me, her teeth glinting silver in the starlight streaming in through the front windshield. I gnash my teeth but she just grins and holds me down. Her pectorals, under her collarbones but above her breasts, press tight at her sports bra and loose tank top. Each muscle is strong — strong enough to hold me down— and I want to bite, right there—

I slap my palm on the ground in the universal gesture for a tap out. She laughs and rolls off me at once, and I almost immediately regret it. My body feels cold, slick with chilling sweat, with the heat she provided moving away.

"Thank you for teaching me how to fight," Juno murmurs and lays down beside me, collapsed against my arm. I look at her, into her huge, planet eyes, and I feel too much, all at once.

I roll away and pull myself up.

I don't offer Juno my hand.

"I call first shower," I say instead and squeeze into the small bathroom, leaving Juno, warm and pliant, on the floor behind me. I strip naked and stare at myself in the small mirror. There are a few bruises coloring my skin now, red marks and a few darker purple ones across my chest, and I press down on one of them. Pain radiates across my front but I don't wince.

My hair is getting long. I run my palm over the short length of it and finally turn away to turn on the water. I twist the dial as cold as I can without being sent back to Doda and, after unlatching my leg and leaning it against the far wall, I sink into the chair I built myself and shut my eyes tight.

Between my legs is slick and I feel desperate— *Wanting*— in a way I don't like to be. I like being attracted to people. I even like sex— it's not like I haven't slept with people before. What I don't like is this lack of control. This hot, sudden, embarrassing *crush* that makes me feel like a goddamn marionette. I rub the tops of my hairy thighs with my hand and try to calm down.

The cold water helps, but I turn it colder still.

I wash my body until my skin shines pink and raw.

6
CONTROLLED MASS MEDIA

When we get to Tortoiseshell, it's clear that the efforts to bring in Juno have at *least* doubled. Every screen surrounding us is toting a three-dimensional hologram of Juno on the day I rescued her from Janus. Only a few days have passed, but I swear she looks older since then.

Because of this, we stick to the shadows. I've relegated myself to only speaking to Juno when it's necessary, and she seems content to mostly stay in silence. With the mask covering the bottom half of her face, round, black sunglasses we picked up from a street vendor covering her eyes, and a black beanie on, she's unrecognizable.

Well. Not to me.

We've barely known each other a week, but I think I could pick her out of a crowd in a heartbeat.

We buy our rations. Juno picks them, and I pretend not to notice that she only chooses ones that I have had stocked on the ship while she's been on board. We get food— there's a taco stand here that sells us each three tacos for eight credits a piece — and then we head back to the ship. They're backed up with the amount of ships here, apparently many others seeking refuge after Doda as well, so they aren't done with our docking maintenance.

I pull the ladder down and prop myself up against the third rung, one foot still on the concrete floor of the dock yard. It's steep enough that I can't quite sit, but it'll do for the few minutes it'll take for us to eat and for the little, buzzy robots to finish up our refuel and maintenance. Juno sits criss-cross on the floor beside my feet and tugs her mask down to eat.

Even though we're pretty well hidden underneath the Gemini's landing gear as the ship casts a large shadow under where it sits six feet off the ground, I still feel a shard of anxiety pierce my chest. I turn my gaze from the distant stars visible through the refuel station's glass ceiling and instead start scanning the faces of those who pass us, searching for any glimmer of recognition.

Everyone passes without incident, and we take off a few minutes later with full bellies and a lingering question hanging in the air between us. I stay in the cockpit for longer than is explicitly necessary after taking off, listening to Juno puttering around in the main cabin behind me. I'm only drawn back into the ship when I hear the TV click on.

"*Welcome back to HAZARD*!" the speakers say, and of *course* she puts on my favorite trivia show. I almost have the self awareness to be embarrassed when I sulk back into the cabin and sink into my seat, peering at the TV while ignoring Juno entirely.

It's trivia. My one weakness.

"*Which refuel station, found in the Williamsburg system, is home to the largest ball of twine, rescued from Kansas when old Earth began to fall to climate death?*"

"Lionfish," I mutter.

"It didn't fall to climate death. Humanity killed it," Juno says at the TV.

The first contestant guesses refuel station Harlequin, which isn't even in the right system. I snort and shake my head before shifting to be more comfortable in my seat. The second contestant gets it and sighs deeply in relief when three hundred credits are added to their total score.

The host, Janice Starr, is an older woman who started as a 'lovely assistant' on another trivia show and eventually started producing HAZARD, all of which happened before I was even born. She was deemed 'too old' or 'too unattractive' to maintain her previous position, but she does more worthwhile work on HAZARD than she ever did on whatever her other show was.

Her long white hair is pulled up in a sleek, straight ponytail and, as she turns back to the board, it swings in a wide arc behind her. The second contestant chooses a spot on the board and the card flips, only to reveal—

"Hazard! Oh, too bad," Janice titters in her accented voice and turns to the wheel behind her. "Looks like its time to spin the Hazard Wheel!"

The hazard wheel is the show's schtick, but I couldn't care less about it. If the contestants could just answer trivia all episode long, I'd be content, but every game show or reality show has to have some kind of twist these days.

It's a huge wheel in alternating stripes of black and yellow, each panel labeled with a 'hazard'. These range from 'BACK-PACK', which gives the contestant a thirty pound backpack to wear for the rest of the game, all the way to 'WHAMMY', which takes away all the money the contestant has earned so far. Some of them are stupid, but others are just hurtful.

Normally, I use the hazard wheel as an excuse to check my messages, but my pad is back in the cockpit.

Janice grabs onto one of the pegs and pulls it hard, spinning the dizzying wheel hard. The music amps up and the crowd begins to chant— Hazard! Hazard! I sigh and tap my fingers against my knee until it lands on the slice that says 'DOUBLE OR NOTHING'.

The crowd goes wild. I roll my eyes, but this one means they get a tough question, so I lean forward.

Janice does her little intro, and then reads from the cards in her hand. "Which galactic president was elected with the biggest majority vote of all time?"

I groan.

"You know it?" Juno asks quietly, and it's the first time she's spoken to me since we sparred. Some part of me wants to be petty and stay silent, but HAZARD gets my blood boiling in a way nothing else does.

Well, nothing excluding my present company.

"Bridger," I answer, "Not like that election was anything close to legitimate."

"Yeah?"

"Yeah, it was a shit show. A couple systems' votes weren't even counted, another system was legislated into a new galactic district so their votes would barely count for anything. Bridger is a fascist who isn't afraid to use every inch of his governmental power to keep the people from having any say in what he does," I explain and turn to look at Juno. She has an expression on her face like someone tied a string to her eyebrows and tugged until she relaxed. "You knew all that, though."

Juno shrugs. "I can always use another perspective," she says and her face shuts down again, guarded and composed. "Though, with how much you know about Bridger, and Marwood, and the law, it's shocking how you refuse to use it for anything."

I groan and turn back to the TV, completely ignoring her sentiment. What part of 'we are shipmates, cargo and smuggler, nothing more' does Juno not understand? She's not going to be able to change me. If I was going to be radicalized, it would've happened when I saw my brother ripped in two bloody pieces.

The contestant doesn't answer the question correctly and his money is set back to zero. I don't feel bad for him.

As soon as the camera cuts back to the view of all four contestants standing at their podiums, the audio cuts out and is replaced with the scratchy inhale of the ship's radio.

"*Come in Gemini,*" the radio gurgles, a stately, confident voice gritting out through the waves of reverb and tinny echo.

I hop up and move into the cockpit and press down on the button to activate the radio. "This is the Gemini," I say. My voice comes out steadier than I feel and I turn around, transmitter in hand. I point at the grate in the floor and she nods, immediately beginning to quietly pull it up.

"*Gemini, this is the Intergalactic Police Force.*" Juno gets the grate up and wiggles into the storage area, tugging the cover shut again behind her. "*How many passengers are on board your ship?*"

"Just me, sir."

"*And you are?*"

I grit my teeth. "I'm Castor Quasar, the owner of the Gemini. I'll send over my license and registration."

"*We await your paperwork.*"

I release the transmitter and turn back to the main cabin. I peer down through the grate and don't see or hear her, so I grab my pad and use it to send over my paperwork. When I return to the cockpit, I can see the ship flying parallel us, the IPF officer speaking visible in the windshield.

"*We have received the necessary documents.*"

I sink back into the pilot's seat and fidget with the metal buckles that make up the harness. It's quiet for a moment and I rub my palm against my head again. My hair is getting too long.

"*Miss Quasar, where are you headed?*"

I wince at the title. It's been a long time since anyone has both known my name and also deemed it appropriate to misgender me. It's not uncommon, but it still hurts.

"I'm a junker, sir," I say into the mouthpiece. "I'm headed to a planet nearby that I heard had a crash site on it."

"Which planet."

It doesn't come out like a question, like they just expect me to tell them whether they're asking or demanding. In this galaxy, it doesn't make a difference.

I glance at the coordinates I picked up on Tortoiseshell and then at the navigation still pulled up on my pad. "Anat-3," I answer. The other end is silent for a few minutes, probably searching for any evidence I could possibly be lying. The longer they're silent, the more anxiety brews in my gut. By the time the radio clicks back on, my toe is tapping repeatedly against the ground.

"You're clear to continue," he says, *"But go straight there. We have reports of dangerous fugitives in this quadrant."*

My heart sinks.

"Thank you, officer," I manage with a clear voice. The cruiser speeds off and I lean forward until I can press my forehead against the dashboard. I stay there for a second, just cool pleather against hot, nervous skin, and once I'm sure they're gone, I jump up and go over to the grate.

I pull it up quickly and drop into the storage area.

"Juno?"

The lid of an old crate pops up just an inch and I see two glistening beetle eyes glint back at me in the low light. "Junker," she whispers.

"How much of that did you hear?"

She lifts the lid of the crate off and shakes her head. "None of it, not any— Are you okay? What did they want?"

I nod. "We're safe, Juno." Her name feels too warm in my

mouth, like honey on fresh bread. It feels nothing like the cold, oppressive words I forced out to the IPF. "They know you're in this quadrant, though."

She pales even further. "I—"

"It's okay. They've cleared the Gemini, so we shouldn't be stopped again, okay?"

Juno climbs out of the crate and lunges forward, enveloping me in a hug. I freeze at the contact but her body is warm and she's trembling so I rub my palms over her shoulders again and again and again.

"It's okay," I repeat. She breathes against my collarbone and I hold her tight.

"I wish my brother was here," she whispers. "He'd know what to do."

"Where's he?"

"Adrestia," she sniffs. Her hair is in my face and normally the loose, wispy fluff on my cheeks would make me need to rub at the skin until it's red, but something about Juno's green hair against my nose makes me want to bury my face in her and never leave. It's the same dangerous train of thought that's been chasing me since we met— The same thoughts that, since yesterday when we sparred, I swore I wouldn't have anymore. Here it is anyways, baby soft and vanilla scented.

"We'll get there," I promise her. "Two and a half more weeks, and we'll be there with your brother."

She nods against my shoulder and then pulls back. Her cheeks are pink and her nose is red and I want to tug her close again. I want to hug her and promise that it'll be okay.

"Sorry," she says, and climbs out of the storage area.

By the time I have it in me to follow her, she's locked in the bathroom. HAZARD is still on, buzzing quietly at low volume, but I turn it off and go back into the cockpit. I press Apollo's rabbit to my mouth and breathe in the familiar scent of old fabric and fifteen years of wear and tear.

My mind feels fuzzy. Every time I think I understand the depth of my feelings for Juno Marcus I turn around and feel more, feel deeper, and I hate it. I shouldn't feel anything for her at all. I should treat her like any cargo, but then her dark lips curl up in a sweet smile and she says something clever, something teasing, and I want to reach out and pull her to my chest.

I set my prosthetic down on the floor of the ship and roll over, tugging my blanket tight under my chin.

I don't sleep much, but it's safer to pretend I am, so I don't have to look Juno in the eye again.

The crash on Anat-3 is less picked over than the last crash that me and Juno checked out. This is great, because it means there's more to scavenge, but it also means we have to start by wrenching pry bars into gaps in the metal exterior and popping the fuselage free. It takes us close to an hour but by the time there's a hole big enough for both of us to fit through, I'm almost entirely certain that we're the first junkers here.

Juno is equipped with my spare gear again, so I show her a panel to start on as soon as we get inside. I do my own exploration of the ship and she begins to hum a quiet song that echoes throughout every corridor. It's not too big, just a central loop with some offshoot rooms, the cockpit buried in the center. I've seen this kind of layout before, but...

The door to the cockpit is blocked. It looks like the storage area just across the way had a faulty door and a half-dozen heavy, metal crates have slid out into the walkway, pinning the door shut. It's feasible to get it open again, it'll just take an hour or two I'd rather spend junking.

Each crate weighs at least fifty pounds. I'm sure I could unload them and move the pieces on their own much easier, but Juno and I can only spend a day here, so I can't take that kind of time. Juno's quiet singing rings in my ears and I find that it helps me pass the time quicker as I hoist the weighty boxes back into the storage room.

By the time the crates are out of the way, my back is sore and I'm dripping with sweat. The other hemisphere of Anat-3 is chock full of tourist opportunities due to the hot springs and towering mountain cities spread across steel platforms stretching between peaks, but if you're here for work, the mugginess is a bit unbearable. Not to mention that sweat under my clothes is one of my least favorite sensory experiences in the whole fucking galaxy. I take a second to wipe my brow with a bit of cloth tucked into my bag, and then I finally head into the cockpit.

As always, I head straight for the dashboard and start pulling up panels. They come up easy and I turn my focus to the wires, chips, and other bits of computer scrap hidden in the body of the ship. Juno starts whistling a song I know and I hum along under my breath. I like how the vibrations feel in my chest. I pull another of those small, blue plugs carefully from the motherboard and squint at it, but it doesn't reveal anything new to me. I put it in my bag anyways.

Now, deep in the dashboard, is a bit of glistening silver wire. I've found this before in a couple of newer ships, and even one intact strand can bag ten credits. It's like gold sitting down there, barely illuminated in the dim light of the ship.

I stop humming to hold my screwdriver in my mouth and reach back in, stretching my fingertips all the way down to the bottom until I feel the edges of the soldering holding the wire in place. My nails are a bit long, so I pick at the edge until I feel a bit of give—

Distantly, I notice that something has changed. I can't put my finger on the disruption, but I *can* put my finger under the silver wire, reaching so carefully— Aha! I pull my arm out and examine it. Perfect condition. I grin and tuck it into my bag.

I should show Juno so she knows what to look for—

Juno.

The quiet voice that had been reverberating through the interior of the ship, carrying a quiet, rounded tune— It's gone. A pang of anxiety surges through my chest.

I pull my bag tighter up my shoulder and turn around, heading for the hole we carved in the metal exterior of the ship, hurrying but not running— "Juno?"

I turn the corner where I left her, and the breath is punched out of my chest.

Her borrowed bag is splayed out on the ground, bits of wire and makeshift tools spilling out onto metal flooring.

"Juno!" I yell and scoop up the bag, squeezing out through the hole we carved to get in. The light blinds me for just a second, but as soon as I blink it away, I look out to see two International Police Force goons shoving a handcuffed Juno into a ship half the size of the Gemini. I cry out and run, sprinting towards the ship. I reach out, my fingertips smeared with grease and dust—

Juno's brown eyes are wide and scared and they're the last goddamn thing I see before the bastards take off with her. I slow to a half and watch them fly away, through the atmosphere and into open space. I could swear, just for a second, that I see a flash of green hair in the icy glass window before they disappear.

I fall to my knees. "Juno," I pant and press my palm to my own heaving chest. "Fuck!"

I keep looking into the sky, into the spot in the atmosphere where the cruiser disappeared, but nothing I do will reverse what has happened. It's gone.

Juno is gone.

My chest aches with the loss and I swallow hard, managing to force myself to my feet.

"I won't let you keep her," I say to the sky.

The Gemini is parked a bit away from the crash behind an outcropping of rock. I run to it and yank myself up and into the hatch, shutting it quickly behind me. As soon as I'm in the cockpit, I strap myself in and turn the ship on. Within ten seconds I'm in the sky and within thirty I'm in open space, turning until I see a wisp of a contrail heading off towards the galactic east.

"Verita," I gasp, panting still from my desperate sprint to the ship, "What is the closest government holding facility in that direction?"

"Fort Harrison High Security Prison," Verita parrots back.

"Fuck!" I cry out again and press my face into my hands. The high security prisons, the ones built in the last forty years or so, are all literal mazes. Every inch of the space is used for cells, kitchens, exercise rooms, whatever, but they are, in essence, enormous metal discs floating in space with only one path from either of the two entrances to the central control room. There's basically no way to find your way around without knowing the layout of each individual prison. That, or just committing to trial and error, which is sure to waste just enough time to get you killed.

I realize vaguely that I'm smacking my palm dully into my temple, the pressure and impact soothing the urge deep inside me to scream, to hit the wall, to pull my own hair out. I hit harder until the sound of my palm against my skin makes a louder noise, until the skin is surely reddened under my touch, and then I force myself to stop. I pull my hand down and look out the windshield.

I know there's a refuel station nearby. It's the one me and Juno were going to swing by after we finished junking to sell our scrap. It's a decent size; there's a definite chance I might be able to bribe a cop, or pay someone off to get me a map of the prison.

It's unlikely, but it might be my best bet. I don't have contacts, not besides the odd fence I've sold to more than once, but Luka is days away and surely wouldn't have anything to help me break Juno out, which feels like my only option.

I let my gaze wander, stopping on tiny pinpricks of light, distant stars and planets swirling and shifting, the calculations Verita projects onto the screens in the dashboard, an old gash in the leather from when I tried to teach myself how to flip my Equinox knife—

Oh.

My gaze lands on a small, round sticker pressed into the dashboard. It wasn't there before I picked Juno up, but I recognize it all the same. Rainbow pixels form her name in all caps on a white background: merchandise turned revolution signaling. Right underneath it, her jacket is on the floor, discarded beside the pilot's chair. The patches face up, phrases Juno painstakingly embroidered into her favorite black jacket, phrases meant for kindred spirits to read and respect.

I bite my lip. I know there are others out there that want to help her, would do anything to help me save her at a moment's notice. Nova and Mars enter my head, from back on Janus. I know they would help.

Instinctively, I push it away. I should be able to do this on my own. I've done everything my whole life on my own. I've gotten Juno this far on my own. I know, logically, that this is when I need to ask for help, but everything in me down to the very makeup of my being says isolate, isolate, isolate. I can do it on my own.

For Juno, though.

I can't let her down.

I pick up my phone and stare at Nova's number. I look at Pollux, who is bubbling around in his aquarium, and I tell him: "For Juno."

✦——

Nova picks up within two rings. "Hello?"

"Nova," I say, "This is— This is Castor Quasar. You helped me and— And a *friend* get off Janus around a week ago."

"The junker," she says, "Aye, I remember."

"I need your help."

"Again?"

"It's important. It's for Juno."

Nova falls silent. It's quiet for almost a full minute, only soft shuffling noises and skin on skin coming from the other end, and I realize somewhat belatedly that she must be signing to Mars.

Finally, she sighs. "What happened?"

"She's been taken. I think she's at Fort Harrison."

Nova whistles. "That's tough. Yeah, Mars, I know. I— I know, Mars."

"What?"

"Mars— Fine, we'll help."

I exhale in relief. "Thank you. I'm on my way to refuel station Goliath. Where can I meet you?"

"How handy, we're in the same system. Meet us at the bao place by the body mod parlor on Goliath in a few hours," she says.

"Okay," I say, but I don't hang up. "Nova?"

"Mmm?"

"I... Thank you."

It feels strange in my mouth, but I think she's earned it. I hear more rustling, like she's signing to Mars.

"Yeah, yeah. Be there. We'll leave if you aren't."

Nova hangs up.

The Gemini is so quiet it's loud, every little noise of the outside vacuum against the fuselage of the ship deafening, even as we go barely a third of the Gemini's highest speed. We— I, I amend— can't draw attention. It'll ruin any chance I might have of saving Juno.

"Verita, put something on, please," I ask, and Verita turns on HAZARD. "Not that!" It switches to the news, but what plays on the screen isn't much better.

There, two bruised hands cuffed together with gleaming metal, is Juno. Her temple is bleeding and one of her lips is split. She wasn't hurt, at least not on her face, when she was thrust up into the cruiser on Anat-3, and the sight of her wounded now makes my blood boil. They had her tied up, they had her captured, and they still saw it in themselves to hit her until she bled, until she looked like *this*. I want to cry, both for her and for everyone she's been the face of a movement for, but my throat is dry and so are my eyes.

"Juno," I murmur. As if responding to my voice, the Juno on the screen looks at the camera and, despite everything, grins. Her eyeliner is smudged under her eyes and her lips are painted the same deep green they were when we walked onto that crash, matching with the shining emerald of her hair. She's surrounded by a dozen guards as she's walked from the docking port outside Fort Harrison to the gate, and then the news cuts back to the anchor with a picture of Juno overlaid on the display.

She's younger than she is now in the image. Her face isn't as soft yet, still angular from the childhood she didn't get to have. Her hair is dyed green still, but only the bottom half; the rest is her natural dark brown. It makes her similarly warm eyes sparkle like she's up to something.

Knowing her, she probably was.

She's wearing a black long-sleeved shirt with cutouts on the shoulders revealing pale, unmarred skin. Her tattoos must have been a later addition, once she and Gideon had officially left their parents. Her legs are made longer by dense, black criss-cross patterns covering every inch of them under a short skirt. She looks so young but so much like her, like Juno, that I catch myself reaching out towards the screen.

It cuts to a clip from one of Juno's videos. She's sitting in front of a plain backdrop with a rainbow flag hanging just out of focus to the side. The anchor is saying some bullshit about Juno spreading dangerous rhetoric, turning kids of tomorrow into cultists— I block her out and focus on the video clip. Juno gesticulates wildly and her lips spread into a wide smile as she talks. The video is muted though, surely to keep her from further spreading her 'groomer agenda'. Stars, how I wish I could hear her voice.

Juno looks so starkly different from all the other trans people I've known. She's confident, even when her legs under her tights are fuzzy with hair I know she shaves near-religiously, even when her eyeliner smudges into dark circles under her eyes, even when the cops are sneering her deadname and hoisting guns into the air.

The look in her eye when she was taken, pulled into that prison with chains between her legs and her skin gripped so tight it's pure white by fists that, if given the opportunity, would surely pummel her skull in— That look, that *light*—

It isn't fear.

It's *spite*.

My mouth twists up until I can feel it in my ears, through my jaw, at the corners of my mouth. I grin, freely and openly.

"I'm gonna come get you," I whisper into the quiet ship. "I'm coming, Juno."

I beat Nova and Mars to the refuel station. I don't know how far out they are, so I just pay my stupid docking fee and fidget restlessly with my clothes until I decide on something neutral, something that looks like everything else I wear.

The jacket I leant Juno is still draped over the second chair and, after a moment's hesitation, I throw it on over my shirt and head off onto the refuel station.

My face is covered by a black mask, but I still know better. I keep my head tilted down to avoid any and all facial recognition software from cameras. If they caught Juno on Anat-3, they almost certainly tracked us from when they pulled us over. That means they know the Gemini, they know me, and they know where we're going.

Thankfully, this refuel station is set up in such a way where the shops and outlets are set up in a massive circular structure with the docks in the center, meaning you can keep an eye on your ship from almost anywhere on the station. I go to a small cafe and order a coffee because who knows when I'll be able to rest next. I find myself at a table near the glass railing and peer over, seeing the Gemini untouched. It'll probably stay that way, but it doesn't hurt to check. I know realistically that they just wanted Juno. If they wanted me too, they would've taken me.

I can still be arrested for aiding and abetting, which gives them full ownership over my belongings, unless I make bail.

That can't happen.

I pull out my pad, intending to pull up my notes app to make a list, but I stop. They can almost certainly access my notes and data and this is something I don't want them to see.

There are napkins on a little table next to the trash compactor and I take a couple. I keep a grease pen in my bag for junking purposes, so I pull that out and start scribbling on the napkin.

GOING OFF GRID:

1. reregister ship
2. new bank account, withdraw cash
3. change appearance?

The third one is easy enough, I could buy a wig right now. Nova did say we're meeting next to a body mods shop. With some light tinkering, I'm sure I could change my retinal scan, at least in my left. Keep the face masks, maybe pick up a balaclava for full coverage.

No more junking, at least not on government or Zephyr— not that they're much different— ships. I have enough credits for us to easily get to Adrestia. If I stop at refuel stations, with new registration, I can pay for gas in cash. Plenty of people do that on refuel stations. The far-right have leaned so heavily into Marwood's bullshit promises of safety and security that they're fully inundated with his all-digital worldview. That, combined with Zephyr owning most of those platforms to begin with, means that a lot of more left-leaning pilots stick to cash exclusively.

Two women sit behind me speaking a language I don't understand. I could turn on Zephyr translate if I wanted to understand, but I don't. All I do is glance back to make sure they're not a threat.

They're both older women with big cups of something warm and sweet smelling and they don't even spare me a glance as they sit down.

I scan the opposite side of the refuel station across the wide open center. I see an ATM, good. That'll help knock out pulling as much money from my account as I can without getting flagged. I keep looking until I find the body mod parlor, and the restaurant right beside. A disguise is a good first step.

I shovel my napkin scraps into my bag and pick up my mediocre cup of coffee. ATM first, then body mods parlor.

The maximum amount of credits the ATM will allow me to withdraw at once is a thousand, but there's no limit on transactions. My bank account is through an unregulated credit union, so I shouldn't be flagged, so I perform ten withdrawals of a thousand credits each. I shove the thick bills deep into my bag and clutch it tight to my side. That'll get us pretty far.

The body mods studio has tinted windows and a thick metal gate rolled up by the entrance that they can pull down if they're closed. The door is closed and most of the windows are blacked out, but there's a green neon sign barely visible through the dark window declaring them OPEN, so I head in.

Inside, it's brightly lit and clean. It's split into a couple of different spaces, some shut off with doors and the others open, revealing leather benches and heavily tatted employees leaning over sketchbooks, other people's bare skin, and even, I see through one small window, an open wound.

"Can I help you?" a low voice says. I turn to see a woman sitting behind a counter. She turns as I look and finally I can see her face. It's sharp and angular, her jaw cutting a sharp profile in all the right ways, and her chin-length straight hair is bleached ashy white with faint streaks of pink and blue throughout. She's easily a foot taller than me, quite possibly more, and her name tag is printed in clear script with blue, pink, and purple stripes: CHELL. Underneath, even smaller, it says 'she/her'. Behind her, the wall behind the checkout is papered in stickers, pinned notes, post-its, and business cards, but my eyes don't focus on any of those.

Instead, I focus on one small round sticker right beside Chell's head, declaring Juno's name in colored font.

"I think you can," I say. "I need to change my appearance."

"Permanent or temporary?" she asks and examines her nails. They end easily a half inch beyond the tips of her fingers and they're painted in an opalescent, swirling color that changes every time she moves her hands. Matching her nails is a chunky necklace around her neck, silver with a milky gem set in a round charm.

"Temporarily, probably. I also need hair dye."

It hurts to say it, and it hurts to think of Juno without her green hair. It's part of her identity at this point, and I know she'll hate the idea of coloring it. It's just a fact, though: once we've saved her, they're going to want her more desperately than ever.

"Color?"

"Brown, I think. Dark," I say. Chell's bright blue eyes flick up to my own hair, which is already dark, muddy brown, and I add, "It's not for me."

Chell squints at me for a second, but then she nods and ducks into a door behind the counter. With her gone, the room feels quieter, and I notice for the first time a small television hanging above her counter. I sigh and pull up my collar, trying to feel smaller, but then I realize— It's not playing any Zephyr sponsored channel, or at least not any that I get on the Gemini. Instead, the news that's playing is hosted by a man with half-dyed blonde hair piled up on his head in a messy bun. The information at the bottom identifies him as Seth Cooper, he/they.

Yeah, not a Zephyr sponsored channel.

"Can I help you?"

I spin away from the TV— almost certainly too frantic for

the circumstances— and see a fat woman with long red hair smiling kindly at me.

"Chell is helping me," I respond and gesture to the door. "Thank you."

"Of course." She smiles even wider, if that was possible, and a wave of deja-vu rings through me— she reminds me distinctly of my mother.

"*Breaking news,*" the TV crows and we both turn to look at it in sync. "*Activist Juno Marcus has been arrested by the IPF. Reports say that the charges against her include aggravated assault, evading arrest, and intention to incite violence, all of which we know is bullshit. Well, except maybe the evading arrest part, but she wouldn't have to evade arrest if the IPF didn't try to kill her every other fucking day.*"

I let out a long breath. Chell exits the back room with two boxes of hair dye in her hands and follows our gazes to the TV.

"Shit," she hisses and sets the boxes down on the counter. The TV changes to another picture and I freeze.

There, with my shaved head and face mask, mismatched eyes and hands clutched close to my chest, is me. It's clearly a security camera screenshot. Juno is next to me and I realize it was taken from the casino on Doda before the shooting, when the two of us were walking to the bar.

Juno is wearing the same jacket I'm wearing now, slightly blurry in the forefront of the shot, but I'm crystal clear.

Chell turns to me at once. "You."

"*Castor Quasar, a known ally of Marcus, has been named as an accomplice and is officially also wanted for arrest. Castor, if you see this,*" Seth Cooper says on the TV and it cuts back to his face. "*You have more allies than you know.*"

My feet carry me towards the door of the shop in jerky, backwards steps. My chest feels tight and there are words ironed into the creases of my skull, desperate pleas not to turn me in, but then Chell reaches into her pocket and pulls out a vibrating, old school phone.

"What is it," she answers in a deadpan tone. The other woman, the redhead without a name tag, is watching me. She shifts slowly until she's in between me and the door.

Fuck.

Neither of them seem like they're leaping to call the IPF, and I'm almost certainly safer in here, with the alternative-looking trans woman, than I am out there, where my face is almost certainly on every goddamn screen by now.

"You know, I think I know the one," Chell says into her phone and turns back to study me. "Meet me at the shop." She hangs up and slams the phone down on the counter. "Alright. Jules, can you close down the shop? Nova is on her way here."

"You know Nova?" I blurt out.

"She's my girlfriend," Chell answers and flicks a stray piece of pale pink hair out of her face.

"And my sister," Jules adds.

"I'm supposed to be meeting her here," I say. Jules face splits in a wide grin and I start to see the resemblance between her and Nova. Both of their noses are upturned at the end and Jules has freckles littering her cheeks just like Nova had back on Janus.

"Well then," Jules says and claps her hands together. "Looks like we're in this together. Where do we start?"

7

OBSESSION WITH NATIONAL SECURITY

Behind the pale blue painted door Chell disappeared into before is a cavernous room lined wall to wall with metal storage racks. Each rack is completely full with equipment and product, including hair dye, tattoo ink, a wide variety of different leather straps and harnesses. I pause next to the hair dye and drag my finger along a dark green that reminds me of Juno's. It's surrounded by other unnatural colors spanning everywhere from pure white to electric blue.

"We're trusting you a lot, here," Jules says and ducks around a shelf to a large stack of crates, not unlike the ones on my own ship. "But..."

"Juno Marcus trusts you," Chell says quietly from behind me, "And she's the only person in this galaxy who can change it."

"It's my fault she was arrested," I reply. My voice comes out flat and numb, like an AI reading from a textbook.

"Castor," Jules says and shakes her head. The word sounds odd in her mouth. It's strange, to feel a disconnect to the name I chose, but Juno calls me Junker. I never trusted her with my name, and now it doesn't even feel like mine. "We're going to get her out."

"We have to," Chell adds and picks up a crate, shuffling it to the side until I can see what she is revealing: a small trap door in the ground with an old-fashioned keyhole right in the center. Chell reaches behind her head and unlatches her necklace. "Juno Marcus is the face of the silent resistance that has existed for decades. She's the catalyst that has brought on our first measurable success in a hundred years."

"We have to," I echo, but I don't have words for what it is I want to say. How do I impress upon them her strength? Her stubbornness, her sense of adventure, her beauty? The way she's the only one who has ever made me feel normal, feel welcomed into her life without a caveat?

We have to save her because she's Juno Marcus and I'd never be able to forgive myself if something happened to her? We have to— *I* have to— and that scares the shit out of me?

Instead, I say nothing, and Chell slides the small jeweled charm into the keyhole in the trapdoor. She fiddles with it for just a second before the door clicks open to reveal a dark opening. Chell climbs down first and then Jules gestures for me to go next, so I do. My Equinox knife sits heavy in the side pocket of my bag and I pat it once, feeling the familiar grip through the fabric.

Chell doesn't offer me a hand when I hop off the ladder, but she does offer Jules one.

"Welcome to Goliath Underground," Jules says as Chell unlocks another door, this time black and unmarked.

The space inside is enormous. It must span the space under multiple stores. The walls are papered with flags, some of which I recognize— pink, white, and blue for the transgender flag, the rainbow Juno has printed on her stickers— and some I don't. There's one in the same colors as Chell's name tag, one in purple, yellow, black, and white, and another in pinks and oranges that reminds me of a sunset. There are probably a half dozen others, some centered around white stripes and others around black, but they all have the same effect: the room is safe and colorful.

It's the complete opposite of the Gemini where the extent of my decor, even after living on the ship for years, is a new plant in Pollux's tank every once in a while. Juno's sticker is the most color in the whole place besides my blue bedding, and that I only bought because it was on sale.

"We'll wait for Nova and Mars here," Jules says and throws herself down into something I've only ever seen in daycares at refuel stations: a beanbag chair. However, this one is easily four times the size of any I've ever seen. It's squished into the corner of the main room next to a door labelled 'RESTROOM' above a symbol I recognize from one of Juno's tattoos, a single circle decorated with the markers of Venus and Mars.

Chell sits down at a long desk with five monitors. She starts tapping at a clunky mechanical keyboard, her fingers moving faster than I've ever seen before. I watch her for just a moment before excusing myself to the restroom.

It's easily three times as big as the tiny cubicle on the Gemini. There's a toilet that I'm sure flushes easier than mine, a urinal, a wide sink, and a shower-tub combo. I relieve myself quickly and stand in front of the mirror for a long time after washing my hands.

The circles under my eyes are dark, prominent smudges of purple and brown that I rub at with wet fingers. My face hasn't changed, which feels odd when my life is nothing like it was even a day ago. My cheeks are still soft and freckled, my lips are still crooked, and the light scarring across the left side of my face still gleams pale in the harsh lighting of the small room. My left eye is still green and my right is still brown, but I feel distinctly different despite any outward signs.

For fuck's sake, if you had told me a month ago I was in an underground resistance base figuring out how to break the modern face of anti-fascism out of prison alongside a bunch of other gay and trans people, I would've completely disregarded the idea.

I know Juno is the reason. She's changed me— No. I've always been here, I've just been locked away behind apathy and desperate solitude. Juno saw something in me and, within a week, pulled out a level of empathy and care I didn't think I had the ability to feel anymore.

Not since the accident.

Not since I had to grow up.

She took me by the shoulders and shook me, told me that neutrality is compliance, and for some odd fucking reason I listened to her.

I splash some water on my face and wipe my hands off on the thighs of my pants. When I exit the bathroom, there are twice as many people in the saferoom than there were before.

"Junker," Nova says and takes a step towards me. "I'm glad you're okay.

She looks about the same. Her long, red hair is up in a long ponytail and she's dressed in shades of green and grey, a knee-length thick coat hiding her form.

"We have to get Juno back," I tell her.

Nova nods. "Of course," she says. "Come on." Jules and Mars are leaning over Chell's computer. Jules and Chell are talking quietly, Jules signing along in fluid, easy motions, as Chell types furiously. Mars gets Jules' attention and signs something to her, and she nods and turns to me and Nova.

"Chell is the best hacker we've got. We have blueprints for a similarly set up prison complex, but she's going to try to get us Harrison's layout. Noves is a hell of a pilot, and Mars can do just as well, plus he's strong as shit," Jules says and claps a hand down on Mars' shoulder. "The four of us should be able to get Juno out no problem."

"Five," I reply. "I'm coming too."

Mars immediately erupts into a series of signs so quick I'm surprised Jules even manages to follow. She signs back and they converse for a moment before Jules sighs and nods.

"Fine, yes. Five of us."

Mars shoots me a thumbs up and I can't help but smile.

"I don't know why I thought you were the quiet one," I remark. "Thank you." Nova snorts and translates quickly and Mars shoots me a small, crooked smile. He makes a rude gesture at Jules that even I understand and she shoves him.

They're comfortable together. It feels somehow like I'm intruding, like they found a stray and brought it home for family dinner. Mars touches Jules' waist and hugs her to his side, while Nova and Chell lean over the computer together, heads bowed.

I don't belong here.

"Look," Nova says and presses a wet kiss to the side of Chell's head. "We got it." Sure enough, the screen is displaying over thirty security feeds from the inside of Fort Harrison in tiny little repeating boxes, each flickering with movement.

"Give me an hour or two, I can get a full floor plan put together," Chell says and starts typing again almost immediately.

"Where's Juno?" I ask and lean in close. Chell clicks on a square and it expands to fill the whole screen. My mouth falls open.

It doesn't take carefully inked tattoos and green hair for me to recognize her. I'd know her shape anywhere. Anywhere. She's facing away from the camera and she's barely clothed.

She's only wearing a pair of purple brief-like panties and a black sports bra, and a half-dozen guards are standing around her, most behind a row of thick metal bars.

Everyone jumps at a loud *smack*. I realize belatedly that the noise came from me and my palm stings where I slammed it into the table. The image of Juno shivering and exposed plays on loop in my mind as I step away, pressing my aching hand to my sternum. I press and press, harder and harder, but it doesn't calm the fluttering in my chest. Neither does slamming it down, deep thuds reverberating through my chest, but I do it anyways.

"Castor," Jules says softly and reaches out for me, but I jerk away. "We're going to get her out of there."

"I shouldn't have let her out of my sight," I gasp and spin around, my fingers grasping desperately at my own throat. "It's my fault she got taken." Everything is so fucking loud and so bright, the station closing in around us, a high pitched ringing that has taken up residence in my eardrums— I hum low in my chest and close my eyes.

A hand rests on my shoulder. I jerk away instinctively, but when I turn and see Chell standing there, I feel a little bit of tension leave my body. In her hand at her side is a small plastic fidget of alternating pink and blue segments that she curls around her fingers at the base. It loops around her thumb and she crooks each finger into it, the same way I seek comfort in twisted bits of chain and metal.

"It might've been," Chell agrees, and somehow that makes my anxiety ease up. They weren't there. They don't know what happened. Any assurances she might've tried to make, any promises that it wasn't my fault, would've rung false. "But you're also going to be the one to save her."

I wrap my arms tight around myself and take a long breath.

She's right. She's right. Even if it was my fault, all I can do now is try to get her back. I nod, and Chell nods back. When she returns to her computer, she sits, adjusts for a moment, and rests her fingers back on her keyboard.

"Alright," Nova says and claps a hand down on her girlfriend's shoulder. "Let's go over the plan."

Preparation takes a full twenty-six hour cycle.

Chell helps me report the Gemini as stolen and then re-register it under a new name. Nova helps me pull out the meager remnants of my bank account and start a new one with an under the table, non-Zephyr company that she and Chell both swear is safe. They work together to jailbreak my watch and reconfigure it the same way that, apparently, everyone else's around here is as well. There's nothing to be done for my pad, so that gets tossed in a trash compactor and I'm provided with an identical old-school burner phone to Chell's and a new one, supplied by a smaller company with no ties to Zephyr or the government.

Jules helps me pick out a wig. I choose a shoulder-length, mousy brown thing that matches my eyebrows well enough to blend. I try it on, but one glance in the mirror makes me want to dig my nails into my scalp and pluck out each hair one by one. My hair hasn't been long since I was ten, and I'd like to keep it that way.

I nap on a beanbag chair with my nose buried in the collar of my jacket, Juno's faint vanilla shampoo and hair dye scent still clinging on just enough to help me rest.

She's on the news again— the good news, not the Zephyr-sponsored propaganda they call INN— when I awake. The only camera angle they seem to have is a blurry shot of her through a cloudy window. She's only identifiable by her green hair, marking the first time in over a week I've been grateful for the bright color. They don't show the picture of me on Doda again and I thank the stars for small miracles.

By the time we're ready to go, I'm restless. I want to get Juno out *now* but apparently there's much more preparation involved with breaking someone out of prison than I previously knew. Who would've thought?

What I know about the plan is this: We're taking the Gemini and Mars' four-seater Voyager class called Echo. Chell and I will take the Gemini, and Mars, Nova, and Jules will come in Echo. We'll dock at the loading bay using some false credentials Chell whipped up. We have approximate blueprints of the prison that we can view through our watches. Beyond that, we're figuring it out as we go along.

Great. No plan, no schedule.

Sounds great for an autistic person who is always one unexpected sensory input away from a full-blown meltdown.

When we leave, it feels like we're preparing for battle. In a way, we are. All of us are clad in identical black clothes layered with pieces of IPF armor and uniform, bulletproof vests tight underneath our shirts. We're ready to win the latest fight in a war Juno has been waging since she was fifteen.

I strap myself into the pilot's chair of the Gemini. Chell is in the backseat and the other three are in the Echo. It feels odd, having someone other than Juno in the back chair. I don't know when it became hers, I just know that it is.

I'm not wearing the wig Jules got me. Instead, I have a skull-tight knit cap pulled down underneath a riot helmet Nova dug out of storage. I turn Apollo's rabbit over in my hands and take a deep breath.

"Clear," I call back to Chell. She unbuckles as soon as the artificial gravity surges on and comes into the cockpit. She has to duck a little to get in. I never have— Nobody who has ever been on the Gemini has. Not that that's many people.

"Did the Echo get out okay?" she asks over her personal radio, clipped to the collar of her chest plate. Her hair is still loose, but she pulls a ponytail holder off her wrist and starts to tie it up.

"Copy, this is Echo," Nova's lilted voice comes through over the radio.

"We'll check in again once we're in comms range, alright?" Chell says, and Nova chirps something back. She leans her hip against the metal frame that separates the cockpit from the main cabin and crosses her arms. "You doing alright?"

"Hm?"

"You. You're so tightly wound I can practically feel the tension in your shoulders from here," she says and tilts her head to the side. Her jawline is strong and I notice two rings through the lobes in her ears for the first time now that her hair is up. She's pretty, in an elfish kind of way.

"I just want to see Juno. I want to get her out of that prison," I answer.

"I worked for Zephyr, you know," Chell says without prompting and looks out the windshield. We're flying fast— Not light speed, but still fast— and there's no other ships around us, save for the faint blur in the distance that makes up the Echo.

"Why?" I ask, and I don't try to, but the disgust I feel for the company is clear in my voice. Even with all I preach about remaining neutral, all the effort I've put into flying under the IPF radar as a non-binary person, I could never talk myself out of my hatred for Zephyr. They're scum. They pay their employees pennies and sell all their clients' information to the galactic government, all so they can put their company AI in more ships and make more profits. Everything you do on the galactic web is tracked and stored by Zephyr, and people like Chell wrote the programs to make it happen.

"Money," she shrugs. "Healthcare, mostly. They paid for my FFS." It must be clear that I don't know what that is, because she clarifies, "Facial feminization surgery."

"Zephyr covers that?"

"It took a fight," Chell replies. "It took months and months of paperwork, and letters from my therapist and doctor. They refused the first dozen times, I eventually had to threaten to file a lawsuit for them to follow through."

"Shit."

"Yeah," she chuckles.

"Why'd you quit?" I ask. "I'm sure you made good money with them."

"Oh, I did," Chell confirms. "Really, really good money."

"But you left."

"I did." She smiles, but there's an air of sadness to it. "I couldn't stay. I worked in their research and development division, specifically working on developing Bellona. I saw how much information they were gathering, how they sold people's data to the highest bidder when the things they sold could ruin lives. They had lists of people like me, people who had gotten FFS, or a prescription for testosterone, or any transgender surgery. Lists of people who let it happen, of parents of trans kids, of doctors. It was a watchlist. A warning. If we were willing to seek out gender affirming care, we had the capability to do worse."

"That was all? I—" I cut myself off and swallow.

"No, say it," Chell replies in her raspy-sweet voice that

reminds me all too much of Juno, vocal chords worn away at and softened by years of work.

"I know all that, and I would never work for them. I never would've even thought about it," I say honestly. "Zephyr is ruining the galaxy. You must've known that the work you were doing was harming people."

"You're right," Chell says and smiles. Her teeth are perfectly straight and white— Surely she also had an excellent dental plan with Zephyr. "I turned a blind eye, because I was making good money. I decided, for me, that prioritizing my own comfort, my transition, over the deaths of my siblings was okay, and I still regret that."

"What changed your mind?"

"I met Nova," she says. It comes out like a confession, something whispered to a holy man behind taut curtains in the dead of night. In this galaxy, it might as well be a sin. "I met Nova, and she *hated* me."

"But—"

"But we're together now? But we seem inseparable? Yeah," Chell says and chuckles dryly. "I... I've known Nova for six years. It took me one to realize she would never trust or believe in my intentions as long as I worked for Zephyr, and another one to quit."

"Why so long?"

"Hm?"

"Once you decided to leave," I clarify, "Why did you wait a year?"

Chell's smile turns sharp. Her eyelashes are dark and long and she peers at me through them, dark curtains covering ice blue eyes. "It's more elaborate than you'd expect to hide hundreds of triggers for encrypted DDoS attacks and information leaks, but I got it done."

My mouth falls open. "That data leak, last year—"

"There have been six leaks in the past four years that I can directly track back to my work in those two years before I left," Chell says and her grin is giddy. "Every time, it makes me feel like I'm flying. Nova isn't my reason for caring about Zephyr's misdeeds, or the galactic government's bullshit, but she was the catalyst."

Something in her tone makes me think there's an underlying message, something I'm not grasping, and I turn back in my chair to look out the front window, biting back the familiar feeling of being out of the loop. "Why are you telling me all this?" I ask.

"You'll figure it out." With that, Chell returns to the main cabin of the ship. "I'm buckling in. Let me know when we're close."

I ball my hands into fists and press them into my chest, right above my incisions. I remember before I got top surgery, how my breasts made me so uncomfortable I couldn't work. How my binder dug into my ribs and made them ache, but not wearing it made my skin crawl and throat close up. I remember how I was on a waitlist for over a year before I even got in for a meeting with the surgeon, and even that was in an underground clinic run illegally by other trans people. It was the first time I saw anyone who reminded me of myself and allowed myself to think so— A boy with short hair and soft cheeks named Noah. He had wide hips and wore a binder that didn't match the color of his dark skin, instead closer to my own pale complexion.

He asked me for my pronouns, and I told him "They, please." It was the first time I let myself have that. It was the first time I let anyone's perception of me match what I felt— No, what I *knew*— I was inside.

It hasn't come up much. It's not like I know anyone well enough to be anything other than 'Junker'.

Even Juno doesn't know my name.

I curl my hands into fists until I can feel my nails digging into the soft flesh of my palm. Juno doesn't even know my fucking name.

"Was it easy?" I ask Chell as I spin around to face her. My voice comes out steadier than I expected it to.

"No," she replies. "I had to rewrite everything I had ever known. For a while during that first year, I thought I'd be able to help people from the inside. I tried to talk my colleagues into being better people, into seeing if there was anything we could do, but there was no chance. Most of the people there were there for the same reasons as me. Money. They don't want to help anyone, or change the galaxy. Nobody does."

"Juno does."

Chell smiles, big and genuine.

"See? You're already most of the way there."

"*Gemini, come in Gemini,*" Nova chirps in her lilted accent.

"This is Gemini," I manage after a breath's hesitation.

"*We're approaching Fort Harrison. Be ready to dock in two minutes.*"

"Copy." I spin to face forward and grab my harness. Juno's jacket brushes my ankle before I can slide the two pieces of the metal clasp together. It's rough under my fingertips when I pick it up, rougher even on my face when I press it there. Vanilla and soap fills my senses and I squeeze it tight. "I'm coming, Juno," I whisper into the fabric before discarding it onto the ground again and buckling in.

"*We're landing.*"

"Cameras will be disabled as soon as we connect to the router. We should have around five minutes of loops before anyone realizes," Chell says into her personal comm.

"*Copy.*"

"You guys ready for this?" Jules asks. There's a distinct moment of hesitation from everyone.

"Ready as I'll ever be," I finally say, and steer us towards the docking bay.

Once we're landed, getting in is easy. Many IPF agents fly personal ships and the Echo and Gemini are untraceable enough to blend in with the others. I'm a little short for an IPF officer, but they wedge me, Jules, and Nova in between Chell and Mars, and we walk in unquestioned with one careful swipe of Chell's forged credentials.

We're all wearing small earpieces that mush down into shape inside our ear drums, and as soon as we enter the prison, I understand why. Immediately inside the doorway, the corridor branches off in two directions. To our right, a curved hall disappears around a bend. To our left, it deadends twenty feet in at a huge door and splits off into another wide passage. In front of us stands an identical, open, door.

"This way," Chell murmurs and turns right. The rest of us follow, a little group of ragtag, mismatched guards in bits and bobs of unkempt armor, and I'm so tense my shoulders ache. When the first convoy of real prison guards passes us, Mars simply nods in their direction and continues walking, and they do the same. I let out a quiet puff of air that fogs up the plexi-glass shield in front of my face. My gun is a comforting weight at my hip and I rest my palm on the grip.

I've always been a good shot. Anywhere inside these hall-ways, with my target within twenty feet of me, I know I can hit them. I know I can kill them.

I would, too. For Juno.

Chell guides us down two hallways. As we walk, I turn my

head minutely to peer through the small glass window in each door we pass. Most of the rooms— Cells— are empty, but we do pass a few that contain evidence of life. Scattered blankets on the floor, a single chair— Through one, I even see a woman holding a set of dice. We pause right beside the door to let another patrol by and I watch as she rolls them, scoops all of them into her hand besides one, and rerolls. Her mouth moves like she's talking but I can't hear anything through the soundproof walls.

"Shit," Nova mutters beside me when we turn down another long, white hallway.

"What?" I breathe back.

"It's an old model. Chell and I went over a few possible layouts, but this one was the worst case scenario," she whispers. "We're going to have to split up. There's a lock to the override that requires two people to press a switch at the same time at opposite ends of the facility. It's supposed to keep things like this from happening, but most places use biometrics now."

Chell leads us down one short staff-only corridor where, I note quickly, there are no cameras. She gestures to Mars and the four rebels sign furiously to each other for a moment until Mars and Nova both nod and split off. I raise an eyebrow at Jules.

"They're going to go press the switches. We're going to head for the control room," she explains. "It's the only place to access the records, which is the only way we can find out where Juno's cell is." We narrowed it down to a few areas back on Goliath: she's probably in either high security or the isolation ward, but those both boast dozens of prisoners. By the time we find her, they'll have noticed our presence.

"C'mon," Chell says and rests her hand on my shoulder. Her touch is gentle, and I get the distinct impression that if I asked her to stop, she would immediately. "Let's go get your girl." I open my mouth to argue, but nothing comes out. Claiming distance from Juno feels dishonest.

Before we can move, a loud noise makes us both jump. I spin around, my gun already halfway out of its holster, and see that the small glass window in the door beside us is covered by a small hand. Chubby fingers and a sweaty palm slide away after a moment to reveal—

A child.

A girl.

She can't be more than twelve, maybe even younger. Her face is gaunt, skin pulled taut over small cheekbones and stretched just as thin over the rest of her body. When she opens her mouth, there's a tooth missing. She calls out to us, deafened by the high-tech soundproofing that makes the entire prison base feel stiff, and thuds her palm into the door. I take a step closer and push up my face shield to reveal myself. A long strand of matted, greasy blonde hair falls in her face as she rushes to the door.

"Chell," I whisper, "Who all is kept here?" Her fingers are so much smaller than mine, even with the distortion of the glass between our hands.

"Anyone they deem an enemy to the state."

"Fuck," I hiss. Juno would tear this place to the goddamn ground, rip it up into pieces until there's not even anything to junk.

"C'mon, Castor, we can come back. We don't have much time," Jules says quietly. "I know. We'll come back for her."

She doesn't know that. I reach into the pockets of my pants, searching— Aha. I pull out a small grease pen I use for junking and write in shaky, backwards lettering on the glass: 'I WILL COME BACK FOR YOU'. I point at it until she nods, and then wipe it away with my sleeve, leaving a blurry smear behind.

"Let's go." I push my face shield back down.

Chell leads the way back into the maze-like halls of the prison. I follow close behind, Jules at my side. We turn through a couple more hallways, and then Chell stops around a corner so suddenly I almost run directly into her back.

"This should be it," she murmurs and points at a door.

"Is it not?" I respond. It looks the same as all the other doors: a metal door with a small glass window in the center and a rectangular control panel built into the wall beside it. It's clinical and cold, but not abnormal. "Are we in the wrong place?"

"No— This door should go to the control room," Chell says and reaches out to touch it. "It's a bigger door, normally, more industrial. No windows." I frown and step forward, peering in through the window much like I have with many other viewports into the barren prison cells that make up Fort Harrison. Something feels different, but I can't place it before Jules chimes in.

"You're sure it's here?"

"Look," Chell says and points to the ceiling. A small metal sensor with lights blinking yellow and green hangs down a couple of inches. "Solid green means you're in the innermost circle. It's the best way to find your way around. The entrance to the control room should be here."

I frown and feel along the edge of the door, but it looks and feels the exact same as any other door. My gloves are too thick to get a good grip, so I tug one off and tuck it into my belt. The metal vibrates from the artificial gravity field being projected from deep inside the core of the prison, but that's not uncommon. Most galactic government ships feel the same, as their gravity fields are powered with small nuclear reactors built so deep into the ship that keep them anchored in space. It's much the same technology as a refuel station, so their galactic coordinates aren't always changing. But while a refuel station is all but a floating city, this is more like a parking lot. All one level, a waste of space—

The vibration stops as I slide my fingers from one panel to the other.

"This isn't a wall," I say quietly.

"We only have a minute and a half left of looped footage," Chell whispers. "If we're in the wrong place, we need to go, *now*."

"Give me a sec," I reply and pull out my Equinox knife. The hilt feels good in my palm, the only familiar feeling in this entire operation, and I flick out the screwdriver attachment. It makes quick work of the screws on the very bottom of the panel and within thirty seconds the panel comes off. I set it aside and peer into the three by three foot gap I've created in the wall.

"It's a doorway," Jules realizes. "They sealed it off."

"Get in," I tell them and crawl in myself. "Pull the panel back up behind you."

The crawl is short— not even five feet of claustrophobic tunnel I know Juno would *hate*— and we pop up in a large room filled with computers and desks. I hear distant typing, but there doesn't seem to be anyone in this room.

"How'd you tell?" Chell breathes once she's standing beside me again.

"I'm a junker," I respond simply. "Go. Find Juno."

"Nova, Mars, you two in place?" she asks into her earpiece and presses a button on the outer ridge that makes all of our communicators vibrate faintly. Nova confirms quickly and then it vibrates again, signalling Mars' response. "Alright. Go."

An alarm begins to blare at once. I press my fists into my ears but Chell just starts tapping on one of the computers, bypassing a login screen and skimming through data impossibly fast.

Under the din of the alarm, metal scrapes against metal in a high-pitched screech and Chell turns back to face us, a huge grin visible even through her disguise.

"Let's go," she says, or at least, I think she does. I'm almost entirely relying on reading her lips, and I've never been very good at that. She turns and pulls Jules back towards the crawl-space, but I feel rooted to the ground.

My skull feels rotted through with the reverberations of the tinny, blaring alarm. It riots through each of my bones from my vertebrae to my feet and I feel *crushed*. Each breath is sharp and shallow, piercing through something in my ribs, and I try again and again, but they're so small and I'm not getting enough oxygen—

Chell taps my shoulder and holds out a hand, offering a pair of earplugs.

Thank you, I think as loud as I can, and then, *sorry*. My mouth stays still even as I take the earplugs and cram them into my ears as fast as I can.

I feel better almost immediately. The sound is still there but it sits in my chest instead of my head, vibrating through my organs and letting my limbs stay loose. I shake out the tightness in my arms and give Chell a sharp nod.

"Always come prepared," she says, gestures to similar plugs in her own ears, and I follow her out of the control room, knife in hand.

The moment we emerge, a group of four guards turns the corner. Chell draws her gun and says, in a low, growly voice that feels false coming from her throat, "They're in the control room!"

I run, but I don't make it far. The biggest guard in the group grabs my shoulder and slams me into the wall, pinning me and sending a shock of pain through my arm. I thrust my knife into the spot underneath his arm where his armor doesn't quite cover. He cries out and loosens his grip on me—

BANG. *BANG.*

I spin around and see Chell holding her gun out, the guard who was holding me at the floor in front of her with blood pooling around his head, a single hole splitting it in two. Another is on his knees clutching his shoulder where her other shot went through, and the third is pinned against a wall with Jules' pistol at his spine.

The fourth drops his gun and falls to his knees, hands up.

"Coward," I spit, but we don't have time for this. I slam the butt of my gun into his temple and he crumples onto the ground. Jules does the same to the back of the third man's knees, and after we take their guns, we run off down the hall before any of them can get their shit together.

We pass two more groups of guards but we're still dressed much like they are and, with Chell in the lead holding a gun, nobody stops us. We cut back the way we came, and every door we pass is wide open allowing people in identical, ratty jumpsuits to hesitantly step out of their cells. The woman with the dice decks a guard so hard he falls to the floor and I don't bite back my grin.

I follow as close to Chell as I can, but her legs are so goddamn long and Jules and I are both short, so we mostly just try to stay together. Chell turns a corner and then, ten seconds later, Jules and I do too, and there's the girl.

Her blonde hair and white jumpsuit are streaked with blood now, but she looks uninjured. I pull away from Jules and rush to her. I throw my face shield onto the ground.

"You!" she calls and rushes to me.

"Go," I scream back over the noise, so much *fucking* noise, "Go outside. Get on the voyager class ship, the two seater parked in the very back of the lot. If you see a girl with red hair and a big, bald guy, go with them. We'll meet you there, I promise." I hand her the gun I took off the guard. "Do you know how to use this?"

Something hard passes through her gaze. "Yes."

"Go," I say and touch her shoulder again. "I promise we'll be there."

We need to keep moving, but I stand there just long enough to watch her run towards the exit. Gunshots echo through the endless identical hallways and, as soon as she turns the corner, I turn back to Chell and Jules at a dead sprint.

"We're close," Chell pants into her communicator, "Nova, find Mars and get to the ships."

"I'm with Mars, we're heading out— There's a girl—"

"Take her with you, get her on the Gemini or the Echo, please," I manage, and then the facility grows deathly quiet. Our comms cut out and the alarm stops all at once, turning the deafening noise into a sickening silence.

"Right around here, Castor, we don't have much time," Chell says and yanks me by the hand around one more corner and there she fucking is, green hair flying as Juno throws a punch at the guard in front of her, another already unconscious on the ground.

Her face is bare, her war paint stolen and wiped away, and she's just wearing a tank top with her white prisoner's jumpsuit knotted at the waist. Chell draws her gun and shoots the guard Juno is fighting with in the back. He crumples to the ground and Juno spins, her bloody knuckles held high and proud in front of her chest.

"Junker," she breathes, and it washes over me like a revelation. "You came."

I rush forward and grab her jaw, turning her face to see the long cut on one cheek and the dark, bruised skin on the other. "Are you okay? I demand and pull my glove from my belt to wipe away the blood. I toss it to the ground and cup her jaw in my hands.

"I am now," Juno says and smiles as bright as a dozen suns. A stream of blood trickles out of her nose and she licks it away. "Let's get out of here."

"We have to go, *now*," Chell calls from the end of the hall.

I drop her face to instead grab one of her hands, holding my gun tight in the other. We run for it, Chell leading us through the twisting maze, until we burst out into the docking bay.

Dozens of bodies litter the ground outside. At least a third of them are guards, but too many are clad in white jumpsuits with numbers across the shoulders. Chell is in front of me, but then she darts to the right—

"JUNO!"

BANG.

Chell crumples to the ground. Behind her, an IPF guard stands, rifle pointed directly at Juno, barrel still smoking. I don't think; I shoot him.

He falls. Chell doesn't get up, but neither does he.

"CHELL!" Nova screams from the Echo, across a battlefield coated in slick red blood. I scoop her up into my arms and run. The scent of death and coppery fresh blood sinks into every pore, every orifice, but I don't stop, not even when I realize she isn't breathing anymore. Mars is holding Nova back, the blonde girl peering out from behind her, but they all step back when I bring Chell to them.

"She's not breathing," I gasp and lay Chell down in Mars' arms, but there's no time, and I'm not leaving my ship behind.

I sprint for the Gemini, for my home, for the only place I've ever felt safe. Juno is right behind me and I throw myself into the pilot's chair, yanking up hard on the steering. Within seconds, we exit the gravity field and burst into light speed, the Echo right behind us.

"Junker," Juno whispers, standing just where Chell was on our way to Fort Harrison, her hands trembling and speckled with blood. "You... You came for me."

"My name is Castor," I tell her and she exhales, the blood splattered on her face a rotten ruby in the low light.

"Cas." She says it like a test, like a challenge. I meet her eyes and I don't waver, not until she sinks down to sit against the dashboard. "Thank you."

8

RELIGION AND GOVERNMENT ENTERTWINED

Juno sleeps on the floor and doesn't wake until we land on Goliath.

I carry her inside, and Mars carries Chell.

She died immediately, Jules tells us. She didn't even feel it, she says.

I sit at Juno's bedside and let Nova, Jules, and Mars grieve. The air is heavy with it, thick with Nova's sobs and Jules' quiet words of comfort to her sister. Even the blonde girl is silent, curled up with Mars, resting in a beanbag chair that nearly swallows her.

I only leave Juno's side once, and I only do to wash Chell's blood off my skin and change into clean clothes. After that, I stay beside her as she sleeps. I hold her hand, bare skin on bare skin, and I watch the rise and fall of her chest to reassure myself that she's alive.

Relief comes with guilt, and guilt comes with a suffocating itch to run.

Why should I care so much to feel bad? I've known these people for all of two days combined. Chell was funny, and clever, and a whiz on the computer, but Juno is my job. Juno is my responsibility.

"She's exhausted," Jules rasps when she finally emerges to treat the cuts on Juno's face and hands. "She'll be fine, she just needs to rest.

Jules says it all to me like I'm the only one who needs to know, like I'm her next of kin. It feeds the flames of instinct, screams at me to go, go as fast as I can, get as far away as possible, but I stay. I stay at her bedside until she wakes up four hours after we escaped Fort Harrison. It's silent, save for the quiet, wet sound of petered out crying from a small side room where I know Chell's body still lays.

I've seen people die. I've killed people— I killed one today. Why should Chell feel different? Why would she feed this soggy, dense quiet in my chest more than anyone else's death would? It hurts, but it's the kind of dull ache I feel every day in my knee, and my back. Grief is chronic. It never passes entirely.

However, with Juno as purple and bloodied as she is, I can't help the relief that sugarcoats Chell's murder.

At least it wasn't her, I allow myself, and feel awful for it.

"Junker," Juno slurs, startling me from my thoughts.

"Juno," I breathe and lean forward. She blinks at me a few times, clearing her vision, and tries to reach up, but our fingers are still entwined.

"Junker," she repeats and looks away from my face at last, peering around the room. "Where are we?"

"Shh," I murmur, "Rest." I squeeze her hand and she complies, laying back down and letting her head fall into the dent she's made in the couch pillow.

"Cas," she says, and it's almost startling. It makes my stomach turn with anxiety, but there's also something else cutting it, making the stress feel lighter somehow. My name in her mouth feels like home, like it was always meant to live there.

"We're on refuel station Goliath," I say quietly and reach up with my free hand to smooth her green hair down away from her face. "Remember Nova and Mars, who helped us get off Janus?"

Juno nods and looks back at me. "Yeah."

"They have a place here, a secret place where we know you'll be safe."

"That woman," she says and stares right at me. "She died for me."

I'm silent for a long moment. I push a final strand of hair away from her face and rest my fingertips on her cheekbone for one fleeting moment. "She did," I finally say.

"Sleeping beauty awakes," Nova's voice says from the doorway, and I turn to see her and Mars standing there.

"Nova," Juno says and tries to sit up again. I lean forward and help her prop herself up against the back of the couch.

"You two have to go."

"What?"

"Your faces are on every news channel as of ten minutes ago. We need to get you off Goliath or everything Ch— Everything we've built here could be destroyed," she says quietly. "We scrubbed your ship, right? You two head straight for Adrestia. That's where you were heading, right?"

"Yeah," Juno says and looks at me. "The Gemini is gone?"

I shake my head. "We re-registered it. Got rid of anything that could possibly trace it back to ever being the Gemini— Though I guess we didn't repaint it. You're riding on the Jupiter, now." Juno's brow furrows and she looks at me confusion plain on her face.

"You're still taking me?"

"You thought I wouldn't?"

She drops her gaze down to our hands, still entwined, and shrugs. The movement seems to cause her pain, because she winces and presses her other hand to her ribs. Mars offers her an icepack and I help her get it settled against her ribcage.

"I don't know," she says at last. "It seemed like an easy way out, after our fight." Her voice melts me, so quiet and resigned, the opposite of everything that's *Juno* to me. Everyone in her whole life sees her as a figurehead, a leader, or an enemy. To me, she is just a girl, and I treat her that way. Maybe that's not worth nothing after all.

"I was wrong," I tell her, and I mean it. "You were right. You're helping people, and that's the right thing to do. I—" I look across the room at where the girl is still sleeping, wearing a spare t-shirt that Mars leant her. It falls nearly at her ankles. "I want to be brave like you. I want to help the next generations like you do. I want to understand how to feel compassion for people I've never met."

Juno surges forward and hugs me tight, wrapping her arms around my neck and pulling me in close. "You're like no one I've ever known, Cas," she whispers, and I feel her lips brush against the shell of my ear. I hug back, gently resting my hands on her waist to avoid her ribcage. "Thank you for coming for me."

"We're in this together," I say simply.

In reality, the thought of not saving her after her capture never occurred to me. She was taken, and within seconds saving her became the number one priority. I don't know when Juno's life became so entwined with mine, when her safety and presence became something I needed above all else, but when she was gone, I felt her absence like my left leg.

"When are we leaving?" Juno asks and pulls away from me. The spot on my shoulder where her hand was resting stays warm long after she pulls away, emanating heat from just one touch, and I want to crawl up onto the couch just to be closer to her.

"As soon as you two can," Nova says. Her mouth is set in a

firm line. "Jules said Juno is good to go as long as you keep these clean," she adds and gestures to her knuckles and her cheek, the two wounds bad enough to need proper bandaging.

"I have a first aid kit on board."

"Good. I trust you to know what you're doing, Castor," Jules says, Nova's hand tightly twined in her own. Their complexions match, and so do the bright green of their eyes brought out by the red rims of their eyes. Their mirrored freckles sparkle with old tears and I feel their sadness deep in my stomach.

It's strange, to care.

"Get her to Adrestia," Nova says.

"If it's the last thing I do," I reply and, for once, I mean it.

I leave the rebels' underground bunker to collect supplies for the rest of the trip. We shouldn't have to stop again, except to refuel and refresh our water. Jules, who I've found out is a nurse, gives me a bag of medical supplies despite my promise that I have a kit on board. I sit with the girl while Juno speaks with Jules. She doesn't remember much before she was in prison, not even her name, but she tells me about her sister who she hasn't seen in years. Nova promises to take care of her, and seeing the sharp glint in her eye, I think it might be good for her to have someone, have a mission.

When we head out, the girl runs up to me and holds my hand, staring at me with an expression far beyond her meager years.

"Thank you," she says, and I squeeze her hand.

"Be good for Nova," I murmur back, and then Juno and I are off. We leave the body mods shop with two bags: one full of bandages, antibiotics, and other things Jules thought we might need, and another full of hair dye and other disguise pieces.

Mars offered us a hoodie to cloak Juno temporarily, and it reaches below her mid-thighs. The hood offers a sufficient shadow to hide her face, and she lets the wrists fall to cover her hands.

Her fingers are bare, now. The long, shiny black nails that captured my attention before are gone.

"Made a friend, I see," Juno says to me on the walk towards the central dock.

"She's a kid," I reply. "It's my responsibility."

Juno stops. She looks at me with her unpainted face, unlined eyes. She clearly remembers the words coming out of her own mouth, remembers that this is what led to our fight on Anat-3, but I don't see any remainder of the resentment that filled her eyes then.

"Castor," she says, "You don't have to say that."

"It's true," I say, and it is. "I... She reminds me of Apollo, and I had to. I couldn't leave her, not like—" I cut myself off.

Juno pulls me by the hand into a dark corner of Goliath's walkway. It smells like chicken and fresh tortillas. "Explain," she says and turns to face me, her hand still in mine.

"If Apollo was still alive, he wouldn't want me to sit around and waste away. I have the kind of money now that he never saw, I have—" I cut myself off and clear my throat. *I have you.* "I survived. He would want me to use that to help other survivors, other people that have been fucked over by the way this galaxy is run. There's no future if we don't fight for it."

Juno isn't looking into my eyes anymore. Instead, she's staring at my lips like every word out of my mouth is a goddamn revelation, even though I'm just repeating her doctrine back to her. She's looking at me like I'm everything she's ever wanted, galactic change be damned.

Ah, fuck it.

I kiss her.

It takes her a second to kiss back, but she does so with a fucking vengeance. She pulls away first, leaving me leaning forward to chase her sweet mouth, and an aborted breath lingers in the few inches separating us.

"Castor," she breathes and holds my face in both her hands before she leans in and kisses me again. I spin us around, one hand cradling her skull with my knuckles roughing against the concrete wall and the other on her jaw, tracing the long, slim line there, wishing I could be impossibly closer even as the heat of her mouth breathes into mine and her tongue brushes my bottom lip.

I'm trembling, I realize, but she is too. We breathe each other's air, taking fast, shallow breaths between desperate kisses, but I don't open my eyes. Juno kisses me again, and again. She doesn't smell like vanilla, not anymore, but her mouth still tastes like her.

My cheeks are wet, and still she kisses me.

"I thought you were gone," I whisper when she pulls more than an inch away. "I never thought I'd see you again."

"I didn't think you cared," she replies, breathless.

"Juno," I murmur and surge forward blindly to kiss her again, almost missing her lips. "I didn't think I did either, until you were gone." I open my eyes to shadow cloaked in emerald green, all hopeful eyes and slick pink lips.

"And then?"

I cup her beautiful face in my hands and smooth her bangs away with my fingers.

"And then I cried and thought about getting you off Janus, and how—" A sob heaves itself out of my chest and I blink away the tears welling up in my eyes. Her hands are so warm.

"Shh," Juno breathes and a fat tear rolls down my cheek. "I'm here now. I'm here now. You saved me, Cas."

I kiss her again because I can and now that I can, I'm not

sure I'll ever be able to stop. She kisses the corner of my lips, my jaw, the spot in front of my ear covered in fuzzy brown hair, and then she pulls me in close and hugs me tight.

"Don't pull your stitches," I murmur through tear-sticky lips and she laughs in my ear. It's the most beautiful sound I've ever heard.

Back on the Gemini— I know it's officially the Jupiter now, but I know I won't ever be able to think of it as anything but the Gemini— we buckle in and get into open space as quickly as possible. I set a course for a refuel station in the general direction of the way we need to go, and then I pull up both of our chairs and set my tablet down on the table to make a new plan.

"We need to go straight to Adrestia. If they find out how I re-registered the Gemini, they'll be on us within an hour or so. I'm going to reroute us," I explain to Juno as I begin to draw a new line along the map of space. "We're going to have to cut through the Montgomery system, but we shouldn't have to stop if we refuel... Here, and here." I mark the two refuel stations on either side of the system with waypoints.

"How far out are we? Total, I mean?" Juno asks and leans in to look at the map. Her hair tickles the back of my hand.

"A week or so," I answer and mark another waypoint. "We'll stop here, here, then the two before and after the Montgomery system, and then it should only take three more stops."

Juno taps on a planet along the route. "I know here is safe. I've been there dozens of times."

I nod and mark it as well. "Good. Nova told me about another outpost like Jules' shop on refuel station Calico, I figure we can stop there, and..." I scroll and click on Calico, right off Kohzikode, and set another waypoint. "And maybe here." I tap on Adrestia's twin planet, Anderos, which is just under a day's flight at light speed from Adrestia.

"That sounds good," Juno says and nods. "If we run into any problems, it's not like there aren't plenty of other stops."

"Mmm," I hum and drag along the route one more time. It's nearly a straight line, with the biggest detours from a direct line being the refuel stations surrounding the Montgomery system, but that's just common sense. Everybody in the galaxy knows that the Montgomery system is one of the most concentrated areas of Marwood's influence and propaganda. Every planet is suffocated by his supporters with the *others* there, the people like me and Juno, drowning in hate. I know surely people build lives, people succeed, but they're hard to spot under all the noise. It's dangerous enough for me to junk on a moon in the system, let alone bring someone like Juno Marcus through. If we're just passing by, though, we should be okay.

We'll be quick.

Juno is still looking at my pad, so I push it into her hands and stand up. I dump out the bags we brought onto my bunk to go over inventory. There are four boxes of hair dye, a few scattered credits I missed when we deposited all my money into a new, anonymous bank account, a rubber-banded stack of round JUNO stickers thrust into my hand by a tear-stained Nova, and a little box containing vials of estrogen and sealed injection needles given to us by Jules.

The credits get tossed into a small jar in the storage above my bunk containing a couple dozen more. I put the green hair dye in storage as well, but set the brown boxes on the table. I stuff the JUNO stickers in my pocket and head into the bathroom to secure Juno's HRT safely in the medicine cabinet. When I re-enter the main cabin, Juno is staring, pale-faced, at the back of the box of brown dye.

"Juno?"

"I've had green hair since the day after I realized I could live as a girl," Juno says and tugs at a loose strand. "Gideon helped me dye it. It was short, then, like..." She trails off and makes a gesture right above her ears. "Short. It was the first thing I did to my body that made it feel like mine."

I sit next to her. Our shoulders barely brush. "I cut mine all off after the crash."

"Jules gave you a wig, right? I... You don't have to wear it if you don't want to. You're non-binary, right? I had assumed," Juno says, looking at me with something like kinship in her glossy eyes.

"Yeah." It's the first time I've admitted it out loud. My body has always been mine and mine alone. It still is, but my identity feels like something worth sharing now, at least with Juno.

The girl beside me rubs at her temples. "Will you help me?"

"With what?"

She prods the boxes of hair dye towards me with two outstretched fingers. "This. I... Can I tell you the reason I chose green, I mean, besides it being my favorite color?" I nod, and she continues. "Green is the least common naturally-occurring color in the galaxy. Even on most inhabited planets, plant life is contained, or monitored. Green doesn't exist naturally on ninety-eight percent of the planets we've colonized since the death of Earth." She picks at the ends of her hair. It's fading a little bit now; the roots are brown and they flow smoothly into dark green in the middle, but the tips are a lighter, more artificial color, like neon.

"You wanted to stand out."

"I wanted, at first, to be noticed," Juno admits, "and then I wanted to be visible. So many people were saying that girls like me didn't exist, or we were— We were predators. Hurting kids."

I scoff at that and fold my arms on the table, pillowing my

cheek against my forearm. "Stupid," I murmur. Juno's lips quirk in a strained little smile.

"I know that, and you know that, but... Do you remember that outbreak of smallpox on Janus a couple years ago?"

I nod.

"I didn't pay much attention at the time, but the media told everyone it was an STD, and only gay men and trans women could pass it on."

"What the fuck?"

Juno huffs a quiet laugh out through her nose. "Yeah. Smallpox doesn't know your gender, or your sexuality. It's bullshit. The only reason those groups were the first to report it is because they've suffered from similar diseases, with no fucking support from the government, as far back as we've existed. We're more likely to get a weird spot or rash checked out by a doctor, a doctor from our community, and that's how the outbreak was found in the first place."

"Hell," I mutter. "They just wanted a scapegoat."

"Mmm," Juno nods and rests her head on the table next to mine. Her hair splays out in little rings and one strand brushes the back of my hand. "Anyways. That was disproved with any semblance of common sense, but the rhetoric spread. When kids got it, it was because us big bad evil trans people were abusing them."

"You were a *kid*, Juno."

"Thirteen," she breathes. "Barely through first puberty, let alone second."

"*Shit.*"

"I wanted people to see me. I wanted the people I knew and trusted to see me and know that I was a girl, know that I was part of that population they were vilifying on the news, so I dyed my hair green." Juno closes her eyes and I can imagine her, younger even than the clip I saw on the news, even younger than the day she led her first rebellion, with wide eyes and shaky hands being told she was a predator.

"Is that why you started making videos? Got famous?" I ask and reach out, brushing my thumb against her cheekbone, against a pale little mole there. Juno hums softly and leans into the touch.

"Yeah. It started as a way to be myself, talk about... Video games, or whatever," she says and tilts her head closer to my thumb, so I keep tracing the soft lines of her face. "Then I started HRT, and... It was vitriolic, the response people had. I was a fifteen year old kid. I was old enough to join the IPF, but not old enough to make my body feel like mine."

"You kept going, though. You kept making videos." I've never been into influencers, or content creators, but I know Juno is successful. She has millions of subscribers, millions more followers on other social media platforms. It's how she started her revolution, and why people follow her still.

"Of course I did. I couldn't let them win."

She says it like it's a fact of life, like it's her purpose to make change. I lean a little closer until I can brush my lips against the very top of her cheekbone, right under her eye, right on that mole.

"You're a supernova," I whisper before I can stop myself. Juno opens her eyes with a flutter of long eyelashes, but I'm already pulling away. "C'mon. Let's dye your hair, and you'll see that you stand out no matter what."

"If you say something about how it's not what I look like on the outside, it's what's in your heart that counts..." Juno mutters, but there's a flush on her cheeks and she follows me into the bathroom.

"When have you ever known me to be so sappy?" I ask and gesture for her to sit down on the lid of the toilet. She sighs deeply but she's smiling now and that feels like a win all in itself. I tear off the top of the box of hair dye and drop it in the bathroom trash compactor. Inside, there's a pair of rubber gloves and a little squirt bottle with a set of instructions wrapped around it. I skim the directions and then turn back to Juno to see that she has taken her shirt off and draped a towel over her shoulders.

"It's easy," she says and takes the squirt bottle, showing me how to mix the dye together. "You're mostly going to use your hands, anyways." I shake it up and she settles in facing away from the mirror. She's fidgeting with the fabric of her shirt in her lap, and I rub a hopefully soothing hand down her arm.

"You're sure?" I ask. "We can just get you another hat, or a wig—"

She shakes her head. "No, this is smarter. It'll keep us safe."

The thought of there being an *us* at all makes my chest buzzy and I press my palm hard to my heart until it calms down a little. I swallow hard and run my fingers through her hair.

"Alright."

With that, I begin to rub the brown dye into the green length of her hair. It takes both bottles, but we manage to cover her whole head and wrap it up in a little plastic net that came in the kits. I fix the cap to her head with some little clips, and Juno stands.

She looks at herself in the mirror for a long time. Finally, she wipes a smudge of dye off her jaw and looks at my reflection.

"Thank you," she says softly. I pull the gloves off and jam them into the trash as well. "Do you want me to help you shave your head?"

I look at her and my expression must be pretty horrible, because she holds her hands up in a defensive posture.

"I noticed you keep tugging at it, I assumed it was getting

kind of long," Juno says and shrugs. "Quicker and easier than the dye, at least. It's the least I could do."

"I..." It is getting long. It has been bugging me. The fact that Juno noticed... "Sure."

I take my shirt off too to avoid getting little scraps of fuzzy brown hair all over it while Juno grabs the clippers from the cabinet under the sink. She is methodical and quick, making sure to get around my ears and the back of my neck. She's careful around the delicate parts, swiping her fingers over each spot to dust away the shorn hairs. The vibrations feel good on my scalp and she does gentle but firm passes over my whole skull with a short guard clipped on.

When she's done, she brushes a few spare clippings off my shoulder and looks at me in the mirror.

"I'm going to take a shower to get the bits off," I say and stand up. With us both upright, it's clear how small the bathroom is— The toilet on one side, the single tile shower on the other, and just enough standing space between to look in the mirror above the sink. It's really not meant to fit two people at once, but Juno and I are both small, so we fit.

For the most part.

The proximity is made even more stifling when I bend down to take my leg off. When I stand up straight again, Juno's body is against mine and there's nowhere to retreat to.

"Castor," she says, and I don't hide the little shiver that goes down my spine. "Can I kiss you again?"

I don't think my name in her mouth will ever feel like anything less than a promise. I lean in and kiss her without answering, hoping this is enough. She grins back against my mouth and I press her into the sink by her hips, my mouth moving hesitant against hers until she pushes the towel off my shoulders and starts to touch my chest.

"'S this okay?" she murmurs against my mouth. I drag my lips over the corner of her mouth and nod.

"Is this?" I respond and brush my hand over her breast, which is still covered by a black sports bra. Instead of responding, Juno just pulls my hand off and leans away from me to yank her sports bra off over her head. She immediately leans back in, one hand sliding down to cup my hip— I can feel her hard against me, and I have to admit, it's intoxicating to feel desired— and help me maintain my balance against her.

"Please," she responds and kisses me again.

The plastic on her head crinkles softly as I cup her jaw, brushing my fingertips against the shell of her ear, and I can't imagine anywhere else in the galaxy I'd rather be.

✦

We rinse Juno's hair a while later, watching the brown suds rinse down the drain together. We use half our water tank, pausing every few moments to kiss, or touch, and I can't bring myself to care about the waste. Her hands are soft on my hips and her collarbones are purple from my teeth, each bruise glistening with minute droplets of water. When we leave the shower, Juno still has a soft, calm expression on her face, even as she looks at herself in the mirror.

"It's a bit lighter than my natural color," she comments after a few seconds, "But it'll do."

"That's all we need," I nod and rub at my own hair with a towel. It's been half an hour since we washed mine by now, but Juno kept pushing me into the shower, under the spray, so she could fall to her knees before me. "Once we get to Adrestia, we'll dye it back."

Juno nods and turns away from the mirror. She smiles at me,

but this one is sad and a little droopy at the corners. I kiss the spot between her eyebrows and tug her out of the steamy bathroom into the main body of the ship. Still just wearing a towel and my leg, I go over to the cockpit and check our route. We're still on course, but I change our objective in the GPS to the first refuel station I plotted out for us. The ship shifts incrementally as Verita adjusts our trajectory and I return to the main cabin.

Juno is dressed now in comfortable looking pajamas. She's wearing one of her black tank tops with nothing underneath and a pair of grey joggers that I'm almost entirely certain are mine. Her tattoos are bright and stark against her skin in the low lighting and I can see more of them that I've ever deigned to look at before.

Before I realized who Juno was, both to me and to the galaxy.

"How far out are we?" she asks as I pull on a t-shirt and then a pair of soft, cotton shorts.

Grimacing, I reply, "Twenty-one hours. By the time we get there, we'll need a full refuel."

"Shit," she sighs and flops down into what has become her chair at the little fold-up table in the center of the small area. "What do you do to pass time? Normally, I mean."

"Read," I offer. "Watch TV. Tinker, box, sometimes. Check out Junker forums."

Juno sighs and stretches out her legs. Her bare ankle brushes against my own hairy calf and she doesn't pull away. "Well. I, for one, could use a nap," she says and looks wistfully at my bunk. "Care to join me?"

"In a little bit," I nod, even though the idea of Juno's soft skin against mine in the warmth of my own bed— after so long sleeping upright in the pilot's chair— is extremely enticing.

"Okay," Juno says and moves from the table to the bed. She

rolls onto her side, still facing me, and pulls my blanket up over her shoulders. "Cas?"

"Mmm?" I hum as I dim the lights and turn up the visual brightness on my own eye, looking over at my small tinkerer's table crammed into the corner of the cabin. The little blue plugs I've been collecting are still sitting there, clinking together in a little box magnetically attached to the wall of the ship. I pull my chair along its track until it sits in front of the table.

I rotate around to look at Juno, who seems stiff under the covers, and then she speaks.

"What was her name?"

"Whose name?" I respond.

"The woman who died for me. The trans woman, with the white hair."

Oh.

"Chell."

"Chell," Juno whispers and then pulls her blanket tight and relaxes into the mattress. "Goodnight, Cas."

"Goodnight, Juno."

I shake off the tension that had settled in my shoulders. It isn't worth worrying about now. The small screen built into the wall beside my workbench lights up when I press a button on my pad. I turn on the game show channel and pop in some wireless earbuds I normally don't use. Typically, I'm the only one on the ship, so there's no point. However, with Juno's breathing starting to even out in my bed behind me, I push the rubber tips tighter into my ears and get to work.

The modules are identical, so I choose one at random and set it on the magnetized workspace. With a pair of needle-nose pliers, I start poking at the casing. It comes off easily and I set it aside. Inside, I can see that the blue color on the outside is both from the small light on the end of the powered body of the cell, and also from a tint in the blast-resistant glass encasing the mechanics inside. I set the glass casing aside and pull over my magnifier. It makes it easier to see the inside now that I've pulled it apart successfully, but what's left is still soldered together too well to see what's really inside. I frown.

Most batteries— Or any sort of power cells, even converters — are as open as possible in the center to avoid overheating, especially when the casing is made of glass. I pick at the soldering and try to pull the two halves apart, but they're too well-crafted. I hum and pull them even closer to the magnifier.

There aren't any markings on the outside of what the cells contain, but what I can currently see after opening it up are the backs of two small computer chips shoddily fused together with a soldering iron. It looks haphazardly made, and the chips look like any random computer piece I could pull from any crash. I set it down and grab another one of the cells to pull it apart the same way I did the first.

Wait.

I pause the show that's playing idly in the background and hold the two now-open mechanisms up to the magnifier together.

From every single angle I look at them, the messy soldering is identical.

The 'scrap' they used to make these are cut in the exact same crooked shapes. The soldering is jagged, but in the way a stream turns, following what was already naturally there. The edges of each piece are smooth and carefully cut. I open the third blue plug, just for good measure, and it's the exact same. They're mass-produced, designed with care and intention, and then made to look as if they aren't.

I pull and pick and scrape, but I can't get the pieces any further apart.

A frustrated sigh erupts from my mouth and I shift over so I can get the piece, maybe the size of my first two fingers held together both in width and length, wedged into the bench clamp on the side of my work table. I push my chair away so I can get at the best angle, then grab my miniature conduction blowtorch and head up the soldering lines on each edge.

Metal touches bumpy, connective metal. It heats up just as quickly as I expect, but it doesn't show any sign of melting. If anything it seems to grow stronger.

I set my blowtorch down and peer at the scrap. I bet, with a hotter tool, or some industrial level machinery with stronger clamps, I could get it apart, but for now, it's a lost cause.

"Damn," I breathe. Pulling my earbuds out of my ears, I drop them back into their charging case and check the time. It's been about an hour since I started picking at the cells, and I can feel myself starting to get sleepy. The batteries, or whatever they are, can be a problem for later me, once I get my hands on the right tool to pop them open. I turn everything off including my brain and let myself fall into bed beside Juno Marcus, the most wanted girl in the galaxy.

I dream of gunshots and bloodstained armor, white hair splayed out on harsh concrete, and guilt shining bright in blue-tinted glass.

9

CORPORATE POWER PROTECTED

When I wake, Juno already has a light breakfast set out for the two of us. She isn't eating. Instead, she's staring at the TV with her tense body perched on her stool. I blink blearily, the remembered scents copper and death still lurking in my nose, and look at the TV as well. It takes me a moment to register what it means, but when I do, my dream is forgotten.

The current Galactic President, Samuel Bridger, is standing in front of a podium decorated with the presidential seal. His meager hair is combed over his scalp in an attempt to hide the balding patches, and his face is pockmarked with skin tags and wrinkles. He lifts his hand and says something, but I don't hear it. All I can see is the smile curling cruelly on his face, tugging at his hollow cheeks as he speaks to thousands of people crowded in a park, all wearing the bright blue representative of Marwood's candidacy.

"*Today's vote is a step in the right direction,*" Bridger says and his voice washes over me like sewage. "*Now that these murderous procedures are officially outlawed on every planet and refuel station recognized by the Galactic Government, hundreds of lives will be saved every day.*"

The people there to see him, their idiotic figurehead without any intention to ever genuinely help anyone in the galaxy, scream. The camera pans over them, showing pale faces turned red with their cries. It makes my stomach ache.

"Next, we will stop child abusers from forcing children to change their bodies to live as the opposite gender. Next, we will work to outlaw the horrible, disfiguring surgeries that our children are put through every day against their will!"

The camera cuts back to the anchor and Juno turns to look at me. If I'm disappointed, Juno is furious. Her dark eyes are glassy with unshed tears and her brow is furrowed. Her upper lip curls up in and an honest to god snarl erupts from her lips. She slams her fist down on her own leg and gestures to the screen with her other hand.

"This is what they did, this is what they always do," she spits, chest rising and falling faster than normal. "It started in the 2020's and '30s, but for all of Earth's last fifty years, this is what they fucking did. They started by claiming they were saving lives, but only the lives of a goddamn quarter dollar's worth of cells, *fuck* the parent. They made it illegal to get an abortion, and then made it illegal to miscarry. Then it was gender-affirming care, gay marriage, interracial marriage. They wanted their fucking white, Christian hellscape—" Juno cuts herself off with a groan and sinks both her hands into her hair, pulling on the brown strands.

I push myself up on the bed, but I don't touch her. It doesn't feel right to, not when her face is pale and a single tear is rolling down her cheek.

"When the world ended, the atmosphere began to kill them while they were too busy killing *us* to notice," she says, flat and deeply, deeply exhausted. "It distracted them just long enough for those of us who couldn't afford to filter the rotten air to get off-planet. By the time they realized they could still control us, they were rounding up every man who would find us and kill us for a few bucks and recruiting them to the IPF. The few people who we thought had our backs told us to *vote.*"

Juno laughs, but it comes out choked and thick. There are two long, shiny tracks bisecting her cheeks as her face morphs into something else, something darker.

"Then, Bridger got rid of term limits," she hisses and slams her fist into the table again. "He was elected thirteen years ago, and he got to stay in charge of fucking everything until he decided he was sick of it— Which he only did to get Marwood in charge, by the way.

"Cas," she says, "Abortion is now illegal again in most of the goddamn galaxy. I... Me and my brother, as soon as he could fly, we shuttled people to places where they could get the medical care they needed. Whether that was hormones, surgeries, abortions, anything. Everything the government doesn't want us to have. He still does that, and I... I'm the voice of the silenced. Do you understand?"

"You don't have to be," I respond, and as soon as it's out of my mouth, I regret the choice in words, even before I look at Juno's face. "I mean, you're doing amazing work, but you could step down. Someone else will fill in, you don't have to put yourself in danger."

Juno shakes her head. "They won't. Too many people stay silent, stay placid and neutral," she says, and her gaze flicks to mine again. The rest of the sentence is left unsaid, but it hangs in the air between us anyways: *like you.* I'm part of the problem. I always have been. "I have the privilege that most people don't. I'm not targeted for my skin color, I have money, I have a platform. There are millions of people like me, sure, but I have this chance. I have to make the most of it. If I don't keep the fire going while I still can, we'll fall back into the same cycle we've been living in for generations. It ends with me."

I frown. I can't help it. The optimism in her voice makes my heart break. "You don't really believe that, do you?" I ask. Juno doesn't react beyond meeting my eyes, tired brown boring right into my skull. "There are somethings you're changing now, like the public perception of trans people, and shuttling people around safely is genuine, important work, but you don't actually think Bridger and his goons are going to listen, right?"

Juno's face is so stiff I can see her square jaw quivering. Her brown hair makes her face look redder, her eyes darker, and right now, it casts her in a dangerous light.

"Of course I do," she says in a strange voice.

"We've been fucked over by this same shit for centuries, though. Nothing is ever going to change. We have to accept the the little victories and not kill ourselves over change that'll never come."

Juno stands up and walks over to the bathroom. She coats her palms in cold water and rubs her face, muttering something to herself.

"Juno? I ask and move to stand up, but she whirls around and holds out her hand to stop me.

"Don't," she says, steely and dark. "I should've known better. I should've figured— Shit," she hisses and curls her hands into fists at her side.

"What's wrong?" I ask. I don't often feel as clueless as I do right now. I'm missing something big, I know I am, but there's a wall between me and realization.

"You can't kiss me and call me beautiful while you let Bridger and Marwood starve my sisters out, hold our hormones over our heads until we give up and go back to being the fake versions of ourselves he finds palatable. You can't want me and not want change, Castor, because change is all I am," Juno snarls and rips open the medicine cabinet, pulling out the small box containing her estrogen. "I am an enemy of the state. I am the most wanted person in the galaxy, just for existing and doing it loudly. I will never be silent, and I won't sleep with someone who thinks I should be."

Oh.

Oh.

"I..." I start. Juno's chest is heaving and I want to reach out and touch her, remind myself that this is all real, that every word has consequence. I won't, though— Not when she's angry, never without her permission. I pull my knees to my chest and glance back at the TV. It has pivoted to some absurdist news story that hinges on the fact that viewers don't expect success from disabled people. It's something I've always wrinkled my nose at in distaste, but never something I've thought of as anything but inevitable in the galaxy we live in. It's just some puff piece about a girl who uses a wheelchair succeeding at some mundane job— I've never really considered myself disabled despite fitting the legal description, so I've never had much to relate to on pieces like this.

Now, however, I see the girl on the screen moving her body to avoid putting weight on one side just like I do when the feeling of my prosthetic on my thigh is too overstimulating. I see her pull a small stuffed toy out of a bag on the side of her wheelchair and I think about Apollo's rabbit, the way I rub it against my mouth when I'm feeling overwhelmed.

I know I'm disabled, but I don't like to think that it keeps me from doing anything, so I don't put myself in groups with people like this girl.

Now, with Juno sitting next to me with fire in her eyes, I feel disabled. I feel very much autistic, and I don't know how to find the words to explain to her what I want to say. I swallow and look back at the TV as it changes stories, back to politics. A Marwood rally is happening on Dearing, the biggest planet in the Montgomery system, and it looks heated.

"Shit," I breathe as the camera zooms in to show men and women and children alike thrusting their fists into the air and crying with joy as the bodily autonomy of everyone in the galaxy is stripped away officially on a ginormous screen beside them. Juno looks too, but she just closes her eyes. She's mouthing something, but I can't read lips worth shit.

"*Celebrating President Bridger's overturning of 2034's United States V. Grover are an estimated four thousand residents of Roosevelt City on Dearing, Mongtomery led by Presidential frontrunner Walter Marwood,*" the news anchor says. I wince as they pan over a shot of two women hugging and crying with joy, jumping up and down, and as they pull apart, I see the glimmer of two silver crosses around their throats. "*While this ruling has been coming for months, many are still feeling shock at the finalization of this landmark decision.*"

The camera cuts to another news anchor standing in some kind of open auditorium surrounded by cots, hammocks, and bedrolls covering every inch. People are sleeping and others are sitting with bags falling off their shoulders, small paper bowls of steaming soup in their hands. The news anchor turns grimly to the camera.

"Meanwhile, in Universe City, hundreds of Dearing residents are currently trying to catch the next shuttle off planet," he says, the microphone held close to his mouth. "While this is a victory for many, it is frightening for many others."

He holds out the microphone to someone standing beside him, a boy with a shock of blue hair and smooth skin. When he speaks, his voice is rough and warbly, stuck in the mid-tones between a voice like mine and a voice after the long-term effects of testosterone.

"My name is Joey. I had an abortion last year," the boy says plainly. "If I hadn't, I would have died. My body can't carry a child, as much as I wish it could." He gestures to a group of people behind him. "I was just talking to a woman who got an abortion because her and her husband weren't ready to be parents yet, and another woman who was assaulted, and didn't want to bear her rapist's child. These are all valid reasons to need this procedure. Abortion is a human right. Freedom to do with our bodies what we please is a human right." Joey reaches down and lifts up a sign. It's white paint on cardboard, cheaply, quickly made, but the words on it are clear.

Juno lets out a long breath and surges forward, peering at the screen with her eyes blown wide, her anger laid aside for just a moment.

I STAND WITH JUNO MARCUS.

Below the words is a phone number.

"If you need somewhere safe to go, call this number. You have more friends than you know." The boy looks right into the camera and, just for a second, I see the same glimmer in his expression that I see in Juno's eyes every day.

In the very corner of the poster is a sticker, and I notice now that dozens of people in the background are wearing identical stickers, buttons, pins. All in rainbow, all declaring the same thing: JUNO.

"Juno," I whisper and turn to her. There's a fire in her eyes and a determined line tugging at her lips. The news cuts back to the people from before with the female reporter. Her face is pale now and there's a set to her jaw that I've seen hundreds of times as cis men raise their hands to the sky and cry out in joy. "I don't want to be those people," I say and gesture to the screen, "But I don't know how to be you, or Joey. I don't know how to do anything but survive."

"That isn't—"

"I want to learn," I say and press inches closer. I lay my hand on the bed in front of me palm up. Not asking, just offering. "I don't think I'll ever be the type to speak up on TV like this, but I want to be better." I take a long breath before I continue and dare to meet Juno's eyes, if only for a second before I'm compelled to look away. "I was born to two upper-middle class parents and I was sheltered from the evils of the world until the crash. I know that I was only able to do that because I could stay alive despite everything these people are trying to do, because it wasn't directly impacting me, or my family, but... After the crash, I didn't have anything. I didn't have my parents, or my brother, and their life insurance— which I know was a gift to even have in the first place— was only enough for my medical bills and the title to the Gemini off Craigslist."

Juno snorts a quiet, wet laugh and the corner of my lips turn up.

"I know," I say and shrug, "but nobody else would sell to an eleven year old. I was alone, and I was learning how to walk again. I distanced myself from everything, even when when I realized that I'm a lesbian, even when I decided to get top surgery. I was able to be alone, so I let myself. I didn't think about anyone else, and that's been ingrained in my mind and routine so deeply— I knew bad things were happening, but I told myself, what could one person change?"

Juno's mouth opens but I lean forward and lift my other hand up. She closes it again and worries at her lip between her teeth.

"I knew who you were when I took the job, from the news, and your videos. I didn't know you were involved, but when I saw you, I... I panicked." Juno scoffs at that.

"You sure did," she mutters. Her voice is gravelly and tired and I want to make her tea with honey and kiss her adam's apple until she sounds clear and tastes just as sweet.

"Here was one person who had done more good than anyone I've ever known or seen," I say and look at my palm, still upturned on the bed. There are a few scars there, some old, some new. They criss-cross over my fingers and pale skin, marking me with the story of my life. "I was overwhelmed. It was defensive, the way I let myself stay silent, you know? It was how I kept myself alive, and that, in itself, was privileged of me. I took advantage of the activism you, and Nova, and— And Chell do, when I got my top surgery, and again every time I hung around in the backs of bars waiting for women who seemed like they might be... Like me, I guess." My mind is racing, willing the words into my skill as I say them. I know they're true, words I've avoided saying or even thinking for years as I focused on junking, on staying alive.

"That's what it's all for, though," Juno says softly. "It isn't taking advantage of our work if you're the one we do it for."

"I never saw you as an inspiration." It comes out blunt, verging on rude, but I need to say it. "I thought you were an idiot. I thought you were going to get yourself killed, and I barely understood for what benefit."

Juno's expression is unreadable, so I continue.

"Then I met you, and you chased me down, and told me about your brother, and threw yourself in front of an assault rifle to help the shooter." Juno chews on her lip even harder, biting down until when she releases it, there are two small rectangle imprints in the skin. "I still thought you were an idiot, but I started to understand why you'd risk it all, I guess."

"Why are you telling me all this?" Juno asks and looks down at my upturned hand.

"I don't know," I say, and it's the truth. "Context, I guess? I... I like you, Juno. I like you so much. I didn't want to, but when I kissed you in that alley on Janus I felt my resolve begin to crumble. I didn't want to get involved in any way besides as your pilot, and even that was pushing it. I've stayed alone for a decade just to stay alive. It was the easy choice, and I want to make a harder one now. No matter if you want me, or even like me, I... You've changed me, I guess. Just like you've changed hundreds of other people, like you've inspired kids like Joey."

"He's barely younger than us," Juno whispers and reaches out, finally sliding her smooth, unblemished palm against mine. My stomach lurches at the contact in that way I remember from before we kissed, before she was kidnapped, even before I knew Juno at all and she came up to me at the bar on Janus.

"Okay, fine," I concede. I don't move my hand— In fact, I don't move anything. I stay as still as I can, waiting for Juno to make the next move.

"I'm not ever going to stand down," she says like it's a warning. "I've been a public figure since I was thirteen and I'm going to keep doing it, keep speaking out and making videos until things change, or I die."

"Nobody could ever stop you."

"I'd like to see them try, though," she adds, and then threads our fingers together properly. "I... I think I understand where you're coming from more, now. Your whole life has been focused on survival, you didn't ever stop to think that it could be better."

I nod so violently my neck pops. "That's exactly it."

Juno tucks a strand of brown hair behind her ear and glances at the TV, which has moved on to some other propaganda about Marwood's wife's childhood that I instantly disregard.

"Do you actually... Like me? I mean, enough to..." Juno says, so quiet, so hesitant.

I shake my head. "This, what I've said, what I know, now.

It's because of you, but it's not for you. If you left tomorrow, I'd still be changed. I... If it was, would it even mean anything?"

Juno's lips curl up in a self-conscious smile. "Selfishly, yes," she admits, "but I see what you mean."

"I like you, and I want the galaxy to be better," I tell her. "Those two things might influence each other, and I'll admit that liking you came first. This whole activism, let's change things idea is new to me. Meeting Jules and Nova and Chell, realizing that there's more infrastructure than I've ever known, than I've ever thought possible, losing Chell— I realized that there's work for me to do that isn't being you. I don't have to be the face of anything. I can do the odd jobs and help you all from my ship, if you need me to. When you were arrested, my first instinct was to drop my whole life and pay for your freedom with mine. That's not on you, that was my choice, but I weighed the pros and cons already. Change is worth a little sacrifice."

Juno squeezes my hand. I've been talking for so long that my arms are starting to get goosebumps and seize up in a strange sort of anxiety. I think back to the girl using the wheelchair on TV, and I think about my mind in the way I've always seen it: a computer that, unfortunately, feels things sometimes. I may never be strong enough or brave enough to do what Juno does, but I can be like Jules, or Mars. I can be support, and I *will* whether Juno ever speaks to me again after we get to Adrestia. That's what matters.

"I made breakfast," she says finally. I smile, and it feels like sunshine on Doda.

Our first stop goes off without a hitch. We stay on the ship while they refuel us and recycle our water, and then we're off again.

Juno doesn't kiss me, but she asks me to hold her when we rest again, and she sleeps with her back pressed against my chest. She holds my hand when we awake and asks me to spar with her. She spends all day afterwards thinking with her face deep in my tablet.

I wish, briefly, that I could read her better, but the thought goes away before I let it stick. If Juno was easy to read, she wouldn't be Juno Marcus, and if reading people came easily to me, I wouldn't be Castor Quasar.

We stop again after a full 26 hour cycle that we mostly spend in companionable silence with the news playing at a low volume every second that Juno is awake. Riots break out on planets like Janus. In liberal systems, in systems with better infrastructure for medical care— even some places like Dearing that have strong sects of passionate anti-Marwood rebels in the area— protests crop up. We watch people run each other over, we watch IPF and planetary police shoot off smoke grenades, we watch people even younger than Juno climb on top of crates, cars, and anything else that lifts them up to scream into megaphones about bodily autonomy.

I can tell that Juno is itching for a fight, that she wishes she was out there, and for once I feel it too. My hands twitch even after we spar so I spend an hour with the punching bag on my own. My words feel dull and Juno's weak smiles in response to my even weaker offers of comfort are subdued. I sleep more than I usually would in a single day cycle, and by the time we get to the next refuel station, I'm desperate to get my feet on solid ground.

Not that the refuel stations are especially solid, but they feel more stable than the Gemini. I sling my bag over my shoulder, a mask pulled tight around my face and a hat covering my head. Juno elects to stay on the ship while they do our maintenance and I agree, showing her where my pistol is stored just in case.

I head out onto the refuel station and head straight for the one shop I know I need to visit: a tinkerer's shop slash supply depot called THINGAMAJIGS. It's right next to the pawn shop I'd normally stop by if I was selling scrap, tucked into a little corner beside another dingy restaurant that, despite it's mediocre advertising and dimly lit exterior, smells exquisite.

"What can I do you for?" the shopkeeper asks as I enter. I show her my induction blowtorch.

"I'm looking for one of these that gets about twice as hot," I say and push it across the counter. The shopkeeper picks it up and peers at the etched numbers on the bottom with the make and model, max temperature and instructions, and then whistles.

"That's already a pretty decent torch," she says and sets it back down. "It'll be pricey to get anything better."

I nod. I figured as much. "I'm willing to pay it."

The woman's eyes light up. "I'll be right back, then!" She heads through an old wooden door to the back of the shop and I take the opportunity to look around. The shop is small, no bigger than the main cabin of the Gemini, with shelves lining all four walls. There are tools covering where the upper shelves don't reach, but nothing I need. Smaller parts are littered across the shelves and in some buckets on the ground, including another of the small, blue power cells. I glance around quickly for cameras before pocketing it. I'm wanted already, right? What's the worst thing that could happen?

"Here," the shopkeeper says when she returns a moment later. It's the same brand as the torch I already have, but it's slightly bigger and the torch head itself is wider. She offers it to me handle first. "This'll get hot enough to melt nearly anything. Not quite top of the line, but it's what I got in right now."

"How much?"

The shopkeeper's face shifts into a lazy grin, one I've seen dozens of times from people offering me less than I deserve for junk.

"Three hundred."

"No way," I say and shake my head. "I paid seventy for the hundred volt. I'll do 130."

"250."

"150."

"200?"

"180."

"You drive a hard bargain," the woman says and squints at me behind thick glasses. "What did you say your name was?"

"I didn't. Do we have a deal?" I ask and hover my hand over the new torch until the shopkeeper nods.

"Fine. One-eighty and it's all yours," she concedes and pushes over a little tap-to-pay podium. I pay and gather up both torches. "Now get out of my shop."

I smile at her, a false, strained little expression that I picked up while I was still trying to act neurotypical, years ago. She turns and slumps down into a low chair behind the counter, watching me even as I leave her shop. I slide the body of the newer, bigger torch into my empty holster and head out, only stopping briefly to slap a small, round sticker onto the side wall in the alley beside the shop. It sits there, clean and bright white next to a dozen other stickers for artists, shops, websites, influencers, and politicians. I see another blue sticker emblazoned with MARWOOD 2292 and I quickly peel the backing off of another of Juno's stickers to cover it up with. I glance around and, when I'm confident nobody is watching, I take a picture of the two stickers with my pad. Juno will like seeing that, I bet.

With my new torch tucked into my belt and another mysterious blue plug in my pocket, I head back to the Gemini. They're just finishing up cycling our water when I get back and Juno has her legs dangling out of the hatch in the bottom of the ship.

"Hey," I call and wave up to her.

"Hey," she says and leans forward so her folded arms are propped against the other side of the hatch and then rests her forehead against her forearm. Her mousy brown hair falls down in a slight curl, less than it had when it was green, and she smiles down at me. "Got what you needed?"

"Yep. Anything new here?"

"Nah, just taking a break from staring at a screen," she says. A refuel station supervisor— human, for once— walks up with a clipboard in hand.

"Jupiter? You're all set," he says and gestures to the robotic arms retreating back into their wheeled bodies to go refuel the next ship. I thank him and follow Juno back up into the ship.

Within minutes, we're back in open space, flying at the speed of light. I unbuckle and head at once back for my workbench, settling both torches and the blue plug down on my table. Juno lingers this time, but I don't let her distract me. I pop open the newest capsule to see the exact same irregular soldering holding the casing together. I set aside the blue glass and crank my winch until it's holding the small metal mechanism.

"Back up," I murmur and pull on my welder's gloves as she does so, stepping back about a foot. The conduction blowtorch heats the metal through touch, so there aren't any sparks or flames to worry about, but it can still melt your skin if you hold it wrong. I'd rather be safe than sorry, so I turn the torch on to a medium setting.

Carefully, I press the tip of the conduction torch to the

soldering. Almost instantly, the metal heats up orange and begins to sag under its own weight. I turn the dial on the torch down to a slightly lower temperature and press again, slowly heating the metal until I can wedge the tip of a screwdriver under and start chipping it away. Within minutes, I have the little device open and I set aside the blowtorch. After twisting the last bits of metal until the outside panel snaps off, I can finally see what has been so carefully shielded from view.

"Oh, shit," Juno breathes against my head.

"What?" I ask. The little piece inside isn't something I've ever seen before. It's a lot like the computer chips that had concealed it, but much smaller, and the wiring is much tighter and carefully produced. I look at Juno and see that she has gone pale.

"Where did you get these?" she asks and gestures to the identical devices.

"Ships," I answer, "And I stole this one from the lady who sold me the blowtorch. What are they?"

Juno turns to me with her bare lips set in a tired line. "This is techno-terrorism. I've seen these before. If the person who put it there so chooses, they can hack into any ship with these devices installed and see their location, vitals, and even control their Bellona."

"Who uses these?"

"Small sects, before. They're hard to make, so not many groups have even tried," she says and leans in even closer to look at it.

"These are identical, though. Every single one is the exact same, down to the nicks in the metal and the amount of soldering."

"So it has to be a bigger operation than some rinky dink freelancer."

"Exactly. I found one in that crashed Zephyr hauler."

"Zephyr can afford to mass produce these into the millions. It has to be them, doesn't it?"

"They have it set up so they can take over any ship they've produced in the last decade. If this works with Bellona, or it's installed on Bellona ships, that number has to be in the billions," I say quietly, and Juno sucks in a sharp breath.

"Fuck," she hisses. "Thank fuck the Gemini runs on Verita. You haven't gotten any of the motherboards replaced recently, have you?"

"I do all my own repairs," I tell her. "There's no chance we have a bug."

"Not a bug," Juno says grimly, "A kill switch. If they have access to tech like this..."

"Well over half the ships in the galaxy could be completely taken over, entirely on a whim, with the push of a button."

"*Fuck.*" Juno reaches out and touches the piece. "It can't do anything from here, not to us, right?"

I shake my head. "I think, once it's been disconnected from the motherboard, it can't do anything. I think they're electrified too, once they're plugged in, to dissuade people from unplugging them."

"That's definitely illegal," Juno snorts, "But I suppose it doesn't matter when you're the ones making the laws."

"Zephyr has had a near-monopoly on ships and most parts for decades already, and they all but own Bridger and Marwood, too. If there was an issue, they could pay to just legislate right over it," I say, and Juno snorts.

"We should check the Gemini too, just in case," she decides, and I agree. I pile the disconnected bits of metal and technology back into my magnetic bin and turn my light out, leaving my gloves loose on the workbench.

I grab my multitool and head into the cockpit. With the screwdriver attachment, I remove the metal panel protecting the brains of the ship. No blue light. "All clear," I call to Juno. I poke around with my penlight, looking deeper, but there's nothing. "They've gotta be installed during manufacturing."

Juno sighs and sits down on the bed. She sinks her fingers into her messy brown bangs and groans.

I replace the panel quickly and lean against the doorway between the cockpit and the main cabin. "What are you thinking about?" I ask her.

Juno looks up at me. She's taken to not wearing any makeup on the ship when it's just the two of us, and I realize I haven't seen her touch her eyeliner since we broke out of prison. "This. It's so, so far out of my wheelhouse," she admits and lets out a little skittering laugh. "I don't know anything about tech, not really. I've always been the wordsmith, the legislator— Even then, my brother is the one who knows the law inside out. You know the tech, but what happens when the tech becomes the oppressor? When the legality of it is the only thing we might have against them, and I'm not an expert in either? I feel like I'm floundering. Without the freedom to speak up, I feel useless."

"Why not make a video?" I suggest. She looks up, a curious look on her face— the same glint I saw in her eyes when I kissed her on Janus. Juno loves a scheme. "I mean, you have the reach to make change no matter what. Forty million people isn't something to sneeze at. Maybe don't talk about the bugs, not yet, but about what you've seen, what you would say if you could hold a protest right now."

Juno is silent, staring into middle distance a bit past my shoulder.

"What are you thinking?" I ask again, and she meets my eyes.

"Can I? Record here?"

"Of course you can. Use my workbench, if you want."

"What if they recognize the ship?"

I shrug. "They already know what kind of ship we're on. They have no way of tracking us, not anymore, so they'd be relying on good old fashioned word of mouth to find us," I say and sit down beside her. "Unless they put out an emergency alert, there's no way they could disseminate that information fast enough to catch us before we hit Adrestia."

Juno nods and leans to the side until her head rests against my thigh. I card my fingers through her hair and she sighs softly.

"Thank you, Cas," she breathes and closes her eyes. "I... I'm sorry I got angry with you."

I shake my head. "No, don't be. You were right," I say and scratch my fingernails against the spot behind her ear. She hums softly and looks up at me with her warm eyes. My stomach flutters at the attention.

"I know, but I shouldn't have gotten pissy about it." She presses her cheek against my thigh and shifts a little closer, brushing her fingers against my calf. "You're doing more than enough."

"I'm not going to stop when we reach Adrestia," I murmur, and I realize that I mean it. I can't imagine leaving Juno behind and going back to my solitary little life, collecting scrap and selling it for pennies. "I'll stay, and I'll help. I'll junk for you guys, or pick up your ships, I don't know. Whatever you need me to do."

"Cas," Juno breathes and then sits up and kisses me. I immediately sink my hand into her hair and kiss back, pulling her close. She's so warm and so soft and we fall backwards, curling up together in our small bed as we kiss.

"I want to be who you think I can be," I say when she pulls back to breathe. "I want to be better."

"I do too," Juno murmurs. "That never goes away."

"Then I won't ever stop trying."

She kisses me again, and again, and again. She kisses me and I don't think about the kill switches, or Marwood; only the softness of her body and the *want* curling around us to do better, be better, and make the galaxy better.

She kisses me again, and I finally understand why the girl on the news does what she does.

10
LABOR POWER SUPRESSED

THUNK.

I shoot upright in bed, Juno's arm falling limply from where it was wrapped around my bare stomach.

KA-THUNK.

The whole ship shifts to the left, tilting, and I feel the gravity shift too. Dozens of metal scraps fall from my work bench, and even Pollux's water shifts to an uneven angle. I swear and scramble out of bed. I'm barely dressed, just wearing a pair of boxer briefs I grabbed out of Juno and I's shared clothes drawer, but I still bolt into the cockpit.

"We are experiencing mechanical failure," Verita says.

"I got that," I gasp, my voice still raspy and dry from sleep.

"There are ongoing issues with the faster than light engine, gravity emulator, and auto-pilot functions."

"What the fuck happened?" Juno calls and I see her in my periphery wearing shorts and a big t-shirt, holding tight to the handle in the doorway to the cockpit and balancing at an awkward angle.

"The exterior of the ship was struck by an unknown projectile, most likely human-made debris."

"Shit," I hiss and look out the windshield. "We overslept.

We missed the second refuel station, we're in the Montgomery system now, in the asteroid belt."

Juno hisses and lowers herself closer to the ground as the ship shudders and jolts to the right.

"Buckle in, I'll manually pilot us to the closest stop," I yell and throw myself into the pilot's chair. I spare one cursory glance back at Juno to make sure she's secure, and then flip the auto-pilot switch to OFF.

I've piloted the Gemini hundreds of times on my own. I've flown for hours with just my two hands keeping the voyager-class ship from crashing, and I know I'm a good pilot, but as a two meter wide chunk of space rock goes whizzing past the cockpit, I feel my confidence shrivel.

According to GPS, we're less than ten minutes from Dearing, and the intergalactic port on Dearing has a full aero-shop. I swear under my breath and look over at the small sticker stuck to the dashboard, and then back at Juno in the small rear-facing mirror. Dearing is a smaller planet of only around fifty million, but that's still fifty million people that, more than likely, want Juno and I both dead.

I hesitate for just a second, and then I switch the ship into first gear and turn us to the left. Dearing is right there; our original route had us narrowly avoiding entering the gravity pull of the planet, but now... I steer us towards the intergalactic port.

We leave the asteroid belt just before we feel the edges Dearing's gravity tug on the ship. I begin to adjust our speed to make up for drag upon entering the atmosphere. It's something I've done dozens of times, but my palms sweat through it anyways.

Once we're safely in the atmosphere, I feel a heavy THUD somewhere in the body of the ship as the artificial gravity kicks off. I feel myself raise in my harness and I hear a quiet, surprised noise escape Juno in the back.

"Hold on!" I call and yank back on the steering mechanism, trying to get us to something approximating an appropriate landing speed, and angle us towards the port. It's adored with red, white, and most of all blue as far as the eye can see; a dozen-odd variations of the old American flag and another six Marwood flags decorate the civilian entrance to the port. The ship entrance is wide open on the top and I pull hard on the wheel until we're plummeting towards the docking bay doors.

"Jupiter, this is Dearing port security. You need to decrease your landing speed at once."

"I'm working on it!" I yell back into the comms system.

We're still barreling towards the surface way too fast, so I push my foot down on the emergency break and hols fast, slamming the landing gear button with my free hand. It deploys and we skitter into place with a crash, narrowly missing another docked ship.

When we come to a stop, the ship is upright, so I consider it a successful landing. There are vague streams of smoke visible through the windshield coming from the engine and I wince as I unbuckle myself.

"Juno? Are you okay back there?"

"Peachy," she grits out. I turn around to see her hunched over with one hand wrapped around her stomach and the other hovering over her pursed lips. Her face is nearly as green as her hair used to be. She takes a few deep breaths through her nose and then slowly removes her hands. "Where are we?"

I try to smile comfortingly but it comes out feeling like I painted a grimace on my face. "Dearing."

Her face pales. "No."

"It was the closest stop. We wouldn't have made it any further."

Juno bites down on her lower lip and ducks down to our drawer, pulling out clothes for each of us. She tosses me a pair of joggers and borrows another for herself, then pulls a hoodie on over her t-shirt. "Okay," she says after a minute.

"Our best bet is to ask if we can stay on board while we get repairs, but..."

"Unlikely," she says and sighs. "Yeah. Well, I'll get my stuff together."

"Stuff? We can leave it on the ship."

"Not my estrogen, not my makeup, not..." Juno says and makes a vague hand gesture. "Anything that could out us has to come with us. It's safest on our bodies, not left here."

I nod. She's right. I change quickly while she starts throwing stuff into one of my junking bags, including the thick stack of stickers, her HRT, my old binder, and anything else that could tell the mechanics who we are. When she's done, the Gemini looks barren, and desolate. She hands me my junking bag, Apollo's rabbit sticking out of the edge, and I sling it over my shoulder. I adjust my shirt and jacket to make my chest look natural and she ducks into the bathroom to draw on eyeliner.

BANG BANG BANG.

"This is port security. We're going to need to see identification, especially after that landing."

I meet Juno's eyes in the mirror and she jerks her head towards the hatch, so I nod and head that way, pulling a paper face mask over my mouth and nose as I do so.

"I'm coming," I call and pull out my pad with my fake ID. Briefly, I'm grateful for past me, who told Chell and Nova to mark my fake ID with F instead of X just in case something like this came up. "Sorry for the hard landing, we hit some unexpected debris."

"Identification, please." The port security guard is armored to the teeth and carrying an assault rifle. He's easily the most heavily geared security guard I've ever seen, up there with IPF special ops soldiers. I silently offer him my pad and start climbing down out of the ship, leaving the grate propped open for Juno.

The guard peers at my ID and then flips up his dark plexiglass face shield to peer at my covered face. "Morgan Sawyer..." he murmurs and I tug my mask down briefly. "Aren't you a little young to have a ship like this?" he asks. There's something in his tone that rubs me the wrong way. Condescension, resentment. Like he sees something on my face he doesn't like. I would tell him that I'm twenty, but I don't know what age Chell put on my fake, and I don't want to contradict my forged paperwork. I already don't like being called another name; we might as well get this shit over with.

"Docking fee is ten credits," he says and hands my pad back over. I transfer the money at once.

"We're going to need repairs. Is there a shop nearby?" I ask him even though I know for a fact that this port does repairs in house.

"Mmm," he grunts, a non-reply. "I'll call over our maintenance guy." The guard turns away to speak into a radio clipped to his chest. Juno climbs down now, her hair brushed to cover as much of her face as possible above her own mask, her eyes painted dark and angular with makeup. She has my spare bag slung around her body and I give her a small nod when she settles in close beside me.

The guard turns back around and gives Juno a brief once over before deciding that she's not worth his time. "Rob will be over in a minute to check out the damage. Don't go anywhere until he's done."

He walks off without any more and I grimace behind my mask.

"Dick," Juno breathes into my ear and I swallow a laugh. A couple of small robots scurry around us with magnets and clamps held out, picking up bits of debris that came off when we crash landed. When the ground is clear, they roll away to work on a few other, smaller ships— inner-atmosphere speeders made for travelling on one planet, not going between them. A couple of them are decorated with stickers and magnets proclaiming the owners' political views. I see more than a couple MARWOOD 2292 stickers on bumpers and wrinkle my nose behind my mask.

"What seems to be the problem," a gruff, short man says as he waddles up to the Gemini. I step away from Juno and duck out from under the ship, turning to the right side where the debris struck.

I detail to him what I believe the extent of the damage is, gesturing along the battered body of the Gemini, and he in turn jots down notes on a tablet with a scrappy little stylus. We do a full lap and then pop the hatch that hides the engine. Juno sits on the ladder and waits, clutching her bag to her lap, and after I hesitantly hand the keys over to Rob, I rejoin her.

"It'll take a few hours, and we can't have you girls on the ship," Rob says and scribbles some more stuff on his tablet. He hasn't once made eye contact with me and I can't say that I mind. "It's a safety precaution. We have a waiting room, or you can head out into Dearing City to see the sights. I'm gonna need half payment up front, and then we'll get started. This'll let you know when we're finished." He hands me a small, metal device about the size of my palm.

The quote for the repairs stings. Eight hundred credits.

In another life, that was impossible. Now, I feel the lingering hurt, the learned pain that comes more from having to pay at all than the fact that I can't afford it. I can, now. Thanks to Juno.

Four hundred credits leave my account. I pat the misshapen side of my ship and turn back to Juno as Rob starts instructing the small robots wheeling around us.

"Shall we?" I say to Juno and gesture to the exit of the hangar, where a glass tunnel with a moving walkway ushers travelers further into the city. Juno takes a long breath and looks up at the waving flags above us before nodding. I go to offer her my hand, but stop before it gets close enough. It isn't safe. Instead, I just brush our arms together as we start walking.

"I don't like being here," she says quietly as we pass another half-dozen flags.

"I've been here before," I breathe. "It's a beautiful planet." We stay close together as we step onto the automatic sidewalks, continuing to move even after they propel us forward. I'm sure we're both feeling the same eagerness to get out of the place we landed in. It's easier to hide and blend in among thousands in the heart of the city than it is in a mostly empty dock, save for forty-odd robots and a dozen armed guards eyeing us suspiciously.

"I'm sure it's lovely," Juno sighs. "I wish it felt like I was welcome."

"I'll keep you safe," I say and bump her with my elbow. "There's no gun carrying laws on Dearing." From the bottom of my bag, I retrieve the holster for my pistol and clip it on my belt.

"Shit," Juno breathes and shakes her head. "Insane."

I don't respond to that, especially as we exit the dock and emerge out onto a bustling city street. A man on a motorized bike rushes past us on the sidewalk, calling something unintelligible behind him at us as we're thrown off balance. I pull Juno closer and tuck us into a corner between the edge of the docking port doorway and whatever building is wedged in beside it.

"Let's find somewhere a bit quieter and I can poke at the GPS," I murmur into her hair as she catches her breath on my neck. "Okay?"

She nods and her forehead touches my jaw. I'm suddenly aware of how warm she is and I want to hold her, kiss her, but that isn't safe on planets like Dearing. Instead, I shuffle us out of the shallow alley I pulled us into and resettle her arm in the crook of my elbow. After taking a deep breath, we're off, both of us in chunky boots and masks pulled tight across our faces on the sidewalk of the most dangerous planet in the galaxy.

I find myself grateful for the mask as hundreds of people pass us going the other way with bare faces, some coughing into their elbows, others sneezing into porous cloth and paper. I keep my eyes straight ahead and focus on where we're heading, even though I'm still unsure where that is.

"Look," Juno says, "Bookstore. Don't see many of those these days." She points across the street. Sure enough, there's a little bookstore across the way boasting PAPER COPIES and OLD FICTION in their glass window. Physical books went out of fashion years ago; it's difficult to transport thousands of books across lightyears, but an ebook can be sent in minutes. There's a little neon coffee cup in the front window and curtains pulled tight, save for a small gap where I can see two gleaming eyes peering out over a few leafy plants lining the windowsill. I squint a little to try and make the animal out, only realizing that I've stopped walking when Juno's boots stop stomping along beside me.

"What is that?" I ask and point at the window. Juno shields her eyes with her hand held flat to her brow and looks across the rows of traffic.

"What, the sign?"

"The little animal."

Juno's hand drops and she turns to look at me incredulously. "The *cat*?"

"Is it?" I squint a little more and adjust my eye manually to zoom in— Sure enough, there are two little pointed ears peeking up above the cat's shiny eyes.

"Have you never seen a cat in real life before?" Juno asks and gives me a look. It's one I know well: it says, 'wow, I can't believe you've never done this thing that I consider normal and common'. It's the look that people give me when I tell them I've never learned to ride a bike or smoked an e-cig. My face does something I guess, because Juno's face breaks out of The Look into a wide open almost-apology.

"No, I haven't," I reply. It comes out flat and I look Juno in the eyes as I say it, but I still have to avert my gaze after just a moment.

"We *have* to go over there," she insists as her face breaks into one of those unstoppable, unbelievable grins, the ones where her gums show over the white ridges of her teeth and her nose scrunches up a little more on the left than on the right. Of course, most of it is hidden behind her mask, but I see the crinkles in the corners of her eyes and I feel the self-conscious anxiety ooze out of my bones where her hand grips my forearm a little tighter.

Juno leads me to a crosswalk and we huddle close while we wait for the light to change. Nobody looks at us twice and I'm briefly grateful for my boxy, masculine figure next to Juno's shorter build. Especially with our coats and boots covering most of our forms, she looks like a girl, and I look like a boy, at least to the unfamiliar eye. While it makes me somewhat uncomfortable to be seen as male, it at least offers Juno some protection with her carefully drawn on eyeliner and shaggy bangs covering most of her face. Inside, I know who I am. I'm Castor Quasar. I'm a butch lesbian. Juno knows who I am, and that's what matters.

When the light finally changes, Juno has to tug me along to catch up to her. We cross the street quickly and end up right outside the little bookshop. Juno crouches down to be at eye level with the cat.

"Hello, little friend," she coos in a high-pitched voice. It's a little grey creature with smudges of brown and tan around its face and a yellow collar adorned with a bell and a small metal tag that says MARIGOLD. It has two fuzzy ears and bright yellow eyes and it looks up at us, its mouth opening in a silent noise that exposes razor sharp teeth and a little pink tongue.

It's cute, but Juno murmuring words at it and holding her fingers up to the glass is cuter.

"Do you want to go in?" Juno asks, and I'm nodding before she even finishes the question. She tugs on my sleeve and brings me inside. When the door opens, a small bell tinkles to announce our entrance and the door falls shut again behind us. The space inside isn't small, but it feels almost tiny with the sheer amount of books, magazines, and other physical media crammed into every nook and cranny. There's a couch by the window that the cat is laying on the back of, but when the door shuts, it turns around and trots over to us, its stomach swinging back and forth.

"Welcome to Long Lost Media," a voice calls, "Feel free to pet Marigold, she's quite friendly." I turn and see the person greeting us: a young girl with blonde hair down to her chest and a kind smile on her face. Her voice is accented— I find that I like it. Her name tag says Faith with a little doodle of a plant.

Juno is already kneeling with her hand sunk deep into Marigold's thick fur and, as soon as I squat to join, the cat rolls onto her back with her belly up in the air for me and Juno to touch.

"She's beautiful," Juno croons and scratches her fingernails gently through the whorls of fur on her tummy.

"Isn't she?" Faith replies and comes around the corner of the desk. My hand instinctively twitches towards my gun, but she just leans against the wooden piece of furniture and gestures vaguely in our direction. "She's my mum's. She's lived here since the place opened."

"What a good girl," Juno murmurs and grabs my hand. I startle, but Juno just rests it gently on Marigold's stomach. The fur there is soft and dense, light grey teetering on almost white, and I can see faint pink spots where her skin shows through. I run my fingers through the fur and my face must betray my delight because Juno grins at me. "Isn't she lovely?"

"Soft," I breathe and drop my other hand down to touch Marigold's side. I don't move much, just resting my hands in the warm fur and incrementally shifting my fingers back and forth to feel it brush against my calloused fingers.

"My parents had a cat," Juno says softly. "I had to leave her, when... When Pisces and I left." I recognize the code— Her brother, the other half of her twin swimming fish tattoo. It's probably smart to speak in code on Dearing. I'm almost surprised I didn't think of it first.

"I'm sorry," I reply. I turn to look at her, try to push some sympathy that I really do feel in my chest out, trying to show it on my face, but she turns at the same time, leaving our faces just inches from each others'. My mouth falls open and Juno's gaze flicks down to my lips—

We both turn away simultaneously, suddenly aware of where we are, who we're with. When I look over, though, Faith is looking at a flimsy magazine she grabbed from a rotating stand beside the checkout desk. When I look a little closer, I see that her cheeks are flushed pink and she's trying a little bit *too* hard not to look our way, so I clear my throat and move away from Juno.

"I'm going to go look, at the..." I say and gesture vaguely into the winding, maze-like stacks and shelves of books, DVDs, and other forms of physical media I rarely see. Juno nods and turns back to petting Marigold, and I can't say I blame her. When my hands leave the silky fur, I immediately itch to sink them back in, rub my cheek on the kitty's side until she lets out that vibrating, purring noise I know that cats make.

As soon as I'm hidden behind a shelf of games for a console I've never heard of— PS3?— I reach into my bag and dig until I find Apollo's rabbit, lovingly tucked away. I rub it against my lips, the worn fabric soothing against my skin with gentle, repetitive motions, and let out a long breath. The cars and trucks and speeders outside roar in my ears and the quiet sound of Faith moving around is deafening, rattling through my head—

I reach up with my spare hand and rip off my beanie. The lack of stimulation makes me feel better at once.

"Junker?" Juno murmurs and comes up behind me. Her arms wrap around my middle and I can't help but sag against her chest. The short, prickly hairs on my head brush against her jaw and I feel her lips brush the base of my skull.

"I'm fine," I breathe and squeeze Apollo's rabbit until I feel the seams begin to give under my fingers. "I'm just not used to spending all my time with someone."

"Sorry," Juno hums and starts to pull away, but I shake my head and turn in her arms to grip the lapels of her jacket.

"No," I reply. I glance around to see if Faith is watching us, but I don't see her, so I push Juno until we're in a back corner behind another bookshelf. "You're not someone."

"Thanks," Juno chuckles and I know I picked the wrong words but her face isn't upset, just curious. She tugs her mask down to rest under her chin, tilts up on the balls of her feet, and kisses right between her eyebrows. "Tell me."

"When I'm with you, I don't get tired, or overwhelmed, and when I do, you don't care. When it's just me and you, it's like it's just me, but better." I don't know if it makes sense, but Juno loops a finger in the elastic ear band of my mask and tugs it off so it's dangling from one ear.

"When I'm with you," Juno breathes and I can taste her toothpaste in her breath, her lips just inches from mine, and there's still that little surge of anxiety about being in public but Juno's eyes dart to look over my shoulder, making sure we're safe. She's checking. She's protecting us. "When I'm with you, Cas, I feel like a person again, like a human being, and not just a voice, or a pretty face. When we are together, I feel *alive.*"

I kiss her. I cup her jaw and feel the soft tips of her brown bangs tickle my forehead and I want to press her into the shelves here and always taste that same sweet-mint toothpaste and vanilla shampoo on her lips, on her skin, in my chest.

I pull back and drop my hands, breathing a little harder than I was just a moment ago.

"Ju—"

"Green," she breathes, "for me. Junker and Green."

"Green," I repeat and step back, but I can't stop the little smile tugging at my lips. "Careful."

She grins and pulls her mask back up, then pulls mine up as well. Juno touches her forehead to mine.

Ding! Ding!

I freeze. The bell above the door rings again, and again. A half dozen feet stomp inside, carrying with them loud, deep voices and jingling keys. Juno presses on my flat chest until we're out of the small, secluded nook we stole our kiss in. I pull my beanie back down onto my head and stuff Apollo's rabbit deep down into the bottom of my bag, resting my palm on my gun when I want it to be cupping Juno's cheek, holding her hand.

"Guys," Faith says like she knows them, like they're usuals, and her voice is terse and strained. Nothing like the cheery greeting we received when we entered. I glance at Juno and take a deep breath, my overstimulation almost forgotten. Juno tends to do that. She brushes her thumb over my wrist one last time before pulling further away.

I shift until it could— at least somewhat convincingly— look like I'm genuinely reading the spines of the books beside me. Juno picks up a CD and starts reading the back. I'm grateful for the mask once again both because of the loud, spitty voices of the men trampling inside and also because of the warm flush still coloring my cheeks.

A big, blonde kid maybe a year or two older than Juno and I bumbles around the corner. He's wearing a white t-shirt proclaiming 'PROTECT REAL EARTH KIDS' and a jacket that's made of beige felt with blue leather sleeves ending in an elastic beige cuff. There's an emblem on the breast that I don't recognize, but I do recognize the style of jacket. He's still in high school, or at least peaked then.

He moves with a purpose until he's in front of a wall of DVDs right in between me and Juno. I know I've been staring at him for too long, but he doesn't even spare me a glance as he drags his fingertips along the spines of the DVDs. He pulls one out and looks at the back. It's yellow and pink, but I don't look further. He tucks it into the crook of his elbow and returns to the shelves.

As he does, I see Juno start slinking towards me around the man's back, her brown eyes meeting my own with a vague, wide-eyed look of glittering fear.

"Oh shit!" the guy cries out and pumps his fist, pulling out a DVD and clutching it in his sweaty fingers. Juno barely manages to shift past him before his body fills the spot she had just occupied. "Duke, I found our white whale!"

Juno jerks her head towards the door and I nod in return. As soon as I take a step towards her, though, the narrow opening between bookshelves is filled by two large bodies.

They're both wearing identical jackets and one has dark, curly hair while the other is shaved nearby bald, his hair even shorter than my own.

The darker-haired one gives me a once over and then turns back to his friend, who is holding up his 'white whale'. I shift past him towards Juno, but before I can get out of the nook we're crammed into, I feel a hand wrap around my bicep.

"What's with the gun, Junker?" the shortest-haired kit asks when he yanks me to a stop. "Don't feel safe here?"

"We're just passing through," I grit out and pull my arm out of his grasp. "Excuse me."

"You're not excused," the tallest boy says and shifts until he's between me and the doorway. I clench my jaw shut tight and don't show my irritation on my face.

"Excuse me," I say again and try to push past him. His bigger friend grabs my back— my bag strap, I think— and I'm stuck between three large, angry teenagers and the solid weight of the bookshelf behind me.

"Didn't you hear me, Junker? You're not excused," the boy repeats and shoves my bag off my shoulder, letting it tumble to the ground. Apollo's rabbit spills out of the opening and I wince.

"You're pretty for a junker," the blond boy sneers and I feel something in my body snap, like tension pulling a rubber cord so taut it rebounds. I pivot on one foot and slam my elbow into the shorter boy's nose, feeling it crack under the impact. Blood sprays forward and speckles the front of my shirt but I barely notice, too busy using the inertia to spring my other arm forward and throw a solid punch into the face of the tallest boy. He stumbles back and reaches up to press a hand to his cheek where I hit him, shock evident on his face.

A hand closes around my throat and cuts off my airflow, but

I twist out of the biggest boy's grip just long enough to pull my gun and aim it directly at his forehead.

The other two freeze. I meet both of their eyes and then look past them at Juno, standing in the doorway. Her eyes are wide and dark.

"I think I am," I tell the boys. My gun stays steady as I turn on my heels until my back is to Juno and I can start backing out of the shop. "Leave us alone." I step on the strap of my bag and kick it behind me with my foot. I hear the zipper jingle as Juno picks it up, but I don't look back at her. I only have eyes for the three children that had the audacity to act like they fucking own this bookstore.

"For your troubles," I hear Juno say and place a couple of credits down on the checkout desk for Faith. I grin and cock my head to the side. Adrenaline pumps through my veins— I feel like I'm floating.

"Are you ready to go, love?" I ask Juno, who kisses my cheek and wraps her arm around my waist. I grin as she hums in agreement, and then we slowly back out of the store, keeping my gun trained on the boys the whole while.

The second the door shuts behind us, I take Juno's hand and start running with no destination in mind, weaving through alleys and back corners and in between towering buildings. She's laughing and the peals of it sit light and warm in my chest as we run through the city, not caring where our feet take us.

When we finally hit a dead end, Juno presses me into the wall and latches her mouth onto my neck before I can even stop to think. I sink my hands into her hair, tossing her hat off onto the ground, and laugh, rolling my head back to crack against the brick wall. She nips at the spot right under my ear and my grasp on her turns sharp.

"Juno," I murmur and reach up with one hand to pull my mask down so I can kiss her, slow and deep. "I—"

"You're incredible," Juno breathes into my mouth, kissing me again, and again, and again, like she's fucking drowning. "So good for me, Cas. So strong, so protective..."

I gasp and grip her tighter. "You bring it— Ah! You bring it out," I reply, stuttering in the middle as her hips press forward against mine, as I feel the beginnings of her *want* growing against my hip— I spin us around and push her against the wall instead, my palm between her skull and the wall. "You bring out the best in me." I pull away for just a second, just long enough to see the flutter of her lashes and flushed cheeks, and then a color catches my eye, scraped against porous brick and mortar.

I realize with a start that the wall behind her is painted in an enormous mural. When I pull away, she whines, but I spin her around and walk her back to see.

"Look," I murmur, and we do.

The curve of a cheek, the soft bridge of a familiar nose, pierced with shining gold— Green hair curls across the right-most edge of the wall, fading in the ends of long brushstrokes closer to the cement ground below us. There's a mole on her cheek above plum lips, a mole I know intimately well, and the eyes are so dark they're nearly black.

It's Juno Marcus, larger than life, with delicate rainbow flowers surrounding her, blooming out of the edges where the painting of her pale throat ends.

"Holy shit," Juno breathes and takes another step back to take it all in. The colors are dark in the darker still alleyway, but when she pulls my pad out of the bag still hanging at her hip and takes a picture with flash, I see how bright and vibrant they must be in the light of the Montgomery system's sun. It's a brave statement of alliance, one that could get the artist arrested, and it takes my breath away just as well as Juno's kisses.

"Stand by it," I tell her and take the tablet from her hands. Juno smooths down her shirt and pulls her mask off fully, stepping forward and turning so her face is right beside the painted one, just as brave, just as breathtaking. I take a picture and Juno's face is lit briefly in pure white, making her cheekbones and sharp black eyeliner stand bright and contrast the paint behind her.

She moves behind me to look at the picture, her chin hooked onto my shoulder, and I can feel her smile in her jaw.

"You're changing the galaxy," I tell her simply and she smiles into my neck.

"Change it with me," she says, and it feels so easy to turn around and kiss her, whispering *yes, yes, yes* into her throat.

✦

We're off Dearing two hours later. We find a cafe a good distance away from the bookstore and sequester ourselves away in a little booth. Juno tucks herself into my side and we drink coffee— well, I drink coffee, and Juno drinks an iced matcha latté— until the small metal puck the repairman gave me vibrates in my pocket.

"Is that a commpuck in your pocket," Juno murmurs against my shoulder, "or are you just happy to see me?"

I snort out an ugly laugh and tip my cup, swallowing the lukewarm remnants of my coffee. "Both, if you could believe it," I reply and pull out the puck to turn it off.

"I can, actually." Juno smiles and slides out of the booth, taking both of our empty cups and tossing them into a compactor. "The junker who swore they'd never take a side, holding a teenage boy at gunpoint to save a wanted fugitive..."

"Shush." I take her hand and pull her out of the cafe, using the other to tug my mask back over my face. "You've ruined me,"

I sigh and stop at a crosswalk. "Made me believe in your liberal agenda."

Juno snickers and squeezes my hand. "Sure have."

If she sounds a little proud, I don't comment on it.

When we get back to port, I let go of Juno's hand. The dozen-odd flags flap in the light breeze and I pull my bag tighter to my side as we approach Rob, who is now standing behind a hover-desk with a tablet open to some color-coordinated spreadsheet. A man after my own heart.

I set the puck down on the desk. He just gestures to the payment terminal, so I tap my watch to it and send the payment. Rob waves us off with a receipt sent directly to my inbox.

"We're clear?"

"Mmm," Rob mumbles and goes back to his spreadsheet. I nod and look at Juno, quirking an eyebrow up in silent judgement. She snorts and off we go, back to the Gemini.

There it is, fixed up and gleaming silver in the low light of the landing pad. The sun has begun to rise in the time we spent hiding out in the cafe, and the orange glow makes my ship look better than it has in years. It's next to another voyager class ship, similarly clean and repaired, but the Gemini is easily recognizable due to the symbol painted on the hull: two curved lines, one facing upwards and the other opposite, with two straight lines connecting them. It says the name of the ship in far fewer words and I repaint it every time it begins to fade.

I should probably paint over it right now, but I can't bring myself to strip my ship of all identity.

"Looks much better," Juno comments as we grow close. I nod and hand her the key fob so she can go inside. She hesitates before taking it, giving me an odd look, but I just push it into her hands and step away to inspect the hull.

There's one obvious repair where the metal gave way and a

new piece has been welded on, clean lines separating the new, shining metal from the slightly older pieces around it, and I run my fingers down the bumpy line of the joint. The rest of the hull has been banged back into shape, little bruises in the metal the only signs that the ship was ever damaged.

I check the rest of the fuselage but I don't see anything worth checking over or complaining about, so I climb up into the ship behind Juno.

"All looking good?"

"Mmm," I hum and set my bag down on the bed right beside Juno's. "Let me do some diagnostics in the cockpit, and then we're good to go." Juno nods and kicks off her boots, then shuts and locks the hatch. I sink down into the familiar leather captain's chair and tap through the computer interface until I get to the diagnostics panel. I press start— they should run without requiring any input from me— and rotate the chair to face Juno.

"Where to next?" Juno asks and pulls out my pad to look at the navigation route I made what feels like weeks ago.

"Refuel station Calico," I answer, "and then Anderos, and then Adrestia."

"We're almost done," she says and then grows silent, her face carefully neutral.

"What's wrong?" I ask before I can talk myself out of it. I don't move closer to her, and she doesn't look at me.

"Will you stay? After we get to Adrestia? When your job is done?"

Her face is schooled but there's a hardness hidden behind the mask. The steel there is all I knew before these few weeks flying her across the country, and now it seems almost out of place. I can't imagine it not being softened by the compassion in her heart, or the sweetness on her lips. I don't even digest the question for a second, too distracted by her anxious tone and the warmth blossoming across her cheekbones.

"I'd like to," I finally say. "If there's work for me to do in your revolution. I'd like to stay with you."

Juno's smile is reward enough, promise enough— I could live off her laugh, drink out of the dimples in her cheeks for sustenance, stay on the Gemini forever with her body as my fuel. As if she can read my mind, she comes closer, easily towering a foot above me from my seated position, and cups my cheeks in her hands.

"Cas," she breathes. She tastes like matcha and almond milk as she slides herself into my lap and I have to admit that touching her waist when she's wearing my jacket does more for me than it should. "You will always have a place with me. Even if this—" she cuts herself off and kisses me, sweet and soft, "—Ends, between us, you have saved my life more than once these weeks we've been together. You will always be welcome, and there will always be a home for you."

I kiss her again because if I don't, I think I'll cry, and I don't want to cry on Juno when we're still docked at Dearing waiting for the ship's diagnostics. I kiss her, and I kiss her, and then I pull away and whisper, "I haven't had a home since I was ten."

"You have one with me."

I sink my hands deep into her soft hair, pressing my lips to hers with something not quite resembling urgency, but desperate all the same.

By the time the Gemini's systems beep to tell me that everything's up in working order, Juno and I are half undressed and she has her hand up the front of my shirt.

"We should get off planet," I gasp and she bites down on my collarbone.

"Yeah, we should," she mumbles into the skin and swipes her tongue over the reddened flesh.

I groan and dig my blunt fingernails into her shoulders. "Stop, stop," I breathe and she pulls away at once. "Off planet," I insist and release her. She brings her hand up to cup my face and kisses me again, softly.

"Off planet," she whispers. "Promise?"

I laugh and hold my pinkie up to her chest, right between her marked collarbones. "Pinkie promise. Now go strap in."

She waggles her eyebrows— Oh. Strap in. I roll my eyes and she smiles even wider, impossibly happy. I'm not unaffected by her touch, not by a light-year, but the niggling reminder that we're still on Dearing lurks in my chest and there is every chance those boys recognized us, or at least Juno.

Juno slips off me and pulls her bra strap back over her shoulder, settling into her seat in the back without any argument.

Or putting any more clothes on.

It takes me another second to calm myself down, but as soon as I feel like I can fill my lungs properly, I turn the seat back around and buckle in. I pilot us out of the hangar, out of the atmosphere, and back into open space, and as Dearing disappears behind us I feel a tension I didn't even notice until now ooze out from my shoulders. As soon as the gravity emulator flicks on, working just right after Rob's repairs, I unbuckle my seatbelt and spin around just in time for Juno to settle herself on my lap again.

"How long until we reach the next refuel station?" she asks, bracketing my hips with her knees.

"Oh, love," I murmur, "We have all the time in the galaxy."

11

DISDAIN FOR INTELLECTUALS AND THE ARTS

We don't, actually, have all the time in the galaxy. In fact, we have about twenty-five hours before we have to stop and fill our gas tank, and we spent fifteen of those in bed. Most of it is sleeping, but the rest... Well.

We refuel. Juno stays on the ship, and I only leave momentarily to pay the docking fee and stretch my legs a little. Refuel station Calico is clean and there's a round walkway around the port with thick glass windows showing open space and a few nearby planets. I do a lap, and then another, and by the time I finish my third, the Gemini is ready for the next leg of our journey. My left leg begins to click quietly, the sound vibrating up through my thigh. It gets worse still on the walk back to the ship, and I sigh. I should've known— it's been just long enough since I tuned my prosthetic that of course a break was imminent. I shake it off for now and climb up the ladder, ignoring the pinch and pull.

I find Juno with her fists taped carefully and the punching bag hanging from the ceiling in the back of the ship. I duck out of the way as she swings her foot through the air, landing a solid kick on the pleather bag, and then I put my hands on her waist.

"Hold your weight here," I say and slide my hands down her

hips, "you'll balance better." She nods and shifts to throw another punch. When it falls steadier and connects with a louder smack, Juno hums in appreciation. I let her go and move into the cockpit.

She sits for exactly as long as it takes for me to get us back out into space, and then she's back at the bag, punching and kicking until sweat drips off her jaw.

Conversely, I settle in at the table. I'd sit at my workbench, but the bag blocks the track that my chair sits on, and I don't want to become collateral damage for Juno's training. My Equinox knife has all the tools I need to mess around with the insides of my prosthetic. I pop my leg off and hoist it up onto the table, getting to work unscrewing the plates of resin casing that hold the mechanics in and cradle what's left of my thigh. I find the culprit quickly: a small piece of plastic has come loose and wedged itself between a metal rod and a synthetic tendon. I pull it out easily and set about finding where it came from.

My fingers are deep in the mechanisms of my leg when Juno stops punching and unwraps her hands, and by the time she emerges from the shower with her hair wrapped in a towel, I've replaced the broken plastic spacer with a similar-shaped piece of resin I pulled out of a ship some months ago. Juno falls down into the seat beside me, pressing a brief kiss to my shoulder, and turns on the TV. She flicks through a few channels of nothing until she stops on INN.

"*After the would-be shooting on Doda,*" the announcer— a woman, this time— is saying and I turn away from my leg both to stretch my cramping fingers and also to look at the screen. "*We have seen* ███ *Marcus and another person, now identified as Castor Quasar, in a couple of locations across the galaxy. We believe they are making their way to the planet Adrestia, in the outer edges of explored space.*"

They show a clip of Juno first, leaving the interrogation

room back in the casino on Doda. I'm there too, a bit out of focus, resting on the hard metal bench I sat on for hours while I waited for Juno to be released. I remember this moment, I remember the anger I felt that just barely clouded over something I didn't yet recognize as desperate, aching loyalty, and it plays out just as it did.

"Quasar is allegedly a part of the group that broke Marcus out of Fort Harrison maximum-security prison just a few days ago, alongside two known terrorist leaders and a woman we have identified as Julia Sullice."

"Shit," Juno breathes, "They got Jules."

"She knew this must be coming," I say and shake my head, "She has Nova and Mars, and I bet they're the two they mentioned. They'll be ready for this."

"They should head to Adrestia," Juno murmurs, "It's the only place we can get people off the grid securely. They won't dare follow."

"I have Nova's number, let's call her," I suggest, and Juno nods. I mute the news as the clip shifts to another shot of me, this time on a refuel station from days ago with my head quirked just enough towards the camera to be recognizable. My eyes are the most obvious part: my eye is brown, while my prosthetic is electric green, surrounded by old, pale scar tissue.

It's strange, to see myself on footage like this, but I'm glad at least that my name is changed, and I've gotten top surgery. Seeing my body on galactic television even a year ago, before I was able to customize the shape of myself, would've killed me.

"Call Nova," I tell Verita. It takes a second for the dial tone to start beeping, low and repetitive, and it drones on for nearly thirty seconds before it goes to voicemail. I frown.

"Hmm," Juno mumbles and picks up my pad, tapping on it with a clear purpose. I lean back in my seat and run my fingers across the resin panels that cover the outside of my expensive prosthetic, some marred with old ragged grooves and nicks from mistakes, ships, and injuries. I pick up one of the panels between two pinched fingers and smooth it back into place. Another, and another, until they're all pressed carefully back on, concealing the mechanisms within, and then I scoop the small pile of scattered screws into my palm. Each one fits into place easily, one after another, and then I use my knife to twist them securely back into place. When they're tight and all the panels are locked in, I slide the cup of the prosthetic back over my thigh and stand. After a few steps across the ship, I'm confident that I found the source of the grinding, clicking feeling, so I sit back down.

"I shot her an encrypted message," Juno says and shrugs. "If she replies, she replies. I... I hope she's okay, after Chell."

I take Juno's hand and glance back at the TV. It has switched to something else, some propagandist news cycle about Marwood and his wife's perfect childhood, but it doesn't seem important, especially when Juno starts flicking through channels to find the encrypted ones Chell was able to get us access to before the jailbreak. They're running some footage from the inside of somewhere I don't recognize: a black and white, gritty, wide shot of some small, crowded bar filled with all sorts of people. I see a small stage off to the side with a drag queen performing, her hips wide and waist cinched tight. Right as she kicks one of her feet up, one of the doors explodes open and light comes streaming into the bar.

With it, bullets. Though the video clip is silent, I see sweeping flashlight beams and the bright white shock of gunfire at the edges of the camera's view. Juno winces beside me and I pull one of my hands to my chest, pressing down with my palm right on my sternum. As bodies fall, I press harder, and then thud my hand into my chest repeatedly when the pressure doesn't help anymore. Juno is still next to me but I let myself dully thud against my own chest over, and over, and over until the video clip ends, but even then I repeat the motions.

"I need to hit something," I mutter and stand, but Juno catches my other hand, the one not pressing against my chest, and pulls it. I follow her gaze back to the TV and wince. They're playing a clip now from another influencer's livestream, a girl with long, pink hair being forced out of her comfortable looking desk chair and shoved to the ground by a heavily-armored IPF agent. The chat is still scrolling along the side of the screen and it pauses when one comment pops up.

'I'LL DO IT AGAIN'.

It cuts again to the exterior of an abortion clinic. I can identify it only because of how sterile the outside of it is; the building is unlabelled and plain. There are two dozen protestors parked outside, some with signs and others armed only with crooked snarls. As they hoist their hateful words into the air, a young Black woman starts trying to push her way past them to the entrance.

The audio is silent still under the emotional pleas from the reporter, but even her words go hazy as blood rushes to my head. A female protestor reaches out and grabs the woman's shirt, pulling so hard it tears at the neckline. I wince and look away as the woman falls to the ground.

"This isn't new," Juno murmurs, and I nod. "This is what it's always been like under Bridger, and even before. The fascists were just waiting for a time when they had enough backing they could say the quiet part out loud. It'll be worse still under Marwood, when nobody who does anything worth prosecuting will ever be convicted."

The video cuts again to more blurry security camera footage, this time of a car ramming into a small crowd of protestors. Again, to another angle— shaky phone footage of the same event. I wince at the impact and a small body goes flying over the hood of the car, unmoving after it crashes to the ground.

"I've seen so many people die," Juno says quietly. Her tone is flat. "On TV, in person. I'm nineteen, and people die for my cause every day. It's hard not to think of their deaths as my fault."

I shift in my chair and wrap my arm around her shoulders. "What do we do?" I whisper.

"Same thing I always do," Juno responds with a grimace before burying her face in my neck. "We fight back."

Juno is quiet for the rest of our journey, and by the time we arrive at Anderos to refuel and cycle our water tank, her eyes are bloodshot from staring at my pad for as long as she has. I don't ask her what she's working on, and in return, I get no answer.

We both leave the ship on Anderos. Juno says she wants to stretch her legs and the rations we have left are starting to feel gritty and oily in my mouth, so I readily agree. We find a small hot pot restaurant with a secluded booth in the back and order quickly. Juno orders a drink and flashes her ID just long enough for the waiter to check her birthday and then hides it away with a wide smile. I know it's a fake— Juno is nineteen. You can join the IPF at sixteen, but you can't drink until twenty-one. Mine is fake too, the one I almost always use, but it still has my name on it. I know Juno's doesn't. There's nothing on there that could connect her to the girl desperately running from the law, no more than her face could.

They bring us big plates of par-frozen, rolled meats and sliced veggies that we immediately start dunking into the hot broth in front of each of us. While we wait for it to cook, Juno taps my foot with hers.

"Hey," she says and rests her chin on her palm.

"Hey," I echo and raise a scarred eyebrow at her. She shakes her head and watches me as I pull a piece of still-red meat out of my pot and eat it, savoring the heat and freshness of it all. She does the same, and once she's done chewing, she finally asks.

"Will you tell me about your brother?"

I'm taken aback, and I'm sure it shows on my face, because Juno tacks on an addendum almost immediately.

"If you want, I mean. You just seem so fond of him, I—"

"I will," I interrupt, "If you tell me about yours." Juno's face splits in a beautiful smile and she nods. I take a sip of my water and fish another piece of meat out of my broth. "He was born on Janus, actually, in Fontus. I don't remember that. I was too young, I guess. He was almost four years younger than me, and he was barely nine when he died."

Juno shifts her grip on her chopsticks and extends her other arm to offer me her hand. I glance around us before sliding my palm into hers, reversed so my fingertips can trace along the faint blue veins in her wrist, made softer and less prominent by the estrogen shot she did last night and every shot before that in an attempt to make her body her own.

"We spent a lot of time travelling when I was a kid. Most of my memories of my family are in the old four-seater our parents flew us around in. Me and Apollo had seats in the back. We were close enough that we could reach out and touch each other, but not so close that we fought. He always carried his ratty little rabbit around." I pause at that and take in Juno's soft smile. It feels like a gift to be able to see her in public, her mask discarded in her pocket so she can eat.

The waiter returns and refills our waters without a word,

and I pull my hand from Juno's. Juno sips on her drink: some orange, fruity thing that I was too busy watching her lips to catch the name of. We both softly thank him and, after taking a sip of water to wet my throat, I continue.

"My mom wasn't the best. She didn't really understand why I was... Different, I guess. I was diagnosed with autism when I was two or three, but she didn't take the time to understand what that meant for how we interacted. My dad did more, I think because he was autistic too despite never being diagnosed, and Apollo couldn't have cared less, but Mom never tried very hard," I say. Juno's hand finds mine again and she hums a quiet noise of acknowledgement. "I loved her, though. She was my mom. She held me when I had a meltdown, even when I pushed her away. She was good to Polly."

"Polly?" Juno murmurs.

I huff a laugh. "Apollo. I called him that to annoy him."

"I call Gideon 'Gigi' sometimes."

I grin. "What are brothers for if not to bother?"

"It's in the word," Juno points out and I laugh, full and loud. Someone a few tables over turns their head to look at us, but I don't pay them any mind.

"He was the best," I say. "The best. He... He was smart, and kind. He knew things about the galaxy at five that I wouldn't now, just from reading. He always shared his food with me and he ate my peas when Mom forgot I can't have them."

"Allergic?" Juno asks, "I didn't know."

"No, not..." I think for a second, eating a few more bites of food and trying to come up with the words. "They make my mouth feel like rubber and my whole body itch, but only on the inside. It's like touching them makes me break out in hives on every single nerve, and I have to get away from it. I don't have any actual allergic reaction, but I can't eat them all the same."

"A sensory reaction, then," Juno offers.

"I guess, yeah. I tried to get them down as a kid, because mom wanted me to, but... I don't know. They freak me out," I say and shrug. I got over the embarrassment long ago, or so I thought, but my cheeks still feel warm. It feels silly, but it's a whole lot easier to just avoid peas altogether when you're alone and not fed by two loving parents who take your rejection of the vegetable as a personal failure.

"Noted," Juno says and takes a long sip of her drink, smacking her lips. She leans back in the booth and stretches her feet out so far they nudge against the seat underneath me. "He sounds incredible."

"Best brother I could've asked for."

We sit together in near-silence, just eating and being together. We sip our drinks and smile at one another, comfortable in the quiet companionship. Everyone before Juno has felt intrusive, like I'm being watched. With her, I just feel... Less alone. I nudge her with the tip of my foot before I can get too lost in my own feelings.

"Tell me about Gideon, then."

"I said I would, didn't I." Juno pulls the little toothpick off the top of her cocktail and pops the artificial-red cherry into her mouth. A bit of juice dribbles onto her bottom lip where her lipstick has smeared away and I push my napkin towards her on the table.

"You don't have to, if you don't want to. He just seems important to you, like Polly," I say as she wipes her mouth. More of her lipstick smears and I find myself wanting to reach out and press my thumb to the center of her mouth to touch the soft, pink skin there.

"He is," Juno says and smiles. "We're twins. We don't have, like, telepathy or anything, but he's my best friend. He knows me better than anyone. He's patient when I get angry and forgives me when I get *so* angry that I lash out. He's in law school. He wants to change the galaxy, same as me, but he wants to do it the right way."

"Your way isn't wrong."

"I... I know. It's violent, though, and illegal, and dangerous," she says, lowering her voice so quiet I can barely hear her. She tucks a strand of brown hair behind her ear and chances a glance at the rest of the restaurant patrons. "He wants me safe, and I can't blame him for that."

I frown. It takes me a second to read between her words, but when it clicks— "He doesn't like what you do?"

"He would rather I skirt the edge of breaking the law, instead of throwing myself over it head first."

I snort. "It's a little too late for that."

Juno nods. "He agrees that some laws are unjust, and that what I do with my body is my choice. He believes that I am a girl and understands that I'm a lesbian. He wants people to be free, and he wants Marwood to rot, but... In jail."

"You want him dead."

Juno's face curls in a tired smile. "Mmm."

I think about the familiar weight of my gun in my hands, the recoil of even a shock bullet, insulated rubber sending a jolt through someone so sharp it knocks them out. I rub the pads of my fingers against the leather holster on my hip and I think of the people on TV, the dozens dead in IPF raids this week alone, and I think of Juno and the rest of her rebels. Queer people like me, sick and tired of oppression.

"I'd kill him for you," I say finally, "If you asked."

Juno's mouth falls open and I immediately go to retract the statement, but she just reaches across the table and pulls me by my collar for a kiss. It's over quick, just a fierce little press of lips that leaves me dizzy. When she pulls back, there's a red-hot fire in her eyes.

She opens her mouth to say something, but another table

surges with laughter and we jerk apart, hyper-aware of our proximity, the public space that we occupy, the little red marks dotting Juno's throat from my teeth, and the bright red flush I'm sure is surging across my cheekbones.

"We'll be off planet within the hour," I breathe and Juno nods, running her fingers through her hair. A loose chunk falls in front of her eyes and I almost reach up to brush it away.

"I know," she says, "I..." Juno flushes even pinker and I realize there's something more than the kiss, something she isn't saying.

"What's wrong?"

Juno shakes her head. "Nothing's wrong, not really," she says and picks up her chopsticks again. "Eat, so we can get out of here."

I mirror her actions and we finish off our meal in companionable silence. She offers me a potato from her broth, coated in reddish spice, and I trade her for a piece of overcooked beef from mine, browner than I tend to take it.

When the waiter brings the check, he sets the small leather booklet in front of Juno purposefully with a heavy look in her direction.

"Here's the check whenever you're ready," he says to her. I lurch towards him with my hand curled into a fist at my side at the implications weighing his words down, but Juno takes it without reacting and flips it open.

"Cas," Juno murmurs and I look over at her. She shakes her head minutely and I relax, pinning the waiter with one more silent stare before I turn back to Juno. She reaches into her pocket and pulls out a few credit pieces, tossing them down onto the table alongside the vendor copy of the receipt, tucking the customer copy into her pocket. "We'll be going, then. Thank you."

The waiter nods and pockets the credits before leaving.

"What," I breathe, but Juno just takes my arm and leads me out of the restaurant, pulling her mask back over her face as she does. When we're outside, she tugs me into a corner and pulls out the wrinkled receipt. Scribbled across the bottom of the paper is a short note.

'IPF on their way here, go NOW'

I swallow hard, pull my mask up over my face, and let Juno lead me out of our nook. Within seconds, she yanks me into another dark alleyway as two IPF officers march past us, the straps that hold their guns in place already unlatched. I hiss a swear under my breath and press my mouth against Juno's shoulder until they've passed.

"Quiet," she whispers and I follow her along the sidewalk back towards the enormous port on Anderos. Another group passes us but Juno and I lean against the side of a tall vehicle, our heads ducked together, and they pass us without a word. We make it back to the port even with my heart thudding out of my chest, so loud it must be audible for miles, but there are more IPF here. They're everywhere, covering the concrete in their oppressive black armor and stopping everyone who enters. It reminds me of Fontus, and I swallow hard. I see their leader — a taller man with his helmet discarded and rifle already resting in the crook of his elbow. He's speaking to who I believe is the port master, an older woman with a scar through her eyebrow.

As they speak, her eyes look past his face and land right on us. Recognition fills her eyes, notable even from this far away, and I clench my jaw shut hard. She grabs the man's arm and I grab Juno's—

"Oh, I forgot to say," she says and holds tight, her gaze darting from me to the Gemini and back. "I think you should come over here, this might be helpful." She trails off and leads the commander towards a small outpost, his back still to us all the while, and winks.

Juno sags with relief under my grip, but we don't have time to breathe. I rush towards the Gemini. The ladder is still pulled down but the hatch is closed, and of fucking course I fumble with the key fob, so it takes me a minute to get it to swing open.

When we finally climb inside, Juno collapses to the ground. I kneel beside her at once, turning her over with quick motions, my hands braced around her shoulders—

She's laughing.

"June," I breathe, and she pulls me down on top of her to kiss me. I kiss back once, twice, and then I lean away, hovering over her. "Love, we have to go."

"Love," she murmurs back and rubs a thumb over my bottom lip, pulling it back with dark purple smudged across the pad.

"I—"

"No." She smiles. "Don't apologize. You can call me anything you want, Cas."

"Right now, I want to call you airborne," I retort and kiss her one more time before standing up and heading towards the cockpit. She huffs out a little breathless laugh but I don't turn around, no matter how much I want to, no matter how much I can feel her lipstick on my mouth and my jaw. I strap myself into the pilot's chair and, as soon as she's buckled in as well, we're off.

"At the restaurant," Juno says when I come back into the main cabin, "I... I've never..."

She seems lost for words. It's so unlike her that I sit on the bed, patting the spot next to me. Juno doesn't sit, not at first; instead, she goes into the bathroom and grabs a makeup wipe out of the drawer. The fact that her things are so entangled with mine, that this ship is as much her home now as it is mine, makes me feel warm. It teeters on the edge of overwhelming, the amount I *feel* as I watch her quickly wipe off her lipstick, but it doesn't spill over. I press my first two fingers against my sternum and press. Energy leaves, fizzes out, like pressing down on an oxygen valve.

When she comes back to me, she presses a clean corner of the makeup wipe to my lips and drags it along my chin and jaw. It comes away purple and she tidies up a few more little spots on my face before she sets the wipe down and takes in a long breath that feels like the precursor to bad news.

"I haven't ever dated anyone."

I... What?

"What?"

"I've slept with people, don't worry," she says, letting her hand rest on the wide expanse of my covered thigh. "I just... I'm not used to the little things, I guess. The kisses without any expectation, the pet names..." She makes a vague gesture between the two of us. "I don't know if I've misinterpreted what we're doing here, but—"

"I'd like to date you, if that's what you want, too," I interrupt. The worry lines I hadn't even noticed form on her forehead smooth out.

"Still?"

"What's changed?"

Her face splits in a smile and she reaches up to cup my jaw. "Nothing, I guess," she says. "Will you let me be your girlfriend, Castor?"

"What else would you be?" I ask and lean forward until our foreheads are pressed together, her bangs barely tickling the rise of my cheeks. "My girlfriend, Juno Marcus."

"Cas Quasar, my... My partner," Juno offers, and I shrug.

"Or girlfriend. I think... I like girlfriend, too," I say. "Contrary to what you seem to believe, I haven't dated much either."

"Tell me about them?" she asks and pulls me down until we're laying side by side, hands clasped between us, foreheads still mere inches apart.

"Who, the other people I dated? They were nothing, really. Nothing compared to you," I say, and I don't mean for it to be flattery, but she smacks my shoulder with her free hand.

"Still. I'm curious about you."

I chew on the inside of my mouth for a moment and then think. "I've dated... Two girls, and one other person. Xe were too loud, the first girl was too quiet, and the second didn't like it when I didn't want to kiss her."

"What do you mean, didn't want to? You kiss me plenty."

I feel my neck flush warm. "Sometimes it's too overstimulating, I guess. Too much touch at once, or too wet, or..."

"And she didn't like that you said no sometimes." Juno scoffs and shifts her hand to rest on my stomach under my shirt. The muscle quivers under her touch, but she doesn't move to do anything else, doesn't drag any lower. She's touching just to touch, feeling just to feel me. I smile.

"I guess. We were only together for... Two months, I think, in the end. It was more of a physical relationship than anything else," I say and shrug. "The others weren't much longer, and pretty soon after that, I decided it wasn't worth it."

"What wasn't worth it?"

"Dating." I think back to the list I made in my head when I first started to think of Juno in a context that added her to the string-wound corkboard that then had only contained my previous, failed relationships. "I'm weird. I'm a loner. I've never stuck around anywhere long enough to really get to know anybody."

"You're autistic, and smart, and extremely charming, just in a way a lot of people don't understand," Juno says and moves her hand, brushing her fingertips across a stray scar on the left side of my stomach before stilling. "It's their loss, I think."

"You say that, but a time will come when I do something or say something that you don't understand, or don't like," I say before I can stop myself, "And you'll get it."

"The implication here is that you think we'll stay together long enough for something like that to happen," Juno points out, "and during that time, and even the time we've spent together so far, I won't learn."

"I—"

"Have you or have you not been outright mean to me in the last two weeks?"

"You've been mean to me too!" I retort instinctually, but then her words sink in. "And you want me anyways."

"I like to think I have a pretty open mind," Juno says, "so when that day comes, I'll ask, and I'll try to understand." She shifts until our foreheads are touching again and I close my eyes. "Don't be so afraid to lose me that you don't let me try, Cas."

"Mmm... Fine. You've convinced me," I breathe and lean in to kiss her. "Tell me about the people you've..."

"Fucked?"

"Slept with, is what I was going to say."

Juno snorts and shifts so she can curl up, her head resting on the soft part between my shoulder and my collarbone. "Eh. Two guys, you can guess how that turned out."

"Badly?"

"One of them still has my number," she shrugs. "I figured out the girl part before the lesbian part, I guess. After that... Three girls, only one of which I even tried to date. She said no, it was too much publicity."

"Oh." All at once I remember that Juno was famous long before she became this insurrectionist figure, this anti-federalist revolutionary leading a quiet rebellion that's about to get loud. Before this, she was just a girl with green hair making videos about the books she read, the makeup she used, and the games she played.

"I... I understand, if that's a problem for you, too," she offers and tilts her chin up to look at me. "It's a bit different now than it was then, but I'm still a well-known face. I'm still a public figure."

"I think we're a little bit past that," I reply. If Juno being— well, being Juno— had bothered me, I never would have kissed her on Goliath. I never would've had to make a list reminding myself why I wasn't interested. "They know my face, they know my name. I'm just as wanted as you by now."

"Maybe," she concedes, "but you could cut your losses when we get to Adrestia. Drop me off and within a month or so they'll have forgotten about you. The news cycle works fast. You could go back to being a junker, go back to being a nameless face."

I shift so I can look her in the eyes, propping my head up on a rumpled pillow. "Juno," I say, "You aren't the reason that won't happen. I... I like you. I like you a lot, and that's something I've never really felt before, but more than that, I believe in you. You've made me realize I can't sit idly by while people like me are killed, not anymore. I was living in a haze of apathy where I was the only one who mattered. I hated you for feeling as strongly as you did, and for being willing to speak up when I knew I wouldn't. Then I met you, and... You showed me the point, but the point wasn't you. It was empathy. Optimism, even."

"I'm just a bonus," she whispers, and I grin.

"A very nice bonus, albeit one I never thought I would've let myself have. Even when I kissed you, I didn't think I was going to go through with it."

Juno smiles and nuzzles into my neck, her nose brushing up against the lingering red marks from yesterday. "I kind of got that impression."

"Shh," I mutter and pull her closer, letting my eyes fall shut with her warm body beside mine. She brushes her fingers along the scarring under my pecs. I kiss her forehead, and all I can think is how can so many people in the galaxy think this is wrong? It feels so natural, to be with her. It feels like the easiest choice I've made in my entire life. "Stop worrying. I told you I'll stay, I told you I want you. I don't say things I don't mean."

"Love," she murmurs, and I swear I feel it too.

12
OBSESSION WITH CRIME AND PUNISHMENT

When we finally land on Adrestia, it's with much less fanfare than I had built up in my head. I pilot us onto the only intergalactic landing strip on the planet and engage the parking brake before anyone even seems to notice our arrival, but once we open the hatch and climb out, a group of people walk up to greet us.

Well, greet is a strong word.

"Stop right there," a tall woman calls out, a long rifle held loosely in her grasp. I raise my hand at once and Juno does the same beside me.

"I'm going to pull my hood down," Juno calls to the group and slowly uses one hand to pull the fabric off her head. Her hair gleams almost golden in the light of Adrestia's twin suns and she holds her hands up as well.

"State your names," the woman says. One of the men behind her, a soldier geared out in a mix of IPF equipment and mis-matched bits of other armor, squints at us and raises a hand to block out the harsh sunlight.

"Castor Quasar and Juno Marcus," I call. The woman drops her rifle. She mutters something to the man on her right side, who begins hurriedly speaking into his comm.

"Identification, please," she says and steps closer, within five feet of us now, and holds out her hand. I pull my wallet out of my pocket slowly and then hand my actual license with my real name and age to her. Once she has both of our cards, the woman inspects them carefully. The atmosphere on the landing strip feels like a held breath, every single person tense and waiting. When she finally hands her cards back and flicks up her visor to reveal a wide smile, we exhale as one.

"Diana," Juno gasps and rushes forward, wrapping her arms around the huge woman's middle. The woman— Diana— hugs back, pressing her cheek to the top of Juno's head.

"Juno," she murmurs, "You haven't grown a bit."

"Fuck off," Juno laughs and pulls away. "I didn't know you were here!"

"Who do you think got Gideon to come all the way out here in the first place?" Diana retorts and claps Juno on the shoulder. "We've just been waiting for you."

"It's been... A hell of a month, that's for sure," Juno says and looks back at me. "This is Cas, they're the one who flew me here from Janus."

Diana whistles, low and smooth. "Long flight."

"Good pay," I retort and step forward, locking the Gemini behind me, and Juno reaches out to take my hand.

"They saved my life, and they're going to be working with us from now on," Juno says.

It sounds a whole lot like *welcome home.*

Gideon is about what I expected.

He looks just like Juno, except with a square face, a faint patch of stubble on his jaw, and a thicker, chubbier body. They're the same height and even their smiles echo one another as Juno runs forward to launch herself into his arms the moment we step off of the shuttle to what I assume is the city.

"Thank *stars* you're safe," Gideon murmurs and I turn away, not wanting to intrude. Instead, I walk over to the folks unloading our things from the shuttle.

"Let me help." I grab Juno's small bag, the one that has been empty since the first night she stepped foot on the Gemini, now stuffed with her belongings. I sling it over my shoulder and the kid grabbing our other things nods in gratitude and hands me my own backpack. He jerks his head towards a long building, beckoning me to follow him.

"This is where we're living," he says and walks me inside. The building is open and spacious in the entryway with hallways branching off, clearly built to function as a sort of dormitory. "We've mostly taken over this building since all those right-wingers dropped out last semester."

"Dropped out?" I ask as he leads me down a long hallway lined with dozens of identical doors decorated with metal numbers.

"Of the university. Cybele University, it's where we're staying. When it came out that Cybele had students like Gideon Marcus, brother of Juno Marcus, over a hundred students dropped out or transferred to schools in Montgomery. It left this building mostly empty so, as far as I know, the school basically said 'hey, it's not like it could get much worse', and unofficially let us set up shop," he explains. We turn down a perpendicular hallway and enter a sitting area with somewhere around a dozen people sitting in wait on varying pieces of furniture. They all turn to look at us when we enter, a few even leaping to their feet. "Everyone, this is Castor. They're the one who flew Juno here."

"So she's safe? She's here?" someone asks, a tall, willowy person with dyed red hair.

"She's here."

The room seems to exhale and then tense right back up, walls squeezing and floor quaking, as every single person comes up to me and says their name, shakes my hand, or touches my shoulder. I clench my jaw shut tight, smile, and try to remember everyone— Aurora wears glasses and has purple in their hair, Jesse has a dozen bracelets on his wrist, Kai, Crow, Sarah— but sweat drips down my neck and I have to press my palm to my chest hard to keep from overloading.

"I," I mutter and take a jerky step back. The boy who led me here frowns at me and then looks at everyone else.

"Alright, back off. Let me show Castor to their rooms."

I don't let go of the breath I'm holding until we're out in the hallway and the hubbub of the room fades into my periphery. It comes out in a long *woosh* and I grab onto the wall to steady myself.

"Are you okay?" he asks, "I didn't mean to—"

"I'm alright," I manage to respond and swallow hard. "Keep going."

He leads me down the hallway until we reach a door labelled 134.

"This is Juno's suite."

"Suite?" I echo, and he opens the door. Inside is a sparsely furnished room with a large couch set across from a television screen mounted on the wall. There's a kitchenette, as well; compared to a full kitchen on a planet like Dearing where people wealthy enough can build their own houses, or even on Janus in the tops of the tallest apartment buildings, it's tiny, but if you're used to the mini fridge and reheater on the Gemini, it's generous. I can see two doors on the far side of the main room and the guy opens the first one.

"Bathroom here," he says and gestures inside before moving to open the second, "and bedroom, here."

I poke my head into the bathroom. It's easily three times the size of the cramped bathing quarters on the Gemini. It has a huge tub and shower combo, a sink, and a short wall concealing the toilet from view. The bedroom is similarly indulgent with a bed bigger than even the double Juno and I have shared so far, a dresser, and a sliding closet door that's currently propped open to reveal more space than I'd know what to do with.

"This place is huge," I breathe and set Juno's bag down on the bed. The fluttering in my chest finally starts to calm down and I release my harsh fists, smoothing over the bedding instead. "Are all the rooms like this?"

The boy shakes his head. "No. Most of us live in singles or doubles. There are five of these suites, including this one. Diana and her wife live in one, and I think the rest might be empty. Well, until now, with Juno."

"And me," I add absently and move to look out the window in the bedroom. It's wide and overlooks what I assume is the reason this area of the planet was built up instead of any other area: the lake. It's huge and clear, water shimmering an incredible, unnatural blue with gentle whitecaps lapping at a half-dozen fishing boats docked down the hill from campus. It's surrounded by thick shrubbery and towering trees stretching high into the sky, deep green reaching for the clouds above. "It's beautiful."

"I'll leave you to get settled, then, if you and Juno will *both* be staying here," the kid says, flushing lightly. I shake my head.

"What's your name?"

"Tommy, sir."

I wince. "No, don't do that. I'm not even really in your rebellion. How old are you?"

"Twenty-two."

"You're older than me. Don't call me anything but my name, please," I tell him and hold my hand out for the two bags slung over his shoulders. "Thank you for the help, Tommy." He hands me my two bags and leaves with a small, sheepish smile.

As soon as the door shuts, I feel... Alone.

I haven't been alone in a month. It's stifling, the feeling of open space and silence. I can hear the faint buzz from the generators running this place. I can hear the electricity in the walls. I walk over to the window in the living room and pull it open to let the lakeside air breathe into the suite, but even the light breeze doesn't make me feel calm. I try to go over the people I met again— Tommy, Finn, Amir, Lu— and focus on the solid ground under my feet.

Closing my eyes helps, too. Somewhere outside, someone is grilling meat. Further, I smell... Pine. It stings in my nostrils.

I'm home, I tell myself, but I think about the worn in sheets on the Gemini, the custom shower seat I built, Pollux and his carefully decorated tank, and I've never felt so far from it.

"Castor?" a voice calls, and I melt.

That's home to me.

"Cas, come here, love." Juno pulls me against her chest on the couch. I press my face into her sternum until I can feel her heartbeat just as sure as my own. She pets over my spine and traces little shapes on my side until my breathing slows and I can force words to come out of my mouth again.

"June," I murmur. "I'm sorry."

"Don't be." She shakes her head and kisses my forehead. "What happened?"

I think. I've never had much luck sharing the way a meltdown feels for me, the way it clouds my brain with thunderclaps and shocks of lightning that only soothe after tears, after my throat is hoarse with exhaustion.

"Have you ever been on a boat?:

"Like, a *boat* boat? Sure."

"You know when you get off the water and your legs feel

wobbly and your stomach rolls, your whole body so used to the sea pushing and pulling you that, now that it isn't, it doesn't know how to act anymore?"

Juno presses her cheek against the crown of my head and hums in understanding.

"It's quiet here," I say, and it's not an explanation, but she takes it without question.

"We can plug in your tablet, get some game shows going on the TV," she suggests and shifts so I can lay more easily against her. "Play some music, get your workbench set up."

"A home."

Juno smiles. "Our home."

We only have a moment to ruminate on that before the door to our suite flies open and there's Gideon, his chest heaving, with Tommy behind him holding a tablet in both hands.

"We need you in the meeting room," Gideon gasps. Juno and I both scramble up and I let my hands flap back and forth at my side to release the last remnants of energy from my meltdown.

"What's happened?" Juno asks, but Gideon shakes his head and darts back out into the hallway, leading us down, around a corner, and into a double-doored room. Inside is a long table with a half-dozen people already seated. I recognize Diana, and I assume the woman at her side with meticulously-braided hair piled on top of her head above thick tortoiseshell glasses must be her wife. The rest are unfamiliar and I find myself loitering by the door as Gideon, Tommy, and Juno slide into seats without the same hesitation I feel weighing on my chest.

"A shooting broke out at a Marwood rally on Anat-2," the woman in glasses says. "Forty people are dead, another hundred-odd wounded. The IPF has been given clearance to raid anywhere they think is a threat to galactic security."

The mood drops in the room at once. It wasn't light to begin with, instead fostering a quiet sense of unease, but now it ignites.

Juno surges back to her feet and slams her hands down on the table, and everyone begins talking all at once.

"Who started the shooting?"

"Has Bridger said anything?"

"Did we know any of the victims?"

Diana holds her hand up until the room quiets down. She taps on the pad in front of her until it starts projecting something on the far wall. A news article. The posting is short, barely more than a headline and a half-dozen sentences, but it gets the point across.

SHOOTING AT MARWOOD RALLY - 41 DEAD AND COUNTING

An unknown individual drew an assault rifle at a Walter Marwood campaign rally on Anat-2. Forty-one people are dead. This individual is cited by witnesses to have stated his cause as aligning with that of 'Juno Marcus', also known as [*SUBSCRIBE TO READ MORE*]

I wince. Everyone around me expels anger at their own speed.

"Fuck," Juno hisses.

"Forty people," Tommy breathes.

"How'd he get in?" Gideon snarls.

"Rest in peace," Diana murmurs and closes out of the article as advertisements begin to pop up.

"Who—" I start, but the dark-skinned woman wearing glasses shakes her head.

"We don't know. We're trying to find out right now. We have a group on Anat-2 that we're waiting to hear back from."

"Forty people," Juno echoes Tommy's quiet breath.

Diana's wife's mouth flattens in a grimace as the table grows dead silent, her lip twitching as she looks down at her own tablet.

"What is it?" Diana asks quietly.

"The IPF have raided two bars and a community center in the last hour," she answers. "They're looking for rebels, for LGBT people, and they don't care about collateral damage."

Hubbub breaks out across the table. Even Juno mutters something before leaning against her brother, pressing her forehead to his shoulder. Gideon rubs her back and glances at me— All I can offer is whatever look is currently on my face and a tilt to my shoulders I know looks more like a grimace than a shrug.

I look out the window behind her. The campus is massive and sprawling, spread around the lake like a carefully manicured resort. Dozens of young people, all around me and Juno's age, are walking around with bags slung over their shoulders and headphones in their ears. I see two freeze and huddle around a tablet. They watch for a moment before one of them claps a hand to their mouth and turns, their chest heaving in a sob.

"How many guns do we have?" I ask. It comes out louder than I intend and within seconds the room is silent. Everyone looks at me, their eyes boring holes in my skin, red hot and itchy. I just look at Juno.

"Excuse me?" Diana's wife says.

"Halima," Diana murmurs. Halima shakes her head and looks between me and Juno.

"Who is this?"

Juno stands. "This is Cas, and they're the only reason I'm still alive," she says and holds a hand out to me. It's not for me to grab— No, it's holding me back, like I'm the one who needs it. "Cas, explain." I shift to stand beside her and her arm wraps around my waist at once. It feels both protective and preventative.

I look around at all the faces staring back at me, at the most diverse group of people I've probably ever seen in one place at once. Diana, with her blonde mullet and wife, both wearing rings freely and openly on different shaped hands; Gideon and Juno who, now that Juno's hair is a muddy brown, are the most boring looking people at the table; the pink woman with dark skin and a younger guy with blue hair next to her; Tommy and another half-dozen people around his age. Some have scars, others wear prosthetics much more advanced than my own out of date mechanisms. They're dressed in free-flowing clothes or barely any clothes at all and none are wearing masks besides one person using a wheelchair at the far end of the table.

"How many guns do we have?" I ask again after a few beats too many of silence. "So we can fight back."

"Juno," Gideon says quietly, threateningly, "What did you tell them?"

"She didn't tell me anything," I retort. Juno's grip tightens on my waist and then slips to grab my hand instead. It's a clear show of support and I squeeze around her fingers. "If they're killing us, we need to be ready to fight back."

"There are other ways—" Gideon starts, but Juno shoots him a fierce look.

"There are other ways for laws to change. There are other ways to make a difference, and we can work on those later. The only way to survive a direct attack where their only goal is to kill thirty or forty of us at once is to shoot back. Have snipers in position when they arrive, have guards stationed at the airstrip, I don't know. This planet is mostly insurrectionists, correct?" A couple people cringe at the wording, so I amend, "Anti-federalists, I mean."

"Adrestia is seventy-eight percent populated by people who

consider themself to align that way politically, yes," the pink haired woman says and pushes her glasses further up her nose.

"Why are you assuming Adrestia, or Cybele, at least, is their next target?" Diana asks.

I scoff and gesture out the window, and then around the table at all of us. "Look who lives here. Every other person who walks by is wearing a rainbow pin or has one of Juno's stickers on their laptop. Even just the way we're dressed. Marwood's people don't tend to look like us."

"Are you saying the attack on Anat-2, the massacre, was... One of them?" Halima says. The room feels like a held breath.

"That's exactly what I'm saying," I respond, and murmurs break out between different groups. Juno squeezes my hand.

"Killing IPF officers won't change the galaxy, Junker," someone says and gestures vaguely in my direction. The nickname stings. When Juno calls me that, it's warm. When this person says it, it feels like a title, like I'm below them in some silent hierarchy. "What do you know of rebellion?"

"I'm not saying we should be trying to kill them. I'm not saying we should all be carrying," I say and press my free hand to my chest. "I've been protecting the most wanted girl in the galaxy for weeks," I remind him. "The two of us have evaded capture despite their many, many attempts to get their hands on us. She wouldn't be alive without us being willing to get our hands dirty. Plus—" I cut myself off and root around in my deep pocket until I find what I'm looking for. "I found these."

"What is that?" Diana asks when I hold up the small, blue glass module.

"Bugs. Kill switches," Juno answers, her mouth set in a grim line. "They're in Zephyr ships that run on Bellona. One button and they can activate millions of these across the galaxy, gaining full control of every single ship they're installed in."

The room is silent. The man who called me Junker as if it was a taunt droops, all tension held in his face dissipated.

"We have to be ready to defend ourselves," Halima says after a lengthy silence. "Castor is right. They're going to come here. It's a poorly kept secret that we're here, that we've made Cybele our base of operations, and they're going to come for Juno. They have so far." She turns to Diana, who still has a rifle strapped to her back. There's a hardness in her blue eyes that I recognize— I see it every time I look in the mirror.

"They're a good teacher," Juno says and shifts closer, so close I can smell her vanilla shampoo. "They taught me how to fight, they could teach us how to shoot. How to disarm."

Silence. Again.

"We'll still lose people when they come. We can't fight against even six IPF officers with the kind of weaponry they're geared up with," Diana says.

"We'll lose more if they catch us off guard," I respond. "We need to get people pulling these out of our ships and training for when they come for us. It could be tomorrow. It could be weeks away. They're going to come, and they're going to kill us."

Diana meets Halima's eyes at last and the two of them are silent for a moment. Finally,. Halima breaks their intense eye contact and looks back at me and Juno.

"I agree," she says quietly. "It's useless to be a pacifist when you're being threatened with assault rifles. It's our lives, or theirs, and I personally would like to protect my family."

Quiet murmurs echo around the table, agreements and comments. Nobody argues.

"Is there a way we can get the word out? Tell the galaxy about the bugs?" I ask. "They could kill billions if we let those go unchecked."

Diana is silent and rubs at her jaw. Her eyes dart over the table between me and Juno, searching for something, and then she looks back at her wife. Halima runs her hand between Diana's tense shoulder blades.

"Juno. I'm sure you could use a break," Halima says. "You and— Cas, was it?— You two go and get some rest."

"No, we should be here. Juno is the—"

Juno's hand creeps onto my shoulder, right in the same spot Halima's perfectly-manicured fingernails scratch gently at Diana's. There's a wedding ring on her hand and I wonder if Diana can feel the weight of it, the heft of their committment to each other.

"Cas," Juno murmurs, and then turns to the two women running the meeting. "Thank you," she says and pulls gently on my wrist with her other hand. I exhale and clench my jaw to keep my mouth shut. I've said more to a bigger group in the last ten minutes than I ever have maybe in my life, and suddenly the idea of being alone makes all the built-up tension in my chest dissolve, just a little bit.

We leave the conference room and two other people leave as well— Tommy and the woman with pink hair.

Once the door is shut behind us, Juno lets out a low groan and leans forward until her forehead rests against my collarbones. I pet her hair and turn my gaze on the two others who left with us, noting that Gideon stayed inside.

"We don't need supervision," I snap over Juno's head after they follow us outside, but the pink girl raises her hands in a gesture of innocence and shakes her head.

"No, of course you don't. Tommy and I just wanted to speak with the two of you more privately," she says. Juno pulls away from me— she doesn't go far, just raises her head— and meets the girl's eyes loftily. Pink holds out her hand. "Cressida."

"Juno," she responds, as if anyone doesn't know, "And they're Cas."

"Castor," I amend.

Juno shakes her hand, but I don't. Cressida gestures for us to follow her down the hallway I recognize as the same one we hastily descended before. I fall in behind everyone, Juno and Cressida in the front, and I reach for my bag only to find that I left it in our rooms. I shove my hands in my pockets and find a little scrap of metal, flicking at it with the ragged curve of my fingernail.

Cressida ends up simply leading us back to our rooms. I lock the door once all four of us are inside and go over to my bag at once to grab my Equinox knife. I flick the corkscrew attachment out and dig under one of my nails for a bit of dirt that's lodged there, opting to lean against the wall by the door while the other three settle in on the couches in the living area.

"Juno," Cressida starts and pulls out her phone. "People online think that you're dead."

"Is that not a good thing?" I ask and push the corkscrew back into the body of the knife, instead flipping out the file to fix a nick in another nail.

"They're losing hope," Tommy explains. Juno's face falls. I close the knife and sit beside her. She pulls my hand into hers and threads our fingers together at once, smoothing her pointer finger along the scarred skin on the back of my left hand.

"I... How do I fix that without giving away my position?"

"Post the picture from Dearing."

Tommy squints at us. "Why were you two on Dearing?"

"Long story," I reply, waving off the question.

"Horrible little planet," Juno mutters and squeezes my hand. "Never going back."

"There are a lot of good people on Dearing," I murmur and pull up the picture of Juno on my pad. It's dark and barely lit in the dingy alley we were in, but the mural nearly glows behind her. Strokes of color paint her cheeks on the bricks and her hair in the foreground, some faraway neon glinting green against the strands, just as it should be.

I look at Juno and she's staring at me, her eyes glimmering with something mysterious and warm.

"Look at how you've changed," she says.

My face flushes hot and I hand her my pad. "Go, post it. We're days from Dearing by now. If they know that Adrestia is the unofficial resistance base anyways, they'll know this was where we were headed. It won't make any difference."

Juno takes my pad and releases my hand, pressing a quick kiss to my first knuckle before she does. Cressida and Tommy scoot over to help her, so I let go of her hand and walk over to the massive windows breaking up an entire wall of the living room. The lake is glittering mercury in the sunlight and there are four small kayaks drifting slowly from one side to the other. The trees that spread between the buildings that comprise Cybele campus are thick and old, clearly here since long before the school was built, and few even have huge bird nests in their branches.

It's beautiful, and even as the planet's twin suns glare through the glass and warm up the small apartment, I can't help but think back to when I was a kid seeing planets whiz by at a speed faster than light. The rare green ones were always my favorite, spread few and far between the red, beige, and even blue orbs swirling by. The trees quiver in the breeze, but I turn back to look at Juno.

I like this view better.

Juno and I take the longest shower I've probably ever taken in my life. When we finally shut off the now-chilly water and get ready to sleep at the start of Adrestia's ten hour nighttime cycle,

I help her twist her wet hair into two braids and we brush our teeth side by side.

"I don't remember the last time I slept in a bed that wasn't on the Gemini," I say absently as I toss our laundry into a corner. I'm shirtless and barefoot, wearing a loose pair of shorts only as we start climbing into bed.

"Shit, and that mattress is the lumpiest thing I've ever slept on," Juno teases as she tugs at the strap of her tank top. She smooths her bangs back, tucking the longer pieces behind her ears, and tugs the covers down to reveal pale beige sheets and four pillows for the two of us. I run my palms along the fabric and let out a long breath.

"Soft," I murmur.

"Welcome to the big guns, Cas," Juno says, grinning, and slides into the bed. I follow after a second, plugging my pad and watch in on the shelf beside my side of the bed. I'm situated closer to the door while Juno is by the window, but she did pull the blackout curtains shut before we even showered, murmuring something about privacy into the crease between my hip and thigh.

We're silent for a minute, a foot of empty space between us when before there wasn't room to breathe without touching one another, and then Juno turns to face me. I mirror her movements. Meeting her eyes feels natural and easy, big brown with just the faintest rim of eyeliner still clinging to her lids feeling more like home than this place probably ever will.

"We did it," Juno murmurs, her eyelashes fluttering, "and we're gonna keep doing it. You, me, and the fucking galaxy."

"As long as you're by my side," I whisper back, "I feel like I can do anything."

Juno kisses me and then rolls over so I can wrap my arms around her waist. We fall asleep like that, our bodies falling to the cyclical pull of gravity as the planet orbits its twin suns in a rotational figure eight, and I don't dream.

Our first full day at Cybele University is quiet. I wake to Juno being whisked away by her brother with a brief wave as a good morning. I find breakfast easily once I'm dressed by following the slow-moving hoard of other tired people seeking out coffee. There are plenty of options in the dining hall, and I make myself a little bowl of oatmeal with granola and a sprinkle of brown sugar. There's a massive machine that dispenses all sorts of drinks and, in a moment of impulsive indulgence, I press the buttons for a juice and a hazelnut coffee. Within seconds, I have two paper cups, one cool and one warm.

I sit alone at a long bar that faces out a longer window. The lake is bubbling with people now, dozens of boats zigzagging across, and I drink my coffee and eat in peace. The dining hall still feels heavy with grief, a dense, foggy cloud connecting each of us together, and it keeps me from itching for my headphones. Every conversation is colored by it, quiet and murky words shared between friends. I finish my breakfast in solitude, and I can't say I mind. It's strange to be alone again, but I've been alone since I was ten years old. Alone is safe, and Juno will be there when I return to our bed tonight.

After eating, I do some exploring. The housing building Juno and I have rooms in— I make a mental note to ask someone about the official interaction between the college and the political revolutionaries being not-so-secretly housed here— is on the top of a hill covered in swaths of ancient, towering trees that cast a cool shade over most of the paved walkways. It's clean and, every so often, there's a wooden bench on the side of the sidewalk, each accompanied by a small sign that points out campus landmarks and in which direction you can find them.

I follow the signs down to the lake and I end up sitting in a shady grove that overlooks the water. There's a large, flat rock that gets me close enough to smell the water on the air but not close enough for anyone to notice me, and I settle in to listen to the rowing teams practice and students walk by just beyond a row of flowering bushes.

A massive bird, bigger than any creature I've ever seen before with thick feathers and shiny brown talons lands silently in a tree in front of me, barely six feet away. It looks at me with glittering eyes and I swear it almost looks curious before cocking its head further and flying off, startled by some other sound.

My chest feels lighter than it has in years. Adrestia reminds me of old pictures from Earth of women in high-waisted swimsuits taking a dip in a lake, climbing a tree, or swinging on a rubber tire connected far above with old rope. It's beautiful and nostalgic all at once, a world I've never gotten to take the time to see awake and alive right before me.

I sit by the lake until my coffee is gone and for another hour after that to soak in the fresh air. Birds come and go and I even spy a small rodent with a long, wiry tail scamper up the thick bark of a tree beside me. When I depart, I leave nothing behind. Instead, I find a composter beside a metal door and toss my empty coffee cup before entering the building on a whim.

"Welcome to the Cybele Library," a woman calls to me from behind a desk. I lift a hand in acknowledgement and look around. The library is enormous and beautiful. The building itself is a quarter-circle with the entire curved wall made of glass, cut through with shining silver metal supports. It's three stories tall and the entrance is open upwards to all three, so I can see people sitting against balcony railings twenty feet above me.

The shelves are mixed. Probably a third of the collection is books, while the rest is an organized combination of tablets built into pedestals, computers with pull-out stools, and small cards to take to the reception desk and check out information on your own personal devices. It's massive and quiet and stunning, and it's the kind of place I know I could lose hours in.

I do a full lap of the library, examining some shelves and brushing my fingers against books' spines. When my watch buzzes with a call from Juno, I'm on the top floor sandwiched between a non-fiction shelf and a long row of tablets loaded with information on flora and fauna across the galaxy. There's a view of the lake that is nearly better than the one from our room, and I lean against the railing as I answer.

"June," I murmur.

"Hey, Cas. Do you wanna grab lunch?"

It's been four hours, which is the longest I've been apart from Juno in weeks. Her voice is like a balm. I'm not quite hungry yet, but *Juno*.

"Yeah, sounds good."

"Meet at the dining hall?"

"I'll be there in ten."

"I'll see you there, love," she says, and the phone clicks off. I realize I'm smiling, a big, honest smile with my teeth showing and my eyes scrunched up, and I shove my hands deep into my pockets to keep myself from thudding at my chest. There's a bridge on the top floor, a big glass and metal walkway that connects the library to another building. I know vaguely which direction the dining hall is in, so I meander that way until I see the long bay of windows.

It's busier now than it was this morning and it takes me a few minutes to find Juno and Gideon. They're sitting in a corner at a small table that is clearly meant for two, but there's a third chair pulled up in between the two for me.

"Hello," I say and sink into it, squeezing Juno's knee briefly under the table.

"Castor," Gideon greets, "We haven't been properly introduced. I'm Gideon Marcus, Juno's brother. It's nice to meet you."

"He's also my much smarter half," Juno adds. "He's in law school. About to take the bar in what, two months?"

Gideon makes a face and suddenly I see the resemblance so much more.

"It's good to finally meet you," I say. It feels a little stunted and over-polite in my mouth, but he takes it with a nod.

"Gideon is gonna help me start making videos again," Juno says and grins at her brother.

"Good," I reply, "That'll be good." Every word I say feels wrong, like now that I'm speaking to someone besides Juno— even worse, someone important to Juno— I feel slow. Awkward.

"For me, and for the movement," Juno agrees and takes my hand in hers. Her plate isn't empty, but I'm sitting on her left, so she just keeps spearing pieces of pasta with her fork, held easily in her right hand.

"Speaking of," Gideon interjects and sets down his own fork. "There's a meeting with Diana in an hour that I'd really like you two to be at. I think they really listened to what you said yesterday."

Juno glances at me, but I'm already nodding.

"We'll be there."

The meeting is, for the most part, mind-numbingly boring. Budgets, numbers, views, impact. None of it means very much to me, but I try to focus anyways. Juno has a seat saved beside Gideon and Diana, but the only other open chair is down at the end of the conference table, so I end up squeezed in between Cressida and someone I met briefly yesterday— Crow, maybe? — with long, shining black hair and kind eyes.

Diana is saying something about 'recovering an asset' and 'communicating risk to the youth', and I drag my finger across the whorls in the wooden table. I'm not fully paying attention, but this isn't my area of expertise. Juno is the wordsmith. I'm the junker. When Diana pivots to talking about yesterday, I focus in.

"We've thrown around a few ideas," she says and swipes a list from her tablet up onto the screen behind her. "We—"

She's interrupted by a sound trilling from her tablet, and then Halima's, and then a chorus echoes through the room from divices all over the table. It's not something that's used very often, but it's a sound I know: the Intergalactic Alert System. Diana silently flicks the notification onto the big screen.

CASTOR QUASAR AND ██████ MARCUS CAUSE OF SUDDEN SHIP CRASHES. CONSIDER THEM ARMED AND DANGEROUS. LAST SIGHTED ON ANDEROS.

Diana wordlessly opens a web browser and searches our name. An article pops up at once from ZNN, Zephyr's— and therefore Marwood's— primary news source.

'After an investigation into the shooting at the Gunnar's Big Win casino, we have attributed the massacre there, as well as the shooting on Anat-2 yesterday, to Marcus and Quasar. They are

part of an anti-government terrorist movement that have also claimed responsibility for multiple previous terrorist attacks, including these recent unprecedented ship crashes. At this time, we are unaware as to how they are hacking into personal vehicles. If you see Marcus, Quasar, or anyone baring this symbol, report them at once to the IPF.'

Below the article is a picture of the stickers Juno's rebels have been putting up, her logo depicted in chunky, pixellated rainbow.

"It wasn't a massacre," I say at last, breaking the tense silence in the room. Diana looks at me, her face tense and gaunt. "Only one person died there, and she was one of the shooters. They weren't shooting to kill. They needed money."

"What do we do?" Juno whispers.

"We make a plan," Diana finally says and closes out of the article. "They think we're these violent monsters, but they're deflecting. They're looking in a mirror and seeing someone else. We have to show them who they really are."

"Diana," Halima murmurs and grabs her wife's arm. Diana takes a deep breath and rests her fingers over Halima's. She meets each of our eyes as she speaks.

"We show up when they do. We train everyone who doesn't know how yet how to shoot, and— We can't continue to try to be the bigger person, Halima. We need to do what we need to do to stop this in its goddamn tracks."

"I don't care if they think I'm this— This monster," I say and gesture to the screen, even though the article is gone. "Maybe I am. They're *worse*. Juno and I, we've travelled through half the galaxy in the last month. We've seen people die. We've seen people scared out of their minds, we've been threatened, we've been hurt. We've been catcalled and hate crimed and— And

Juno was *arrested.* They will keep killing us in his name for as long as he spreads his propaganda. Forty yesterday, how many today? We have to fight back."

I ache with the honesty of it. My heart races, my skin is pinpricks of visible anxiety. Juno looks down the table at me, red rimming her dark-lined eyes, and I want to hold her hand.

"We will do what we have to. If they won't listen to our words, they will listen to our bullets," Diana says, and that's it.

"We will fight," I say, "and we will win."

13
RAMPANT CRONYISM AND CORRUPTION

The first ship crashes into Adrestia that night.

We hear it from the dormitories. Not the crunch of metal on metal, not the crush of shatter-proof glass, not even the explosion as a spark catches the dribbling fuel leaking from the tank and ignites it, sending a fireball into the atmosphere.

No.

We hear the screams.

The passengers don't scream; they're already dead. We hear the cries from those rushing from the dorms beside us, the shouts of the rescue crew on their way to rip any unlikely survivors from the wreckage.

Juno and I leap out of bed, but a security guard shakes his head at us as soon as we enter the hallway. Another dozen-odd people poke their heads out of their rooms, but we're simply told to go back to sleep and we'll be briefed in the morning.

There's nothing we can do right now.

We go back to bed, but we don't sleep. Juno stays up sitting at the little bar in our kitchenette pouring over the news, comments on her posts and videos, and any news site she can get her hands on, including INN. Some show the plague of deaths across the galaxy, but those that favor Bridger and Marwood are silent.

When I finally pull Juno to bed, she stares at the ceiling until I press enough kisses into the back of her neck that she closes her eyes and relaxes against me.

Even then, we both sleep in fits. I alternate between staring at the back of Juno's head, finding patterns in the faint brush-strokes on the wall, and dozing. My dreams are full of crashed spaceships and screaming corpses. Body bags, bloody boots. Chell, crumpling to the ground to save Juno's life. Apollo, dead against my fingertips. My leg, severed from my body, bleeding weakly onto ashen metal.

Juno, a bullet between her eyes.

Diana calls us minutes after we give up on trying to rest. She gives us a building on campus to report to and asks that we do so— After breakfast, that is. We find groceries in our fridge and a note from Tommy: 'EAT WELL'. I make us eggs and toast and Juno puts the news on the TV.

It's the rebellion news, compassionate and careful, but it still hurts to watch the coverage of yesterday's attack. There are recordings of it happening; gritty, shaky camera footage of someone being shot in the shoulder, the chest, the leg. Every shot has blood blurred out, but it's still red hot copper in the back of my throat.

It transitions to footage of ships crashing. A family four-seater, a passenger shuttle, a cargo ship, a Voyager class a year newer than the Gemini. There aren't any on Adrestia. Diana knows better than to record which ships come and go from the rebellion's base of operations. Instead, they show a half-dozen on Janus, another two on Sors-3, and two more crumple against moons with no atmosphere, leaving the passengers inside to gasp for breath and die in the cold vacuum.

One refuel station was completely destroyed when a ship

carrying highly-compacted explosive material clipped the edge of the dense shell protecting it from the expanse outside. It went up in flames. Seven thousand people died, their corpses unrecoverable in deep space.

Juno's plate goes mostly untouched. The toast she does swallow comes back up at the sight of a hundred bodies floating in zero gravity.

We dress in near silence. Juno borrows a pair of my cargo pants and they sit low on her hips before she cinches her belt. I dress in similar functionality. We both tie our boots with our hips touching on the couch and Juno nudges my gun towards me. I strap the holster onto my belt and then sit and watch her draw on her eyeliner and lipstick, careful and precise. I watch her fingers tremble as she rolls the tube in her hand to adjust her sweaty grip. A smear of dark green goes outside the boundaries of her lips as she swallows a sob. Wordlessly, I hand her a makeup remover wipe and rest my palm between her shoulder blades. Using one fingernail wrapped in the wipe to make the line crisp and smooth, she drags the smeared lipstick away and redraws it on, perfectly straight.

It contrasts her pale skin like a white moon against the backdrop of space, the difference shocking and stark, yet complimentary. There is no one without the other.

We head to the building Diana told us to meet in. It's a long, nearly windowless building between the auditorium and the lake. It takes up a decent spot. It's too bad that it doesn't have a view. The walk there is lovely despite the scent of carbon in the air. It's early enough that there's still dew on the leaves, still birds just waking up and singing sweet songs throughout campus. Juno holds my hand the whole walk there.

When we enter, a gruff man sitting behind a desk looks us over. "Juno and Castor?"

Juno nods.

"Down that way." He waves a hand down a hallway and the two of us turn that way, following the distant sounds of muffled voices until we reach a door that is propped open.

"Ladies first," I murmur to Juno. She huffs quietly. It isn't a laugh, but it's close. She enters, and I follow with a hand on her lower back.

A shooting range.

There are a dozen-odd tense people milling about, most of which I recognize, at least by face. It strikes a bit of distant anxiety into me— If I recognize them after only being here for two days, there are surely people here who would recognize me, remember me. I remember what I said to Juno: this is my home now. It is okay to know people.

Still, I find myself tucked behind her shoulder. She's an inch or two shorter than me but her presence is enormous even without her iconic green hair.

"Ah! Juno, Cas, you made it," Diana says and greets us with a clap on Juno's shoulder. There's a grim set to her jaw but she manages a half-smile through it anyways. "Juno, head over there with Tommy. I'm going to talk to Cas for a moment.

"Castor," I mutter. I don't fully know why— I haven't been 'Cas' to anyone but Juno and some little part of me wants to keep it that way.

Juno squeezes my hand and departs, leaving me with Diana. She's nearly a foot taller than me and twice as wide, muscular shoulders visible even through the dark blue flannel she's wearing over a Cybele University shirt.

"Me and you," she says and claps her hand down on my shoulder, just like she did with Juno a moment ago, "We're gonna teach these kids how to shoot." I wince and instinctively pull away from the touch. She doesn't seem bothered, just drops her hand and uses it to gesture to the group instead. "After last night, we're almost sure we're next on their list.

They know we're here, and we need to be ready when they come."

"The IPF?"

Diana thinks for a moment, her lips pursed in a flat line. "And Marwood. His cronies. The extremists. We tracked the signal from one of the kill switches— Bugs, you called them— right back to his campaign ship."

I hiss and glance over at Juno, who has plastered her subscriber-winning smile back onto her face as she chats with another girl. "Shit," I mutter.

"Yeah. Overnight, the possible threat you brought us became very, very real. We need as many sets of hands we can get."

"Shit," I repeat and drum my fingers against my collarbone. "We need to open up the dashboards of every intergalactic ship we have, make sure there aren't any bugs in the motherboards."

"We've already got out mechanics working on it. Are you in? I trust Juno when she says that you're a good teacher."

I nod. "I'm in. Can we start now?"

In lieu of a response, Diana just calls out to everyone and starts sorting them into two groups: those who have shot a gun before, and those who haven't. Each group forms a line and Diana pairs me with those who have. Juno stands proudly at the front of the line. There is a long table set up with over a dozen guns laying on it. Some are real, some I can tell from here are props, to learn how to handle a weapon without danger. I recognize a lot as stolen IPF guns, regulation, identical.

"You ready to teach us, Junker?" Juno murmurs as I select an IPF handgun and lead her into the stall.

"You ready to learn?" I retort and pull a pair of noise-cancelling headphones over my ears. Juno mirrors me and then smiles. It's a sad smile, a tired little upturn of her mouth, but it soothes something in me. "Let's do this."

We get in four days at the shooting range. More people show up every day, and Diana silently pulls more stolen guns and walks everyone through how to load them, clean them, shoot them. I spend eighty percent of my waking hours there and Juno does almost as much, only leaving to attend briefings and bring back food for me and Diana.

The first night, another two ships plummet into the planet's surface. Four people die and, despite injuries worse than my own decade-old wounds, one lives. It gives us just enough hope to keep going. We broadcast the names of the dead into the morning air and sit in silence, grieving, before picking up our guns and starting fresh.

The second night is silent, and the third night is as well.

Somehow, that's scarier.

On the fourth day, we all gather the same as each day before. I bring my own gun, shot more in the last half a week than ever before in my life, and clean it at a table while Diana walks the three new people through the basics. We settle in, me in the first lane and everyone else split into a couple of lines with a pistol each, and we shoot for an hour.

I don't notice immediately when we're interrupted by a young girl who runs in, chest heaving, and pulls Diana aside. The near-deafening sound of a half-dozen people shooting at faraway targets slows one at a time until it's silent. I engage the safety on my gun and tug my ear covers off to rest around my neck.

Diana listens intently to the girl, but she's speaking so quietly that all I catch is a few muffled filler words here and there. When the girl stops, Diana looks over and makes eye contact with Juno, then me. She jerks her head, and we both move towards her.

"Another ship has crash landed on the airstrip," Diana says quietly so nobody else can hear. "This one is different. It wasn't killswitched."

"What—"

"We don't know," Diana says with a grim set to her lips. "Cas, you come with me. Juno, get everyone in their gear and keep an ear out. I'll call when we have more information." She gestures past us to the locked door in the corner that leads to what we've taken to calling the armory. Bullet-proof gear, weapons, all safely locked up and only accessible with Diana's keys.

Juno catches them easily when Diana tosses them at her head. I give her a heavy look— I try not to think of it as goodbye, but something about it feels final— before following Diana, my own gun still strapped up to my hip. I rest my palm on the butt, initials C.Q. carved into the ivory grip pressing into the calloused skin on my hand. It's a familiar comfort, the same touch that has kept me safe for nearly a decade on my own, but I'd trade it for Juno's presence in a heartbeat.

We hop on a shuttle, and it feels like a hearse.

The driver takes one look at Diana and rushes us to the airstrip on her command. She produces two bulletproof vests, one bigger and one much smaller, and wince when I see that she's given me a child's sized vest. I try not to think about the children in the elementary school on the other side of the city from Cybele, bullet proof vests tucked under their desks and safety precautions drilled into their heads alongside multiplication tables. Diana undoes the safety on her own rifle as we get close and I pull my pistol out into my hand, adrenaline beginning to thrum through my chest.

When the shuttle reaches the airstrip, Diana leaps off before it's even fully stationary. There's a small group of people huddled beside a metal shipping container and Diana touches

Halima's waist gently to announce our arrival. I avert my gaze and look out onto the airstrip itself, the heat from Adrestia's twin suns making the ship itself nearly impossible to see through the heat waves emanating from the hot pavement. I squint and pull my hand up to shade my eyes, finally managing to make out the ship's shape.

"Diana," I call. "I know this ship."

The group grows silent.

"This is a resistance ship," I say and let my shoulders sink in relief as I holster my gun. "Where is the pilot? Where are the passengers?"

"Here," Halima calls. The group splits up and there's Nova, on her knees with cuffs binding her wrists. "She's IPF."

"No," I say and rush forward, falling to my knees in front of her. Her face is bloody and bruised, some so old they're green. "She isn't. Nova— Where are Mars and Jules?"

"Goliath was compromised," she rasps and turns to spit onto the concrete beside me. "Christ, get me some water and take these goddamn cuffs off. I can't feel my left hand."

Nobody moves.

"Do what she said," I snap, and an armed man quickly hoists her up to her feet and undoes her restraints.

"Jules and Mars had to steal an IPF ship," she says and rubs her wrists. Loose curls of orange hair glint fire around her face, reflecting the sunlight in golden waves. "I was the only one who made it to the Echo in time. I don't know where they are."

"I think I do," Halima says and points at the sky.

A battered IPF ship trailing smoke out of its left thruster barrels towards the air strip. Pieces of debris and metal fall off and twirl away into the sky leaving dust and flame behind in their wake. Over someone's radio, I hear a muffled voice come through over the scratchy speakers.

"Adrestia airstrip, this is rebel cell Goliath— We're coming in hot!"

That's a bit of an understatement.

The IPF ship slams into the runway and skids, very narrowly missing the Echo. Smoke pours out of a gash in the left side of the ship. Diana and another couple rebels rush forward, leaving me and Halima here with Nova.

"Are they here?" she murmurs. "Do you see my sister?" She reaches up and grabs my wrist. Her touch is light, her strength sapped, but for once I read between the lines: *don't leave.*

I stay and watch as the guards pull limp figures from the near-wreckage of the stolen ship. Mars comes out first, bulky and limping but *awake* and *alive.* The girl I rescued back at Fort Harrison crawls out on her own, blonde hair matted with ruby blood, and then Jules is pulled out by Diana.

She doesn't seem conscious. Her shirt is splattered with blood and dust and Nova's grip tightens on my wrist.

"Jules," Nova moans. "Julia, wake up."

For one breathtaking second as Diana lifts Jules up onto a hover gurney, I could've sworn she was dead. Her chest doesn't raise, her mouth hangs open— She looks for all the world like a corpse, and I swallow hard.

When she shudders awake, spitting blood onto the front of her shirt, I exhale. Nova rushes to her side and grabs her round face, smoothing hair back from her face.

"That's right, Jules, breathe for me," Nova is whispering, calming words soothing the trembling reverberating through Jules' body. She takes hold of the gurney from Diana and rushes over to the shuttle, where Mars and the blonde are waiting.

"They're coming," Halima yells. "Look sharp!"

Gunfire rings through the airstrip, bullets shattering concrete just beside my feet. Puffs of dust raise and obscure my vision, but I know the sound well enough to identify it. It isn't the patter of a pistol that I've grown so accustomed to in the last few days, or even the ringing shock of an assault rifle as bulets dig into flesh and tear out the other side. No.

This is a gatling gun attached to an identical IPF ship to the one that just crash landed eighty feet away. Shots ring out in a repetitive rhythm, hundreds fired in just seconds, and I see one of the men I was just speaking with beside Nova collapse to the ground as his thigh erupts in a spray of bright blood. I look up at the ship and see, past the glaring twin suns, the glint of a dozen gun barrels and five more ships hurtling towards the planet with matching smoke trails bleeding from their engines.

Finally, I move. I sprint over to Nova and help her lift Jules onto the shuttle. The quartet of rebels aren't the only people on board— The man dripping blood from his upper leg climbs on board, his hand gleaming maroon in the sunlight.

"Go! Get them to the infirmary and send another shuttle back, we're gonna have more wounded!" I scream at the driver over the tap-tap-tap-tap of machine gun fire and the crushing sounds of a half-dozen ships crashing into concrete. I clap my hand down on Nova's shoulder one more time. "I'll see you again soon. Take care of your family, I got it here."

It turns out, I don't have to wait for another shuttle. The second the first one is gone, another pulls up and a dozen people leap out, all wearing bullet proof vests and wielding pilfered IPF weaponry. I see Juno in the back— she's easy to spot, with how short she stands— and I manage to make eye contact for a split second before the IPF ship finally lands. Officers pour out, guns flashing bright as bullets spray across the air strip. The ground is already stained red with blood as I duck behind a low concrete wall, drawing my own gun. The path you'd usually take from the airstrip to catch the shuttle is wide open, but almost twenty of us are crouched in hiding behind whatever cover we can find. Diana, Halima, and Tommy are all squatting behind the shipping container, just across the path from where I am hiding.

The gunfire comes to a stop. One more crunch of metal on metal, a low moan, and then, silence.

For just a moment, I hear bird calls.

"Surrender the one you call Juno," an officer calls out to us. "We have an arrest warrant. If you do not comply, we have authority to shoot our way through your little terrorist group."

Someone shifts behind me and a hand closes around my wrist.

"Cas," Juno breathes, muscles tensing as if to stand.

"No," I hiss back.

"I—"

"No!" I repeat, almost certainly too loud. Diana shoots me a glare. I suck in a breath and shift my sweaty grip on my handgun.

"Cas, listen to me," Juno whispers and shifts until her mouth is right behind my ear. "I'll pretend to go with them. You and Diana surprise them when they turn their backs."

"It's not safe," I protest.

"Nothing is. Not for me," Juno breathes. I crouch down more and turn to face her. "I trust you, Cas. Trust me too."

I swallow hard and reach up with my left hand to pull her by the back of her neck into a searing kiss. She makes a quiet noise and it's over much too soon— Before I can even catch my breath, she stands to her full five-foot-three height and raises her hands above her head. From my angle I can see the pistol tucked into the back of her pants, but there's no way the officers could.

"I'll come with you if you leave these people alone," Juno calls out. The officers seem to relax and I hear two sets of footsteps approach Juno. "If it's me you want, I'll come. Just don't crash any more ships. Don't hurt my friends."

I meet Diana's eyes and slowly lift my hand up to where she can see it. As soon as her gaze flicks over to my hands I hold up three fingers, then two, then one. As soon as I pull down the third finger, she stands with her rifle situated against her shoulder, just a few inches showing above the barrier we've hidden behind, and starts picking off IPF officers with carefully aimed shots. Juno dives behind a thick-trunked tree just beyond the barrier I'm behind and I fire off a shot at the IPF officer reaching after her. He stumbles and turns to me. His shot misses me by inches.

The firefight is quick. We outnumber them. They're wearing armor, but so are we. I see someone on our side go down, hand clasped to their chest, but their palm comes away dry. Juno is still trembling behind the tree, her unfired pistol held tight in her grip. The person next to me, a young man with bleach-blond hair, is bleeding from his calf and I quickly cut a chunk off his pant leg to staunch the bleeding.

"More are coming!" Diana yells and points to the sky. Another two IPF ships are circling, unimpeded by those damn blue switches killing any other ship that tries to pass through the planet's atmosphere. I swear under my breath.

"Juno," I yell. When she turns, I beckon for her to come closer. "Get him onto the shuttle. I'll do what I can here."

She nods and helps the blond stumble to his feet. He's a good six inches taller than her so he ends up leaning on her shoulders like a crutch as they hobble away together, right as another much larger IPF transport sinks into the atmosphere.

Another shuttle pulls up with more of us, more hodgepodged revolutionaries with stolen guns and barely any training, and skids to a halt. It becomes a makeshift blockade between the cement barricade we had been using for cover and the only spot left visible on the airstrip that could fit the massive ship, right between the Echo and the two smoking cruisers. Thankfully, the transport ships aren't weaponized, so we don't have to hide any more than we did a moment before. We have as long as it takes for them to land to get ready.

I rush forward and take up a new position pressed against the shuttle.

"Are you sure you were never in the army?" Diana murmurs as soon as she joins me. I see Halima helping another injured person towards the shuttle. Behind her, there are two bodies on the ground, both faces I recognize, laying so still I'm sure they're dead. I swallow hard and turn my gaze back to where the IPF ship is slowly landing.

"I'm sure," I answer, even though I'm sure it was a rhetorical question. Diana grabs my shoulder and looks me in the eyes, her blue ones steel with a deep sadness, the kind that only comes with prolonged grief.

"You're a good kid," she says, "Don't get killed."

The transport lands. Within seconds, the side of the shuttle is riddled with bullets. There has to be at least fifty of them pouring out of the side door, and each one has hundreds of shots that could end a life. Those of us hiding behind the shuttle duck down low to avoid the shots.

One person leans around and takes out an officer, getting a bullet through their throat in repayment.

I'm used to blood. I bled heavily every month from ages ten to fifteen when I was finally able to get the implant that stops your cycle. I've cut myself junking. I've hurt people for trying to steal from me, touch me, know me. I've watched men die by my hand.

I've seen a lot of blood.

Yet, when this rebel staggers back, blood spurting from their throat in long, arching spray that stretches so far I swear I can smell the rust of it, I have to turn away. I pull my shirt over my mouth and take a few harsh breaths, but I have to move. I have to move. If I don't, that could be me.

That could be Juno.

I shove my arm through the panes left behind by shattered shuttle windows and aim quickly, the barrel of my gun pointing right into the front of the mass of officers shooting back.

I hit one in the arm, right underneath the hard armor plating protecting his shoulder, and then I duck back down to breathe. Someone beside me cries out and falls to the ground. The scent of blood and burnt ash grows stronger as I take another shot, missing entirely. My left hand flies up to press at my sternum and I breathe. I breathe.

Diana has killed three men by the time I've calmed myself down enough to return fire. Another bullet sinks into the metal beside my jaw and I wince away. One of the officers yells something that comes to me like travelling through water, muffled and slow. Half the men around him swing their bodies around to focus fire on Diana, leaving their backs exposed. I hit one in the back easily and he collapses, but then I hear Diana cry out and fall to the ground. I swear and shoot another one—

"Another ship is coming!"

I don't take the time to look at the sky. Instead, I crawl towards Diana, and—

I stop.

I know that voice. It's so goddamn familiar I could swear it's been carved into my *bones*. I see Juno, hair tied up in a messy bun, standing in front of the near-ruined shuttle with her gun pointed at the array of officers in front of us. There's blood on her vest but she doesn't seem injured; it must be from the man she helped to the shuttle.

I see, almost in slow motion, an IPF officer in the back raise his rifle and aim for Juno's chest.

"JUNO!" I scream. My vocal cords are shredded, raw and hot from the debris catching in my throat. My boots slip on a sticky pool of blood under where I was standing but I manage all the same to throw myself against her side right as the man's finger tightens on the trigger. Juno falls to the ground, winded and confused but *safe*.

When the bullet punches into my shoulder, I stagger, crumpling to my knees.

It doesn't hurt the way I thought it would. It isn't a sharp, piercing pain— At least, not at first. In fact, I barely feel it as I drop my gun and reach up to paw numbly at the spot the bullet sank into. The wound is right between my shoulder and the edge of the vest. Blood spills and my hand comes up red and wet.

Now, it hurts. It hurts like it hurt when my leg was severed from my body and I press my hand to my heart, to my sternum, to my shoulder, but nothing helps. I feel it like a punch to the gut, like a trash compactor crushing my chest, and then the sharp pain comes.

I fall forward onto my chest. My skull hits the ground, smears the blood spattered there, and I don't remember anything else after hands on my back and the noise of rebellion so loud it roars.

14

FRAUDULENT ELECTIONS

I WAKE TO SILENCE SO STILL IT MAKES MY EARDRUMS ache. It is interrupted only by quiet machinery that feels so far away and a low, constant beep that makes my head pound with every tone.

I open my mouth to try to speak, but nothing comes out besides a rasping cry that drags against my throat and dry tongue. There are tubes in my arms and a plastic clip on my finger. The blankets covering the lower half of my body are scratchy and rough and I'm not wearing a shirt or pants, only the loose boxers I only wear when anything tight makes me feel like I'm being choked.

When I'm finally able to pry my eyes open through the sleep-crust around them. I recognize where I am: Cybele Hospital. I've only been here once, a distant memory that feels years old of accompanying Juno to pick up her prescription, but the white painted walls and green tiled floors are unmistakable.

So is the shock of dark green hair, freshly dyed, resting on the bed beside me.

Juno is sitting in an uncomfortable looking wooden chair. Her face is hidden in her arms, pillowed on the bed beside my hip. She's wearing a white tank top— clean, no blood— and no bra over a pair of my sweatpants that she rolled twice at the waistband to keep up. As my ears adjust to the quiet, I hear another sound; Juno is snoring so lightly I can barely catch it. I try to smile but my face cracks and twinges, making me grunt in pain.

"Ah, you're awake," an unfamiliar voice says from the side Juno isn't resting on. I try to turn my head, but the pillow I'm propped against is dense foam that holds my neck still. "Shh, stay still." The person comes into view and I see a man with dark skin wearing pale green scrubs. He's holding a clipboard and there's a badge clipped to his breast pocket but my vision is too blurry to make out the name.

At once, I realize why— My optical prosthetic has been removed.

"Castor," the man says. A distant part of me decides that his voice is kind, that he feels safe. Juno clearly trusts him; she'd never sleep if she didn't. "You were shot at the ambush on the airstrip. Do you remember that?"

I open my mouth with some difficulty and rasp out, "Yes."

"Good, good. Do you know where you are?"

"Cybele." It comes out pained and broken— sigh-uh-lee.

"Good. We had to remove your prosthetic for surgery," he explains as my single eye desperately tries to track his movements. "Your collarbone was very nearly shattered. One inch lower and we're almost certain you would've bled out before Juno could have gotten you back here."

"'Uno," I breathe and flick my gaze back to her sleeping body beside me. She shifts a little but doesn't wake and, even when I try to reach out a hand to touch her, I can barely lift a finger.

"You're going to be quite weak for a while, Castor," the

nurse says softly. "It's going to take a long time to recover from this."

I look at him and swallow to wet my mouth before I grit out the truth: "I've had worse."

When I wake again, Juno is sitting upright and holding a cup.

"Juno," I slur and she turns to look at me.

Her face is a mess. It's a mottled, splotchy mess of purple, red, and fading yellows; her nose is crooked right at the bridge in a way it wasn't before and there's a halfway healed cut on her forehead, still held together with a few stitches.

"Cas," she gasps and surges forward, cupping my face in one hand with an impossibly soft touch. "I heard you woke up, but I wasn't here, I'm so, so sorry, love—"

"No," I croak, "S'okay. You were asleep, but you were here."

"Do you want water? I have— I have little ice chips, it's what Jules and Noah told me would be best," she says and then backtracks, "Noah is your doctor. Him and Jules have been taking care of you."

I don't respond. The effort it takes to open my mouth and gasp out horrible, burnt little words is exhausting, so I just part my lips and let my eyelids fall closed as Juno slides small chips of ice into my mouth. The moisture coats the inside of my gummy throat, revives my tongue and gums and makes me feel a little less like a sponge left out in the sun.

"Thank you," I whisper after Juno has exhausted her cup.

"Cas," she breathes back and presses in to kiss my forehead, barely a brush of lips against the the bruised skin there. "I... I thought you were dead. When you weren't, I thought there was no way you'd wake up."

"Takes more than a stray bullet to put down a junker," I reply.

Juno smiles, and everything feels better.

Recovery takes weeks. I'm in the hospital for three, which is only made tolerable by the news that my bullets put down a half-dozen IPF officers. Juno stays with me almost all the time. She sleeps in a folding cot in my hospital room at first and then, when it's cleared by Jules and Noah, in my bed beside me. We're both small, so we fit fairly easily, but the wires and tubes get tangled in her hair sometimes anyways. She never minds.

I ask Juno about everyone who was hurt and everyone I tried to get to safety. Jules is already almost fully recovered—She's even been helping out at the hospital for the last week or so. She's still in physical therapy, which Nova has been going to with her. Nova is doing well as well, having recovered from her concussion while I was unconscious. Diana and Halima are both alive, but Diana was shot in the stomach and is still in the hospital a few rooms down from my own. When I start walking, I stop by, and she holds my hand and thanks me.

Six of us died, but twenty-six of theirs did before they withdrew. The statistics don't feel half bad to me, but I still spend days mourning.

I never would've cared before. Six people? That's a drop in the bucket. Now, it's faces I knew, voices I'd recognize. People like me, dead, just because Marwood and his people wanted it so.

After I'm released, I use a wheelchair to head back to our suite. Juno pushes me for most of it, as my arm strength still isn't back to where it was. It hasn't changed at all, other than the evidence of Juno stopping by a few times while I was in the hospital. A drawer is left open, my leg is waiting on the couch for me.

"I've been feeding Pollux," Juno tells me as she pushes me over to the couch and helps transfer me from the chair to the carefully-built blanket nest she set up ahead of time. "I got him moved up here. The Gemini is fine, it's parked in one of the hangars down by the airstrip, but he's here now, see?"

Against the wall with the TV is another piece of furniture now, a similar wood blend dresser, but on top there's a large fishtank with my little buddy swimming around inside.

"Thank you." It doesn't capture the overwhelming feeling in my chest, the warmth and brightness that consumes me when I think of Juno carefully moving my fish into our new home, but she just shrugs.

"No need. I'm basically his step-mom," she replies. The joke doesn't really land. I pat the couch next to me and look up at her as she tidies away my chair, tucking it into a corner by the door.

"June," I say. She's antsy, pacing around the living room looking for something to do with her hands. "Love, come sit."

After a moment, she does, but she doesn't touch me. Our thighs don't even touch.

"Juno."

"Castor," she responds flatly. I shift until I can hold out my hand to her, careful to keep my upper arm held close to my chest to avoid strain on my still-healing collarbone.

"Tell me what's in there," I say and gesture to her head.

"I thought you were going to die."

"So did I."

Juno groans and slides her hand into mine. The touch is tentative and slow but I squeeze her fingers. "I thought you were going to die for a cause you barely believe in in the first place, and it would've been my fault."

"Juno," I repeat and wait until she looks at me. Her under eyes are smudged dark and the cut on her forehead is scarring over, still red and angry. "If I didn't believe that Marwood was a fascist and the galaxy is more than likely going to fall apart within this election cycle, I wouldn't still be here, even if I loved you."

Her eyes are glistening with unshed tears but when she looks at me, there's steel in her gaze. "Love?"

"Mmm..." I murmur, a non-answer and we both know it. I lean forward and touch our foreheads together. "You're a hard person not to love, Juno."

She reaches up with her free hand and wraps her palm around my neck. Her thumb brushes the corner of my lips and I smile.

"Thank you for taking care of me," I tell her.

"I always will, as long as you'll let me."

"And I'll be at your side, wanted criminal or famous influencer."

Juno snorts out an ugly laugh and it's like a balm to my broken body. When she pulls back, she's smiling, and it's all I need.

TWO WEEKS LATER

"Crowbar?"

I hand Juno the long piece of iron and she uses it to pull a thick sheet of metal off the wall of the IPF hauler we're in. She sets it aside and starts carefully pulling the innards out, handing them to me so I can sort them into two piles: to sell, and to keep for the rebels.

Noah wouldn't clear me for junking after barely two

months of recovery, but after both of our desperate pleas that I be allowed to do something, he reluctantly decided that if Juno does the work and I just accompany her, it should be okay. I'm still using a wheelchair a lot of the time while my bones stitch themselves back together and I regain strength throughout my body, but it's easy to strap my bag to the side of the chair, a flat piece of metal over my lap like a desk, and sort through the bits of wire and scrap Juno hands me. It's nice to be back to doing what I'm good at, even if it's just clearing out the smashed IPF ships scattered across the airstrip.

We work in silence for a little bit, just the two of us together for the first time in weeks. It's been doctors and nurses in and out, Gideon and Halima and Tommy all checking in on us at least once a day, and it's almost nostalgic to be with just Juno again. It hasn't even been three months that I've known her, and she's changed the entirety of my life. The days of us lounging in the Gemini and watching trivia feels like years ago. Now, our days are filled with physical therapy, filming, and junking. Juno leaves for meetings once or twice a day for a group that's trying to figure out what Marwood's next steps are, and occasionally, someone comes to our rooms to ask my thoughts on how to stop the bugs. Ships aren't crashing nearly as much, not after our decisive victory on Adrestia, but the need to stop it from happening again lurks around every corner.

We've slept a lot. A lot. Showering has been... doable. Maybe even tolerable, with Juno's hands helping me avoid getting water on my still-healing injuries. I can't lift my arms any higher than waist-high, but that's still twice as high as I could this time two weeks ago. I got a lot of practice when I got top surgery and recovered alone in the Gemini, orbiting an abandoned planet for two weeks, and it's much easier with Juno at my side.

Her face is healed but I can tell that she is self-conscious about the new shape of her nose. I catch her staring at it in the mirror once, dragging her gentle fingertips across the bump. I kissed it until she forgot her train of thought, but I still see her look at her reflection for longer than she did before.

Deep down, after everything, I still thought that when we got to Adrestia, Juno would go off to return to her normal life. I would be left behind, and the two of us would grow to be acquaintances, our time together a memory and nothing else. She would remember that there are billions of more interesting people in the galaxy, and I would do my quiet work for the rebels, maybe waving when we passed in the dining hall. It would hurt, but I would survive.

That isn't what happened. We don't spend every waking moment together, but we share a suite, we sleep in the same bed, we shower together. Juno brings me food from the dining hall and turns on reruns of HAZARD when I start getting antsy. I help her edit her videos and run her channel, which turns out to be a much harder job than I would've thought.

She has only posted one video so far. She filmed it right after the IPF raid on Cybele, so her face is still bloody and bruised, barely held together with stitches and butterfly bandages, and her hair is that box brown we used to cover her green. In it, she told the whole story. Everything from me picking her up on Janus, to the three ships full of officers with assault rifles and body armor. It has garnered millions of views. Nova and I took over moderating her comment sections. We delete thousands of hateful comments a week, but they're more than made up for with positive, supportive ones.

Her merch is completely sold out. Pictures of her stickers stuck to walls in dangerous places becomes a trend as millions of people sick and tired of the way things have been post images of them defacing Marwood signs, Zephyr-owned businesses, and even IPF stations. All of the proceeds from the stickers, hoodies, t-shirts, and other merchandise Juno sells goes into a mutual aid fund she has established intended to pay bail for those arrested in her name.

Juno Marcus is a household figure. She's on the news, but she's also a celebrity. Juno wears shirts with her own name emblazoned across the chest with pride as she brings awareness to a government raid of a peaceful college, as well as the other half-dozen they managed to do without public outcry. People are furious. Everyone who has ever supported Juno sees her face beaten bloody and listens to her cry, and it makes a difference.

It's a start.

We held a vigil. Over three hundred people have died since I met Juno on Janus, and it's worth taking time to mourn them all. We lit candles. Some pray. I didn't, but I knelt in front of a picture of Chell, right beside one I dug out of storage of Apollo, and touch their faces in turn. I dream of them both that night.

Ships stop crashing, and the bugs go on the back burner, but I break open ones we recover and try to reverse engineer them. It isn't working, but I don't give up. I haven't solved them yet, but I will.

In my pocket, Juno's phone buzzes.

I pull it out quickly and she glances back at me, raising an eyebrow. I read the text and I smile so wide an old scab on my chin splits again.

"What is it?" she asks and sets down the multitool she bought, almost identical to my Equinox knife.

"Gideon passed the bar," I tell her, "and Marwood is officially under investigation for sending the IPF a false report about the shooting at his rally that led to the attack on Cybele."

"Holy shit," Juno breathes and surges towards me, taking her phone out of my hand and peering at the screen. "Holy shit, Cas."

"I know."

"This— This could be nothing, but it could— Cas, this could stop his campaign," Juno breathes.

"And Gideon passed the bar," I remind her.

"We all know that was going to happen," Juno says and waves me off. She skims the article and lets out a breathless laugh. "God. Cas, this is huge. If anything comes of this, anything at all..."

"It'll definitely influence his campaign, even if it doesn't get him thrown out," I reply and nod. Juno leans forward and wraps her arms around my neck, careful to put her head on the right side of my own to avoid my still-healing collarbone. I can't hug her back, not fully, but she just kisses my cheek and then sits back down, leaning against the wall she was just pulling scrap out of.

"We might actually change the galaxy," Juno says, and I believe, I believe, I believe.

When we get back to Cybele, Nova and Mars greet us on the airstrip, now mostly cleared of debris. Nova calls out to us and Mars waves as Juno pushes my wheelchair off the entry ramp of the ship we borrowed to go junking.

"I assume you've heard the good news?" Nova says when we're closer.

"That Marwood is being investigated?"

"No, that Gideon passed the bar," Nova says, a teasing smile playing at her lips, and Mars snorts. "Yes, about Marwood. Though, I hope you're up for a party. Halima has a whole party set up back on campus. Don't tell Gideon, I think it's a surprise."

Juno laughs and the three of them fall in step behind my chair. "Those two have essentially adopted him, I think."

Mars signs something at her and she hesitates, a little hitch in her step that betrays what's going on in her mind. Juno has taken to learning galactic sign in the last few weeks and promised to help Nova teach me too once I can move my arms and hands all the way. For now, I don't know what Mars is saying, but it makes Juno draw silent.

"What?" I ask after a second.

Juno runs her hand over my shoulder. "He said... He said they've adopted all of us. We're family. We're home."

I rest my hand over hers. Nova chimes in to keep the flow of conversation going as Juno stays quiet behind me as we make our way to the conference room. I squeeze her hand and she presses a kiss to my hair as the door swings open.

Inside, everyone we've grown close to in the past month is there with a huge sign that says '*CONGRATULATIONS GIDEON MARCUS ESQ.*'. The man of the hour is still in his bar exam attire: black joggers and a grey sweatshirt with 'CYBELE LAW' across the chest. There's a table with a vast array of food, everything from cocktail pickles to a huge cookie cake with the scales of justice frosted on the top. Surrounding Gideon are over a dozen people.

Diana and Halima are front and foremost, both wearing little party hats and holding plastic cups full of red... Something. Diana is still leaning on a cane, but Halima supports her on the other side as well. There are a couple of other people I've only met in passing, including a girl named Hisa with dark skin and long black hair that Juno told me Gideon has been trying to get up the nerve to ask out for months. Juno's handler from back on Janus— who I now know is a man named Charles, an old family friend that is one of the last people Juno keeps in contact with from her childhood— stand by Halima, his hand curled around a glass of bubbly liquid.

Tommy is there with the stitches on his face almost ready to be removed, as is Cressida: they're both law students as well, I've learned, which is how they became acquainted with Gideon and Halima. Everyone is smiling wide and the joy erupts in a cheer when me, Juno, Nova, and Mars enter. Juno immediately surges forward to hug Gideon, and Mars takes over helping me with my chair.

"I'm so proud of you," Juno tells her brother. He hugs her back just as tight as I know she always hugs and I can't help but smile at the twins. Mars scoots me over to the food table and gestures at it, raising an eyebrow, but I shake my head and clumsily make the sign for 'thank you'. I can't quite reach my mouth, so it's more of a gesture from my chest outwards, but Mars seems to get the idea as he grabs his own piece of cookie cake.

I look around the room as someone turns on music and the party gets started at last. Every once in a while I catch a whisper of the revolution, the chance that Marwood could be taken down a peg— the mere *hope* that he could be stopped— fills the air and allows us to relax just long enough to have a little party for a nineteen year-old who passed the bar exam so he could try to make the galaxy a better place.

Juno returns to my side after a few minutes and runs her fingers over my buzzed hair, her black painted fingernails chipped but matching her eyeliner, her black lipstick, the black clothes she has begun to don again.

"We might actually do it," she says, an echo of her words back in the abandoned ship we were scavenging.

I look at her, I see the optimism plain on her face, the same optimism and determination I mocked just months ago yet has never faltered even as we were tracked through the galaxy, even as she nursed me back to health.

I think of Mars' words— home, family. I think of Juno's thousands of supportive comments every single day reminding her that she is not alone. I think of the people who risked their lives to help me and my green-haired girl across the galaxy.

"Yeah," I say softly, for Juno and Juno alone to hear. "I think we might."

ACKNOWLEDGMENTS

To my wife, Kit, who has supported me since I was writing Dracula fanfiction on the back of vocab sheets in our high school lit class—

To Levi, who I met on Tumblr in 2016 and now live with, who is my best friend in the galaxy, who will take over the writing world any day now, if only he writes a goddamn book—

To my family— Dad, who sparked my love for sci-fi from a young age; Mom, who has always been my biggest cheerleader; Lydia, who actually kind of knows how space works; and the rest of the kinplampelista gang for all your support and love—

To Lee, Vesper, and Maddie for giving me Hope and the chance to flex my creative muscles while also becoming the best friends I could've hoped for—

To Holly, for being my first supporter back when I had no one else, my fanfic buddy, my twinkie defense bestie—

To Twitter & to Camp Helicon— Kal, Cass, CJ, Miriam, Rose, MJ, Bug, Ash, Kia, Liana, Bethany, Juli, and everyone else; I wrote this book in two months in June/July 2022. You kept me motivated for the long haul, not just for the sprints (those helped too, though!)—

Thank you. Thank you. Thank you.

ALSO BY OLIVE J. KELLEY

REBEL RISING

Book two of the TWIN SUNS DUOLOGY

coming Summer 2024

Olive is a 23 year old, non-binary, disabled lesbian who writes about young queer people finding hope even at the end of the world. When they're not writing, they can be found playing video games, watching Star Wars, or working as a barista.

They attained their degree in creative writing from Champlain College, and currently live in Denver, Colorado with their wife and three cats. JUNKER SEVEN is their debut novel.

twitter.com/olivejkelley
instagram.com/olivejkelley
tiktok.com/@olivejkelley

Ingram Content Group UK Ltd.
Milton Keynes UK
UKHW021007130623
423366UK00015B/493

9 798987 824603